MORE PRAISE FOR
THE KEY WEST FOOD CRITIC MYSTERIES

An Appetite for Murder

"What fun! Lucy Burdette writes evocatively about Key West and food—a winning combination. I can't wait for the next entry in this charming series."
—*New York Times* bestselling author
Diane Mott Davidson

"When her ex-boyfriend's new lover, the co-owner of *Key Zest* magazine, is found dead, Hayley Snow, wannabe food critic, is the first in line on the list of suspects. Food, fun, and felonies. What more could a reader ask for?"—*New York Times* bestselling author Lorna Barrett

"For a true taste of paradise, don't miss *An Appetite for Murder*. Lucy Burdette's first Key West Food Critic mystery combines a lush, tropical setting, a mysterious murder, and plenty of quirky characters. The victim may not be coming back for seconds, but readers certainly will!"
—Julie Hyzy, national bestselling author of the White House Chef mysteries and Manor House mysteries

"Burdette laces *An Appetite for Murder* with a clever plot, a determined if occasionally ditzy heroine, and a wealth of local color about Key West and its inhabitants. You'll eat it up." —*Richmond Times-Dispatch*

"Florida has long been one of the best backdrops for crime novels—from John D. MacDonald to Carl Hiassen—and Burdette's sense of place and her ability to empathize with a wide strata of Key West locals and visitors bodes well for this new series." —*Connecticut Post*

continued . . .

"An excellent sense of place and the occasional humorous outburst aren't the only things *An Appetite for Murder* has going for it, though: There is a solid mystery within its pages. . . . Not only does Burdette capture the physical and pastoral essence of Key West, she celebrates the food. . . . Although you might want to skip the key lime pie, don't skip *An Appetite for Murder*. Let's hope it is just an appetizer and there will be a feast of Food Critic mysteries to follow."

—The Florida Book Review

"Burdette cleverly combines the insuperable Key West location with the always irresistible hook, food. . . . Hayley is a vibrant young character to watch, and she writes scrumptious food reviews as well."

—*Mystery Scene*

"Hayley herself is delightful. Exuberant and naive, rocking back and forth between bravado and insecurity, excitable and given to motormouth nervousness, she's a quick study who has a lot to learn. I'm sure that many readers will be happy to make her acquaintance and follow her through future adventures."

—*Florida Weekly*

Death in Four Courses

"In a crowded cozy market, Lucy Burdette's Key West Food Critic series stands out among its peers."

—The Florida Book Review

"Anyone who's ever overpaid for a pretentious restaurant meal will relish this witty cozy."

—*Publishers Weekly*

Other Key West Food Critic Mysteries

An Appetite for Murder
Death in Four Courses

TOPPED CHEF

A Key West Food Critic Mystery

Lucy Burdette

AN OBSIDIAN MYSTERY

OBSIDIAN
Published by the Penguin Group
Penguin Group (USA) Inc., 375 Hudson Street,
New York, New York 10014, USA

USA I Canada I UK I Ireland I Australia I New Zealand I India I South Africa I China

Penguin Books Ltd., Registered Offices: 80 Strand, London WC2R 0RL, England
For more information about the Penguin Group visit penguin.com.

First published by Obsidian, an imprint of New American Library,
a division of Penguin Group (USA) Inc.

First Printing, May 2013

OBSIDIAN and logo are trademarks of Penguin Group (USA) Inc.

ISBN 978-0-451-23970-9

Printed in the United States of America
10 9 8 7 6 5 4 3 2 1

PUBLISHER'S NOTE
This is a work of fiction. Names, characters, places, and incidents either are the product
of the author's imagination or are used fictitiously, and any resemblance to actual per-
sons, living or dead, business establishments, events, or locales is entirely coincidental.
    The recipes contained in this book are to be followed exactly as written. The pub-
lisher is not responsible for your specific health or allergy needs that may require
medical supervision. The publisher is not responsible for any adverse reactions to the
recipes contained in this book.
    The publisher does not have any control over and does not assume any responsibility
for author or third-party Web sites or their content.

ALWAYS LEARNING   PEARSON

*For John, the chocolate sauce and nuts
on my Mexican Sundae*

ACKNOWLEDGMENTS

I am so grateful to the folks who bought character names for *Topped Chef* in the name of charity. They are such good sports as they have *no idea* what I'll come up with when they write their checks! Peter Shapiro bought an auction item to benefit the Waterfront Theater in Key West, and requested that I put Randy Thompson in the book. I added Peter himself just for fun. Thank you to Randy for allowing the use of his name and for sharing his stories. Toby (Davidson) Scott bought an auction item to benefit our dearly beloved E.C. Scranton Memorial Library in Madison, Connecticut. Thank you, Toby! Though the names are real, inspired by real people, the characters are purely fiction.

Thanks to Adam Boyd for allowing his name to be used; to Tim and Stacie Boyd for their recipe; to Leigh Pujado for details on the gym, which I should already have known intimately—and for her cameo appearance. Thanks to Ron Augustine for his insights on tarot and Key West and to Jane for connecting us; thanks to my wonderful Key West friends Steve, Eric, Cory, Cathy, and Jim, for sharing stories and lives. Pat Cronin provided details about how paramedics would react in a crisis. Huge thanks to Rose Anati for helping me understand the ins and outs of reality television. I would have been lost without her, though of course all mistakes are mine!

I'm utterly grateful to the usual suspects—Hallie Ephron, Susan Hubbard, Chris Falcone, Angelo Pompano, Susan Cerulean, and John Brady, who never let me down when it comes to brainstorming, feedback, and support. My blog mates and dear friends at Jungle Red Writers, Mystery Lovers' Kitchen, and Killer Characters fill my inbox every day with laughter and support. Thanks to all my writing friends in the mystery and cozy community who share tips and encouragement.

And thank you to my fabulous agent, Paige Wheeler, and her gang at Folio Literary, and to Sandy Harding, my amazing editor, who makes every page better, and the supporting cast at NAL. I appreciate you every one, including Kayleigh, Elizabeth, the illustrators who produce my fabulous covers!

But most of all, thanks to readers, booksellers, and librarians for reading the Food Critic mysteries and spreading the word! I hope you'll enjoy this vicarious visit to Key West—all the good parts in the book (including restaurants) are real. The rest of it, I made up.

TOPPED CHEF **KEY WEST**

The Staff
Peter Shapiro, executive producer | director
Deena Smith, assistant to the executive producer

The Judges
Sam Rizzoli
Toby Davidson
Chef Adam Boyd
Hayley Snow

The Chef Contestants
Henrietta Stentzel
Randy Thompson
Buddy Higgs

The Homeless Guys
Turtle
Tony

The Cops
Detective Nathan Bransford
Officer Steve Torrence

Staff at *Key Zest*
Wally Beile
Danielle Kamen
Hayley Snow

Friends at Tarpon Pier
Miss Gloria Peterson
Connie Arp
Ray, Connie's fiancé
Janet Snow, Hayley's mom
Sam Cooper, Janet's boyfriend

Then she also read Sirine's coffee grounds and said she could see the signs written in the black coffee traces along the milky porcelain: sharp knife, quick hands, white apron, and the sadness of a chef. "Chefs know—nothing lasts," she told Sirine. "In the mouth, then gone."

—Diana Abu-Jaber, *Crescent*

1

> "When you wake up in the morning, Pooh,"
> said Piglet at last, "what's the first thing
> you say to yourself?"
>
> "What's for breakfast?" said Pooh. "What
> do you say, Piglet?"
>
> "I say, 'I wonder what's going to hap-
> pen exciting today?'" said Piglet.
>
> Pooh nodded thoughtfully. "It's the same
> thing," he said.
>
> — A. A. Milne, *Winnie-the-Pooh*

Evinrude woke me from a sound sleep, first with his
rumbling purr and then with a gentle but persistent
tapping of paw to cheek. I blinked my eyes open—the
bedside clock read six fifteen. I hissed softly at his gray-
striped face. "I love you dearly, but you're a monster,"
I told him as I rolled out of bed. "Spoiled rotten cat
flesh."

Tail hoisted high, he trotted out of the room ahead of
me, meowing loudly. Miss Gloria's lithe black cat, Sparky,

intercepted him before he reached the food bowls lined up in the corner of the tiny galley of our houseboat. He sprang onto Evinrude's back and wrestled him to the floor. While they boxed and nipped at each other, I poured a ration of kibbles into each bowl, refreshed their water, and then staggered onto the deck to check out the morning.

The plum-colored night sky was shifting to pink to make room for the day, which looked as though it might turn out "glorious and whimsical," as the *Key West Citizen* had promised. A quartet of wind chimes tinkled lightly from the boats down the finger. Had there been a stiff wind or the first spitting drops of a cold rain, I'd have gone directly back to bed. But on a morning like this, there was no excuse to avoid the dreaded exercise I'd prescribed for myself.

Twice in the past ten days, I'd lured myself out of bed to go jogging before work, with the promise of a thick, sweet café con leche from the Cuban Coffee Queen as a reward on the way home. In addition to adding heft to my resume, my position as food critic for *Key Zest* had added a bit to my waistline over the past months; I was anxious to reverse the trend. And besides that, the Key West Food and Wine Festival loomed this week—it promised a series of tasting sessions that could ruin the most stalwart dieter. Which I was definitely not.

And most pressing of all, my first real date with detective Nate Bransford had been rescheduled for this evening. (You can't count a threesome including your mother as a romantic encounter.) So it wasn't hard to convince myself that today should be the third session—not that jogging two miles would magically transform my figure from jiggles to muscles, but I had to start somewhere. And maybe it would help work out the predate jitters, too.

I hurried back inside, replaced my pajamas with baggy running shorts, red sneakers, and a T-shirt that read "Dinner is ready when the smoke alarm goes off." I'd bought the shirt for Christmas for my stepmother— who, while a brilliant chemist, was famous in our family for cremating roasts and burning even soup from a can—but lost my nerve before sending it. Why jostle a relationship that had recently settled into a pleasant détente?

I tucked my phone into my pocket and dashed off a note to my roommate, Miss Gloria, who lets me live onboard her houseboat in exchange for errands like grocery shopping (which I adore anyway), and sending occasional reports on her mental and physical condition to her son in Michigan. I stand between her and a slot in an old-age home—and I take my responsibility seriously. The Queen's Guard of Tarpon Pier.

I wrote: *Jogging—ugh! Call me if you want a coffee.*

Then I hopped off our deck, tottered along the dock, and started grinding up the Palm Avenue hill over the Garrison Bight, which is Key West speak for harbor, toward the Old Town section of Key West. There aren't many changes in elevation in this town, so I was just as happy to get this challenge over with early on. I puffed past the U.S. Naval Air Station's multistory building— *Fly Navy*—and then by the pale pink and green cement block apartments for enlisted folks and their families. I finally chugged around the curve onto Eaton Street, my lungs burning and my thighs cramping into complaining masses. I picked up my pace, pushing harder because I smelled bacon: The Cole's Peace Bakery called to me like a Siren to Ulysses. Stopping for an unscheduled bacon and cheese toast on crispy Cuban bread would devastate my fledging resolutions.

As I hooked right on Grinnell, heading toward the boardwalk that wound along the historic seaport area, I tried to distract myself by thinking about my tasks for the day. There'd be e-mail to answer, as the biweekly issue of *Key Zest*, our fledgling Key West style magazine, hit in-boxes today. And I was in charge of responding to the usual flurry of complaints and compliments. For the first time in my short career, I'd had to swallow hard and write a negative review. This was bound to come sooner or later. Key West is a foodie paradise, but like Anywhere, USA, there are lousy meals to be had, too. As a careful follower of the major newspaper restaurant critics, I'd read plenty of stories about critics suffering through horrendous dinners. Or worse yet, bouts of food poisoning. I'd actually memorized one of the *New York Times* critic Sam Sifton's sharper quotes: "And lobes of dismal-flavored sea urchin served over thick lardo and heavy toast were just dreadful: the eighth band after Nirvana to write loud-soft-loud music and call it new."

But hearing about rotten reviews and writing them were two different animals. I wasn't convinced that I would ever develop a killer instinct—famous critics seemed to enjoy ripping apart a horrible dinner. Me? I could only imagine the chef sweating in the kitchen, slaving over the stove, plating the meal, praying that his special *whatever* hit the mark. It broke my heart to think about dissing some poor chump's food.

My second meal at Just Off Duval a couple nights earlier had started off well. True to its name, the restaurant was located a half block from Duval Street, far enough from the bustle of the town's main party artery to mask the grit and noise. My friend Eric and I had ordered glasses of wine and settled into the pleasant outdoor patio edged with feathery palm plants to enjoy our dinners. The night was cool enough for a sweater, and the scent of roasting meat had my stomach doing anticipatory back-flips. A half loaf of stale Italian bread and a pool of olive oil that tasted almost rancid were the first signs the experience would be a downer. I jotted a few notes into my smartphone, agreeing with Eric: Any restaurant should be allowed a tiny misstep.

But then my chef's special salad was delivered: a small pile of lettuce dog-paddling in thick blue cheese dressing that screamed "emulsifier" and wore powerful overtones of the plastic bottle it must have been squeezed from. On top of that were chunks of pale pink mealy tomatoes. Though the mashed potatoes that accompanied the main courses were creamy and rich, my thirty-eight-dollar fish smelled fishy and Eric's forty-two-dollar steak was stringy. We didn't have the nerve to order dessert. I hadn't actually gotten ill, but my stomach had roiled for half the night in spite of the half roll of antacids I'd eaten. According to a text the next morning from Eric, who generally had an iron constitution, his gut still didn't feel quite right as he and his partner drove to Miami for some much-needed R & R.

I had tried to wriggle out of writing it up. But there wasn't time to substitute something else. And my boss, Wally, had specifically told me this restaurant should be included in the next issue of our magazine. But hadn't I heard former *New York Times* food critic Ruth Reichl warning prospective food critics and writers that the more expensive the restaurant, the more damage a lousy review could do? And mine was definitely lousy. It started like this:

> *All kitchens have an off night. Unfortunately, my three visits at Just Off Duval coincided with three bad nights. JOD, a newish restaurant on a cul-de-sac a half block off Upper Duval Street, has been the site of four failed restaurants over the past six years. Whether this is due to bad cooking juju or simply uneven and over-reaching preparation, I fear that Just Off Duval will be joining their ranks. . . .*

I shook the words out of my mind and staggered past the *Yankee Freedom* ship, which ferries tourists to the Dry Tortugas for snorkeling expeditions most mornings. Then I paused on the boardwalk along the harbor to catch my breath. Several large sailboats left over from the races the previous week still clanked in their slips, alongside catamarans loaded with kayaks and sport fishing powerboats. The pink streaks in the sky had expanded like silken threads of cotton candy, lending enough light that I could make out the details of the early-morning activity. Nearby, a thin man in faded jeans with long hair and a bushy beard that reached to the middle of his chest sprayed the deck of one of the Sebago party boats with a high-pressure hose. The hair around his lips was stained yellow, as if he'd smoked a lifetime's worth of cigarettes, and faded to white at the tip of his beard. His name—Derek—was embroidered on his shirt.

As I leaned against a wooden railing to stretch my calves, a bare-chested, red-haired man skidded around the corner, wearing a long black cloak and a small American flag draped from his belt like a loincloth. He leaped onto the boat, pulled a knife out of his waistband, and, taking a fighter's crouch, brandished it at the man with the hose.

Even under the pirate's tricornered hat, I recognized him—Turtle, a chronically homeless man whose behavior fluctuated with the status of his mental illness. A couple of months ago, I would have backed away as fast as I could. But now I understood more. Since it was the end of the month, he'd probably run out of meds. And if the cops came, he'd end up in jail. Where he'd only get worse.

The bearded man spun around, growled, and pointed the hose at Turtle, who had begun to execute tai chi–like movements, waving the knife in shaky figure eights. My adrenaline surged as I pictured a throat slit right in front of my eyes.

"Listen, man," the worker yelled, "get the hell out of here. You're on private property."

"They can't take what I ain't got," said Turtle, crouching lower and moving forward.

This was going to get ugly unless someone intervened.

"Turtle," I called. "Put the knife down. Please?"

"Avast, ye stinking pirates!" Turtle yelled, swinging around to wave the knife at me. Heart pounding, I stumbled back a few steps.

"I'm calling the cops right now." The white-bearded man sprayed Turtle's legs, now wet to the knees, as he yanked a phone from the back pocket of his jeans.

"Turtle," I said, "I'm going for coffee and a Cuban cheese toast. Can I get you one?"

His pale blue eyes darted from me to the white-haired man and back; the knife twitched in his fingers. Then he shrugged, shoved the weapon into his belt beside the flag, and hopped off the boat. I took a shaky breath and led him around the block to the Cuban Coffee Queen, wondering how to keep him focused in this world, not deep in his own crazy loop.

"I love this weather, don't you?" I asked, glancing over my shoulder. He danced along several feet behind me, fending off imagined dangers by feinting left and then right with his cape. What would it feel like to be inside his head? Awful, I guessed.

As we approached the little white shack painted like an oversized Key West postcard that housed the Cuban Coffee Queen, he hunkered down and pulled out the knife again. A couple with a baby stroller were ordering breakfast at the walk-up window. The woman stiffened and whispered something to her husband. He moved around to stand in between his family and us.

"Turtle," I said softly, "better put that away or you'll scare the other folks. Would you rather have a Cuban bagel or a cheese toast?" I reached out to touch his arm but stopped when I saw his startled face.

"Cheese toast, matey!" he growled, sidling away from me and sliding the knife back into his belt again.

"Why don't you wait here?" I suggested, pointing to a painted wooden bench about ten feet from the coffee stand.

He sat, tugging his cape around his body and closing his eyes. He rocked back and forth and his fingers tapped out a rhythm on his knees to a tune I couldn't hear. I stepped up to the food stand's window next to a large stuffed rooster.

"Two large café con leches and a cheese toast please," I told the woman with dark hair and eyes who appeared at the window. I glanced over at Turtle. "Better make one decaf." She took my money and I stuffed two bucks into the tip jar while the milk steamed and shots of espresso drained into paper cups. Smelled like my kind of heaven. She buttered a slab of Cuban bread, slapped on a layer of cheese, and popped the sandwich into the grill press.

As soon as my order was ready, a police car pulled up and stopped next to the coffee stand. Officer Torrence—a cop who knew my business a little better than I'd prefer for a man I wasn't dating—peered out of the cruiser on the passenger side. His gaze darted from the sodden homeless man to the breakfast in my hands. He rolled down the window and smoothed his mustache. "Everything okay here?"

"Just dandy," I said, forcing a smile. Turtle had tensed, looking ready to spring. My hands trembling, I walked over to deliver his coffee and sandwich. He took off, Torrence watching him as he booked it around the souvenir shop and back to the harbor.

"Where's your scooter?" Officer Torrence asked.

"I jogged here this morning."

"You want a ride?" he asked, gesturing to the backseat of the cruiser. "You look a little pale."

"No thanks," I said with a weak grin and waved them on. I was terrible at keeping secrets—the worst. He'd want to know everything about Turtle and I'd find myself spilling the details of the altercation at the harbor and how he'd scared the little family at the Cuban Coffee Queen and likely Turtle would still end up in jail.

Besides, everyone on Tarpon Pier would notice me emerging from a black and white—I'd never hear the end of it. As I took my coffee and walked out to Caroline Street, a text message buzzed onto my phone.

FYI, Hayley, the owner of Just Off Duval called me at home. Freaking Out. Get to the office ASAP and we'll make a plan.

I almost dropped the phone. My worst nightmare: facing the owner or chef whose restaurant I'd panned. It hadn't taken long to happen.

I flagged down a pink taxicab to carry me home.

2

When he sees twenty-somethings obsessing about foam or rushing around the kitchen in a competitive cooking challenge, it's kind of like watching pornography. I think: I'd love to do that, but I'm afraid I'll throw out my back.

—Rick Rodgers interviewed by
Kathleen Flinn

I arrived at *Key Zest* at eight, damp from the fastest shower on record. The *Key Zest* office sits above Preferred Properties real estate on Southard, more attic really, than office. Danielle, our magazine's receptionist, looked at the clock and then at my overheated face—still red like a tomato the last time I checked in the mirror. She touched a finger to her glossy pink lips.

"I wouldn't go in there," she whispered, pointing at Wally's office. "Not unless he calls for you."

Through the blinds on Wally's windowed wall, I could see the silhouettes of two figures, one at the desk, one in the chair beside the desk. "Just Off Duval?" I asked in a hushed voice.

She nodded and made a quick face. "Livid," she whispered again.

"Shoot." I crept past Wally's half-opened door and slipped down the hall to my nook, which is more like a hallway aneurysm than an office. Leaving my door cracked open so I could eavesdrop, I turned on my computer and pretended to work. Not easy with the raised voices that began to carom down the short hall.

Wally's voice came first, low and controlled. "I'm sorry you didn't like the review. A new restaurant takes its chances. But you've got enough experience to know that already. We have to act like serious journalists or we won't be taken seriously. And that means we call them as we taste them. We're not designing advertising—we publish reviews."

Then came another male voice, loud and furious. "If she'd let them know that she was there, the chef could have done something about—"

"Either the kitchen can cook or it can't," Wally cut in. "A critic's presence at one of the tables in the front of the house shouldn't make any difference at all."

"If you don't care about advertising revenue, that's a fine business practice," the second man said.

"If you wish to take out an ad, we will include whatever copy you choose. But the wording in our review is not up to you. The piece stands."

Wow. He was going way out on a limb for me.

I heard the noise of a chair scraping on the tile floor and then the second man said: "I could appreciate you standing behind an experienced reviewer. But bleeding to death over a newcomer who doesn't know pâté from potatoes? Pure foolishness." He stomped the short length of the hallway and slammed out of the office.

I waited a few minutes to be sure he wouldn't come back with more last words, then edged down the hall and stuck my head into Wally's office.

"That went well," he said, adding a lopsided grin. "Come on in." He waved me in, then ran fingers through his short blond hair until it stood straight up. He had on the same yellow shirt with palm trees on it that Danielle and I were wearing—one of his sort-of-endearing eccentricities was insistence on a company uniform.

"I'm sorry I was late," I said, brushing past the enormous faux palm tree that guarded the door to his office. "I was over at the harbor when you messaged me. I should have been here to help you out."

Danielle rolled her chair down the hall from the reception desk and stopped in the doorway. "No amount of reinforcement from extra troops was going to change that man's mind. He's a bully, pure and simple," she added.

"I should have gone easier on the descriptions," I said. "The olive oil wasn't really that close to rancid, just a little off. And we didn't actually get sick. And it wasn't fair for me to predict the restaurant would fail."

"Diners don't want reviews that are whitewashed," Wally said, sliding his tortoiseshell glasses down his nose and peering over the top of them. "They are spending good money on this place and they deserve the truth. You have to get over this urge to be nice, and go ahead and say what needs to be said."

"But you're always telling me to smile when people come in," said Danielle.

"You're a receptionist, she's a critic," said Wally firmly. "Different job descriptions." He crooked a smile, ran his fingers through his hair again, and pushed his glasses up to the top of his head. "Can I talk to you alone for a minute, Hayley?"

"Of course. Let me get something to write on." As Danielle rolled back to her station, I trotted down the hall to my tiny workspace and grabbed a tablet and a pen from the desk, hoping he didn't have more bad news. Was my trial employment period up? Had I flunked a test I didn't know I was taking? I returned to Wally's office and took the seat catty-corner to his, still warm from the irate restaurateur who'd sat there only minutes earlier.

He smiled and patted his desk blotter. "Don't look so worried. You're doing fine. This is about a new assignment. A real plum. You know the Food and Wine Festival is upon us, right?"

"Of course. I have tickets for the Mallory Square Stroll tomorrow night, remember? And Duval Uncorked on Saturday." One of the first events for the festival involved sampling morsels from restaurants from three districts around town. Diners would rotate among five businesses, tasting their food and drinking wine. It had seemed like a good way to try a few places I'd never visited, fast.

"And maybe you've heard about the Key West Topped Chef contest this weekend?"

I nodded again, searching my brain for the details of an article I'd skimmed in the *Citizen*. "I might have seen an announcement but I don't know the details."

Wally settled his glasses back on his nose and tucked a pencil behind the side bar. "It's a reality TV cooking show slash contest and the winning chef scores an opportunity to do a pilot for a new network show. The producer called this morning asking *Key Zest* to provide a judge."

"A judge?" I cleared my throat, feeling the tickle of an unpleasant assignment coming. "Isn't it a little late to be naming judges?"

He peered over the top of his glasses, frowning. I wasn't demonstrating the old rah-rah team spirit that he wanted in his one and three-quarters employees—me and Danielle. "I'd like it to be you."

I sat back, the frayed nubs of the wicker chair poking my shoulder blades. "I wouldn't have a clue how to choose a television personality. I know how to judge food, not people. And I'm a horrible actress—all you have to do is preview a few of my mom's home movies to know that."

He grinned. "Rain check on that. Do you watch any TV cooking shows?"

"Of course. It's a blood sport in my family."

"Which ones?"

"Rachael Ray, of course. She's not much of a chef, but she's utterly charming—and she makes her viewers feel like they can cook. She makes it all seem possible. That's an art! On the other hand, Mom loves Emeril. Some of the other chefs think he acts too much like a clown, but we think he's a fabulous entertainer. And I never miss . . ." My words trailed off as I realized I'd talked my way into the new gig.

"It will be fun!" Wally said, seizing the opening I'd

given him. "The first session begins in half an hour at the Studios of Key West. Just imagine you're at home on the couch with your mom."

My first instinct was to whine and wheedle. I squelched that and tried to muster a smile. From the look on Wally's face, I could tell the question was settled.

"If you have any questions, get in touch with Deena Smith. She's helping to organize the weekend." He slid a slip of paper across the desk with her phone number on it.

As if it wasn't already etched in my mind for life. Deena was my ex-boyfriend Chad's secretary and I'd called that number more times than was decent after our ugly breakup. In spite of those bad memories, I felt an immediate relief—Deena and I had managed to remain friends in spite of Chad. She was a levelheaded, evenhanded person—how bad could it be if she was involved?

3

The best tools, like the best chefs, are a little offset.

—Michael Ruhlman

I drove my scooter up Fleming Street, buzzed the long block across on White to Southard, and parked outside the cavernous yellow-sided former armory trimmed with turrets that now housed the Studios of Key West. I trudged up the front steps and went inside. The two-story vestibule was jammed with people—some in checkered chefs' pants and white coats, some wearing earphones and carrying clipboards, some in random Key West dress—shorts, flip-flops, and T-shirts emblazoned with unprintable slogans.

Inside the main room—which stretched the full length and width of the armory and two stories high—I found Deena. She looked stunning as always, her thick black hair curling past her shoulders and an extra sparkle in her dark brown eyes. Her red tank top matched her high heels and her nail polish, any one of which would have looked ridiculous on me. Standing next to Deena always made me wish I were a little taller and that I'd dressed a little better—or a lot, if I was honest. Like changed out of the yellow *Key Zest* shirt that clashed with both my freckles and my auburn curls.

Deena offered me a quick hug and ran a finger down a line of typed names on her top page. Mine was penciled in at the bottom. She checked it off with a red pen.

"Welcome to the zoo."

"Thanks. I think." I rolled my eyes. "How the heck did you get roped into this?"

"I took the week off from Chad's office," she said. "I used to work in reality television before I moved down here. I love this stuff. It's too unpredictable to do as a steady diet, but I couldn't resist applying for a temporary job right here in town. It's so much more exciting than the lawyer business." She underlined my name on her clipboard and grinned. "When I called your office yesterday looking for another victim, I never imagined you'd get tapped."

I couldn't keep from rolling my eyes again. "I was the only option. And Wally's a little desperate for *Key Zest* to make a splash."

"Oh, hey, congrats on the review this morning, too." Then her eyes got wide. "You do know that Sam Rizzoli is one of the judges?"

"Are you sure it's *Sam* Rizzoli?"

She nodded. Checked her list and nodded again.

I felt a fist to my gut, but before I could follow up, a very tall man with a mane of white hair, a close-cut white beard, and intense blue eyes clapped his hands and called for attention. The chattering died down to a murmur. He pushed through the crowd and beckoned Deena to join him on the rustic stage that was used for "Old Town, New Folk" concerts.

"Welcome to *Topped Chef*, Key West–style," he bellowed into the microphone mounted on the podium. "I'm the executive producer and director of the show, all wrapped up in one shiny package. Like surf and turf. Or fish and chips or . . ."

Deena put two fingers on his wrist and he stopped and grinned down at her.

"Okay, my assistant says enough with the foodie metaphors. My name is Peter Shapiro. Deena Smith—this gorgeous morsel next to me—will be assisting me with scheduling details. She's my field and story producer, also known as the vice president in charge of difficult people."

He squeezed Deena's shoulder and smiled in a slightly oily way.

"For the preliminary round of this event, this morning our wannabe chefs delivered an original dish featuring the seafood of Key West to our staff. We've narrowed these dishes to six entries and these wonderful contestants are right here in this room."

I glanced around, searching the faces of the people in chef's clothing, feeling my curiosity blossom. Which of them would be disappointed when the contest ended? Only one would be elated—as I'd been when I landed the job at *Key Zest* in the fall. I had wanted the job so badly; actually landing it felt unreal.

"We have selected a distinguished panel of judges who will rate the food purely on appearance, flavor, general excellence of cooking, and evidence of technique, without consideration of the cooks behind them. Once the three winning dishes are chosen, the personalities will be introduced into the mix." He rubbed his palms together, laughing in an evil way. "Then things get wonderfully interesting. Could the judges come forward to the stage?"

I headed to the back of the room and trooped up the steps to join Peter and Deena and three other judges—a rangy man with dark, wavy hair and wearing a paisley shirt, a small woman with an anxious look on her delicate features, and a substantial man wearing a white chef's coat and black clogs and a white toque.

"Sam Rizzoli and his family have inhabited Key West for generations." Peter pointed to the rangy man, who had the kind of muscles that came from regular workouts, but also a small gut that suggested he enjoyed indulging in food or drink, or both. "Sam owns four restaurants in town," Peter added, "including the brand-new sensation Just Off Duval."

Yep. The very same restaurant I had panned. The very man who'd been in our office this morning shouting at Wally about my foodie ignorance. I hadn't gotten a look at him as I'd snuck down the hall, but I'd know his angry voice anywhere. I forced my face to retain the pleasant expression I'd painted on as I climbed the stairs to the stage. Spotlights beat down on the stage and I began to sweat.

"Next to Sam is Toby Davidson." Peter Shapiro pointed to the small woman wearing a brown pageboy streaked with gray. She looked as uncomfortable as I felt—possibly even worse. She waggled her fingers and mouthed "hello."

"Ms. Davidson has written a memoir about how she handled her grief over losing her husband through baking cakes. She is a founding editor of *Bake with Joy*, and has seen her work published in *Gourmet*, *Bon Appetit*, *Cooking Light*, and many other magazines. Her essays have been included in anthologies of the year's best food writing for 2010, 2011, and 2012."

Now Toby flashed a warm smile. I pictured her pulling cake after gorgeous cake from her oven, her spirits lifting as each one baked and was frosted and eaten. I could definitely relate to that coping style—it was only surprising that she wasn't round as a beach ball.

"And next to Toby, meet chef Adam Boyd whose brilliant treatment of seafood has propelled his Key West restaurant onto the top one hundred list of places to eat on the eastern seaboard." The mustachioed young man in the chef's coat blinked his eyes and gave a stiff bow.

"And last but by no means least, please meet Hayley Snow, new food critic for the style magazine *Key Zest*." No accolades after my introduction—I hadn't had time to accumulate any.

I bared my teeth and tried to look distinguished. And tried not to look at Sam Rizzoli's incredulous, outraged face. He clearly hadn't known that I was joining the judging roster.

"After the top dishes have been selected, the three winning chef candidates will be interviewed by our judges. Three cooking challenges will follow, details to come. Are there any questions about that? I hope not because we don't have time for them."

There was a smattering of applause and laughter and

he glanced at his watch. "I would like the judges to follow me. Chefs, please remain here until you're called.
Any pressing questions or concerns, talk to Deena." He
squeezed her shoulder again and she grimaced and held
up her clipboard.

"The bathroom is to the right of the entrance," she
said, and everyone laughed.

We trooped off the stage and exited out the back
door, into a narrow passage between two buildings
that opened into a small courtyard. Tropical plantings
and pieces of abstract sculpture made it look both
homey and artsy. Cameras, lights, and wires spoiled
the effect.

"We'll be filming up here," said Peter as he ushered
us up two steps onto a large covered porch connected
to a darling conch cottage. Inside the double glass
doors, I could see a cameraman filming dishes of food
that had been laid out on the counter, filling most of the
small kitchen. Workers wearing earbuds and microphones buzzed around him, adjusting plates and bowls
and lights. Two more workers positioned us in four
wicker chairs that had been pulled up to the table facing the kitchen, and then clipped microphones to our
collars, wormed wires down our shirts, and fastened
battery packs to the back of our pants.

I could feel my intestines starting to grind. I'd only
appeared on a TV show one other time, shortly after
getting hired at *Key Zest*. I'd come across simultane-
ously wooden and giddy, recalling not one of the talking points I'd memorized ahead of time.

"Welcome, welcome," said Peter, when the sound
checks had been completed. "Do you know each other?"

I looked down the row, at Toby's ski jump nose, Chef Adam's bristling mustache, and then Sam's grim face, and shook my head. The others followed suit.

"Perfect! Then there will be no off-camera shenanigans to queer the contest. Don't worry about the camera and don't worry about us—we are simply white noise. Be yourselves, act natural, talk to each other about food. What could be easier? We are not airing live, but we do not, I repeat *do not* have time to reshoot scenes. So give us your best first time out."

He pointed at a cameraman who stood by the double doors. "Are we ready?" The man with the camera gave a thumbs-up.

"Welcome to *Topped Chef* Key West–style!" Peter said as the camera rolled. "Home of the next culinary superstar. Our judges today are four distinguished guests from the food scene here in paradise—the island of Key West." He stepped aside and introduced each of us, as he had on the stage. The crew in the kitchen began to ferry the dishes that had been arranged on the inside counter out to our table.

"Six seafood dishes have been selected in a preliminary tasting round," Peter told our invisible audience. "Now our judges will have the opportunity to sample them all and narrow the selection down to three. As you can see"—he motioned for a camera close-up—"the dishes are only labeled with the number corresponding to our contestants' names. Let the games begin!"

He stepped to the side and one of his assistants ladled a glob of orange-sauced seafood and rice onto the square white china plates that had been set in front of us.

"Tasters, on your mark, get set, go!" said Shapiro.

"What in the name of god is this?" Sam Rizzoli asked after he'd forked a bite into his mouth. "It tastes like a cross between Russian dressing and Welsh rarebit. Only curdled."

I touched my tongue to the spoon, eyes closed so I could concentrate, wishing he'd let the rest of us taste before he'd trashed it. The sauce was definitely on the oily side, slightly sweet, containing small chunks of what appeared to be stone crab, and maybe a dash of pickle relish. A recipe my old-fashioned roommate, Miss Gloria, might have enjoyed. And actually something that might turn up on Rizzoli's restaurant's menu.

"If you absolutely must sauce it, stone crab wants to be savory, rather than sweet," said Chef Adam. "This is the kind of dish you might expect to find in Ohio. Key West? Not so much."

Toby took a deep breath and raised a finger. "I like it."

"Interesting, but a little odd," I added, feeling utterly lame.

The two male judges exchanged tortured glances, and Chef Adam signaled for the next dish. The plates were whisked away and one of the assistants placed pieces of white fish in a butter and caper sauce onto clean ones. I nibbled quickly so I could come to my own conclusions before the others colored my perspective. Not bad, though the cook had been overgenerous with the capers, so the saltiness overwhelmed the pallid, white flesh of the fish.

"Would you say it's a little salty?" I ventured, wanting to register an opinion but unable to suppress the idea that the creator of this dish would be hanging on our every word. Probably this very chef's family and friends were gathered in the Armory, watching his hopes and dreams get torn to shreds on a TV monitor.

"I would say it's not awful, but perhaps unremarkable," said Chef Adam.

"Remarkable for its pedestrian treatment," Sam agreed, pushing the plate aside. "In fact, the strongest flavor in the sauce is the hint of metal lid from the caper jar. How long do you suppose they were in his refrigerator? Next."

Toby looked as though she'd been about to say something but the plates were removed before she had the chance. Shapiro's assistant placed a small blob of polenta and a pink shrimp on each of our fresh plates. I carved off an inch of the crustacean, drew it through the buttery, cheesy cornmeal, and popped it into my mouth.

"I love this!" I said as soon as I'd swallowed.

"Classic, but unimaginative," said Chef Adam.

"I agree with Hayley—it's a simple recipe but executed flawlessly," Toby piped up.

"Not terrible," said Sam in a booming voice, looking directly at the camera. "But quite the Key West cliché. I know you want a chef who can cook regional dishes, but shouldn't they show evidence of some imagination? Let's sidestep the dishes with 'uneven and overreaching preparation,' shall we?"

I didn't dare look down the table. *Uneven and overreaching preparation* were the words I'd used to describe his restaurant. Along with *bad cooking juju* and some other phrases I wanted to forget.

Assistants delivered the next dish, a lobster salad drizzled with a spicy green foam that looked like something that had washed up on the beach after a storm. It was garnished with a glistening spoonful of caviar. I took one fiery bite and clutched my neck, signaling for a glass of water. One of the assistants hurried over with a glass and I gulped it down.

Chef Adam finished chewing, leaned back in his chair, and sighed in satisfaction. "Nearly perfect. Whereas the caper sauce overwhelmed the other fish with its metallic salinity, the jalapeño foam provides just enough contrast to brighten the fish. And the caviar is both gorgeous and delightful."

Had Chef Adam even noticed the metallic taste of the previous dish before Mr. Rizzoli mentioned it? Their tag-team act was starting to seriously annoy me.

"It tries too hard," I snapped, feeling my throat continue to burn and thinking this description applied to Chef Adam, too. But then I added a softening smile, hoping I didn't sound as mean as the two men. "I like hot peppers, but not so hot I have to call the fire department after I eat."

"Would this fall into the school of molecular gastronomy?" Toby asked. "It's tasty, but I've never quite connected with the foams and fumes and so on. How could a home chef possibly hope to reproduce it?"

"That's exactly the point, then, isn't it?" asked Chef Adam. "To have people introduced to food they wouldn't otherwise experience? Most people can throw a roast in the oven or whip up a skillet of tacos and call it supper. This kind of cooking goes way beyond that sort of thing."

"I'd rate it nine out of ten," Sam Rizzoli agreed.

In the background, Peter Shapiro was rubbing his hands, looking pleased and excited. He motioned for the final dish to be delivered. This appeared to be seafood in a red sauce, served on a tiny nest of linguine. I poked through the sauce with my fork, identifying a ring of squid, a small shrimp, and a mussel. I tasted.

"Wonderful," I said, closing my eyes to savor the spicy fra diavolo sauce. "This is the best so far. Hot enough to tingle the tongue without scorching."

The men weighed in, Chef Adam for and Rizzoli against—though I had the feeling he would have dismissed anything I liked. Toby waffled, enamored of the red sauce but unimpressed with the jumble of sea creatures.

"That's all there is," Shapiro announced to the camera. "And now the moment of truth, in which our esteemed judges narrow the field. . . ."

After five minutes of debate, we settled on three dishes—the homey Key West–style shrimp and grits dish, the lobster with caviar salsa and jalapeño foam, and the sophisticated yet substantial Italian seafood fra diavolo.

"Fabrulous, fabrulous," said Shapiro. "Now we shall briefly meet our chef contestants." He signaled to Deena, who ushered a gaggle of six chefs from the alley to the courtyard.

"Thank you all for your participation in *Topped Chef!*" said Peter. "We so enjoyed *experiencing* your contributions." One young blond man grinned but the other candidates looked solemn and nervous, maybe wondering as I was what was wrong with old-fashioned food *tasting*.

"As certain as we are that all of your dishes were outstanding, our judges have spoken! Will the following individuals please join us here on the set: chef Randy Thompson!" The smiley blond man leaped into the air, clapping, and bounded up the steps.

"Chef Henrietta Stentzel, formerly of Hola on Miami Beach, and now chef-owner of Bad Boy Burritos!"

I blinked in disbelief. Then my heart sank with a hollow clunk as a fortysomething woman with a long braid climbed the stairs, looking everywhere but at me. Food was not the only thing we had in common—though I adored her small storefront burrito shop. Unfortunately, I'd suspected her in the murder of my ex's girlfriend last fall—and from what I could tell, she had not forgiven me.

"And last but not least, meet chef Buddy Higgs!" Peter crowed.

A very tan man with a weathered face and a scraggly ponytail joined the other two as the rest of us clapped. Were Buddy and Randy currently not employed, or had Peter forgotten to mention that?

"That's a wrap. Chefs are dismissed. Be here tomorrow morning at nine sharp." Peter turned back to face the judges. "Not bad for a first day." Sam and Chef Adam got to their feet as Deena came forward to hand Peter a clipboard. "Listen up, people—I have a few tips for tomorrow's taping. First—and this is very, very important, be here promptly at nine." He glanced down at his papers. "No offense intended, but I have a few notes to pass along from our photography director. They are intended to help you show your very best sides."

First he turned to face Chef Adam and gave a little

bow. "We all *know* you're a real chef—not to be confused with Chef Boyardee."

Toby and I snickered, but the chef didn't crack a smile. He adjusted his toque, looking as if he'd like to dive across the table and strangle someone.

"Anyway, my camera people suggest that you lose the white coat. The camera does not love white and it washes out your color and makes you look sallow. And Toby"—he stroked his neck—"a scarf tomorrow maybe? Something salmon-colored perhaps? Our middle-aged quirks tend to show up more distinctly under the lights. . . ."

He smiled regretfully and looked at his clipboard again. "Mr. Rizzoli, watch the loud patterned shirts—they can be distracting to viewers, even make them dizzy. And if they're dizzy, they are likely to flip to another channel. And Miss Snow"—he grinned and patted his belly—"you have an adorable shape; shall we say plump like a guinea hen? Perhaps choose something less formfitting for the next episode? Less, yellow? But definitely no horizontal stripes, darling."

Sam Rizzoli snickered loudly enough so that everyone on the set heard him.

As color and heat rushed to my face, I felt myself shrinking into a puddle of humiliation. Then I got mad. The *Key Zest* shirt might very well be a fashion faux pas, but it was my faux pas. And that of my friend and ally Wally, who'd stood up for me this morning in the face of a raging bully.

"You wanted someone to represent *Key Zest* on your show," I heard myself say. "The shirt comes as part of the package."

Peter looked stunned but then he burst out laughing. "Brava! I didn't think you had it in you." He tossed his head, the white mane flying. "That's it, people. Until tomorrow."

I plastered on a smile, then gathered my backpack and sunglasses, and walked out. Wally owed me bigtime for this.

4

I'll have what she's having.

—Nora Ephron

I was already antsy about having dinner with Detective Bransford later this evening. But even though I'd stood up for myself in the end, Peter Shapiro's "guinea hen" comment magnified my nerves times ten. I tore through most of the items in my closet before settling on black jeans and a black sweater. According to my mother, who knows these things, sticking to one color was supposed to be slimming. And then I added my lucky red cowboy boots, which, as far as I was concerned, went with everything and took five pounds off, too. At least six times I checked my phone to re-read the exchange of text messages I'd had with Bransford last night.

Him: *I made a reservation at Michaels.*

Me: *Been dying to try Michaels. Sounds great.*

Him: *Steak from Chicago and Hayley from New Jersey, a perfect menu.*

He'd even added a little smiley face, which seemed utterly, nerve-wrackingly out of character. Once I was ready—too early—I paced in tiny circles around the living area, yelling out answers to *Jeopardy!* before the contestants could get to them.

"You're making me woozy," said Miss Gloria from her seat in the galley. "Come sit with me and try a bite of dinner. I used to fix this when the boys were little but I couldn't remember all the ingredients. I'd love a professional opinion." She patted the chair beside her, her smile a little quivery.

So I grabbed a fork and a small saucer from the dish drainer, plopped down in the seat at the kitchen table not occupied by sweet old ladies and pushy cats, and nibbled at her tuna casserole.

"What do you think?" she asked, grinning hopefully. Either Miss Gloria was terribly out of practice or had never really enjoyed cooking. I was betting on both, but especially the latter. Mayonnaise, pasta, and dark tuna in oil, all mixed together and heated through—something you might find on a college student's hot plate. Both cats were standing sentinel on the couch, drawn, I was sure, by the fishy odor.

"Delicious," I said, shuttering my eyes closed for dramatic effect. "It reminds me a bit of one of the chefs' dishes we chose this morning. Let's see . . . cheddar cheese, a hint of pickle relish, overtones of mayonnaise, a dash of dehydrated onion flakes?"

She giggled and ladled another spoonful onto my dish. "You forgot the Worcestershire sauce. That's my secret ingredient." She rested her elbow on the table and put her chin in her palm. Her eyes twinkled, set off by the rhinestones on her pink sweatshirt. "Do you think Nathan Bransford is *the one*?"

I shivered and let my fork clatter to the table, then crossed my arms in a big X to ward off that thought. "I have no idea—I'm really bad at this. I thought Chad Lutz was my destiny and you know how that worked out."

Chad and I had lasted five short weeks after I moved to Key West to live with him last fall. But to be painfully frank, I barely knew the guy when I followed him the length of the eastern seaboard—as my mother and my closest friends were fond of pointing out. In the end, I came out way on top, landing in the paradise of Key West, which might never have occurred to me otherwise. I thanked Miss Gloria again for the bite of casserole, excused myself, and went to brush my teeth for the third time this evening and grab my purse.

When we scheduled this dinner date, the detective—Nate, I had to remember to call him—had insisted on picking me up. He was old-fashioned that way, he'd said. Which made me a little more nervous because I like to be able to bolt if necessary. Plus, the idea of arriving at a restaurant in a police car made my stomach turn—and I'd never seen him drive anything else. At ten minutes to seven my phone buzzed with a call from Nate. My mind, programmed to expect disaster lately, assumed he was canceling.

"Sorry," he said. "I need to spin by the harbor and check something out. Do you mind meeting me at the restaurant? I may be a couple minutes late."

"No problem," I assured him, my blood pressure dropping a few points from the sheer relief of taking my own ride—and a little giddiness at knowing we were still on. I grabbed my coat, kissed Miss Gloria on the cheek, and kissed the gray *M* marked on Evinrude's forehead, and started down the dock toward my scooter.

Minutes later, I stood alone at the host's podium outside Michaels on Margaret Street, nervous as a polydactyl cat in a stampede of tipsy tourists. I would not have guessed that this unobtrusive gateway on a quiet residential street opened up into the charming courtyard of one of the best restaurants in town.

"Reservation for two, Bransford," I said smiling weakly at the host. "The other half of the party is running a little late."

"May I seat you outside?" asked the host, smoothing his tie down the length of his crisp, white shirt.

"Perfect," I said, although wondering whether Nate might rather be indoors. January was "winter" in Key West, like everywhere else in the northern hemisphere, and the locals took the season seriously. But the overhead heaters would warm the nip in the night air, and the splashing of the big fountain at the back of the courtyard might take a tiny edge off my nerves. I could see myself hyperventilating if we ended up trapped at a table in the back of the small indoor space.

I wasn't usually quite this nervous about dinner with a new man but Nate and I had suffered a series of ruinous interactions over the past few months, none of which could be properly called a first date. The evening on which my mother had tagged along might have been the worst outing in all of romantic history. Hard not to keep running over the script like a tongue on a rotten tooth. So I much preferred to back up and start fresh. On the other hand, that put all the first date pressure squarely on this evening.

The host seated me and assured me the waiter would be around shortly to take my order. I pulled out my phone. I'd promised myself that I wouldn't consider this dinner as review material for my food-critic job—it would be too easy to overlook important social cues if I was busy whittling clever sentences in my head about the food. On the other hand, eating out was a busman's holiday. How could I ignore it?

I snapped pictures of the fountain and the bar, which was buzzing with customers eating small plates of food and dipping vegetables and bread cubes into vats of fondue, and then jotted some notes on the décor. The rustic wooden floors, the living bamboo wall separating the restaurant from the property next door, the white wooden ceilings with fans, the strings of tiny lights following the line of the eaves, the clusters of tropical greenery with uplighting, all made it feel cozy and romantic. My phone buzzed with an incoming text message from Nate's phone number.

Fifteen minutes. Sorry. Order drink and appetizer. Be there asap.

Oh geez. Now I had the pressure of ordering for him piled on to the pressure of waiting for the date to begin. When the waiter stopped by, I selected "our salad" thick with shrimp, eggs, provolone, pepperoncinis, and salami for Nate because it sounded manly and substantial, and grilled asparagus with ham, roasted peppers, and Boursin cheese for me. And finally, I added a Bloody Mary for my jangling nerves.

I'd finished the asparagus (just a hair too much ham for my taste) and the drink, including licking the circle of celery salt off the rim, and begun nibbling on his salad—delicious, when he texted me again.

Twenty minutes. Order me a steak, medium-rare, and baked potato?

Which seemed odd. How long would it take to cook a steak? Why didn't he order when he got here? Maybe he was having regrets about the entire evening. I clicked back over to the messages I'd been studying all day. He hadn't sounded regretful—more like he was really looking forward to the date. Maybe he imagined we'd gobble the dinner and then go back to my place and . . . forget it. With no privacy to mention, there would be no romance on Miss Gloria's houseboat. Besides, I was nowhere near ready to take that step. I waved the waiter over, explained that my date was running even later than predicted, and ordered the strip steak for Nate, and the snapper meunière for me.

"We have a very popular chocolate lava cake for dessert," the waiter said. "It comes with vanilla ice cream. We like to warn folks ahead because we prepare them individually and they take about twenty minutes to bake. Shall I add that to your order?"

"Definitely," I said, mouth watering at the prospect. Pointing my internal compass toward that dense, warm chocolate would make me feel better, no matter what else happened—or didn't happen—tonight. "And could you bring along a glass of the house red wine and one of the white?" Nate hadn't said anything about alcohol and maybe he couldn't drink while on the job, but the longer I waited, the more nervous I felt. And I hated to drink alone.

After the waiter had cleared my appetizer plate and delivered the wine, I tapped the web address of the *Key West Citizen* into my phone to see if there might be breaking news in the crime report—something that would require the services of the top detective on the KW police force. But the latest entry—several hours earlier—was a story about a homeless man who'd been evicted from an Old Town bar for falling asleep and refusing to leave. I hoped it wasn't Turtle. In any case, that was a bread-and-butter no-brainer for Key West cops: Nate would never have been siphoned away from dinner to handle that.

Twenty minutes came and went and so did the waiter with our main courses. "Shall I keep the gentleman's dinner in the kitchen so it doesn't get cold?"

I glanced around to see if the other diners were watching, probably speculating that I'd been dumped. Not only dumped, but left with a big fat check. "He said he'd be here any minute," I told the waiter, who nodded with raised eyebrows, but then backed away.

Minutes passed, three then four. I hated to let my fish congeal in its rich artichoke sauce. So even though I felt awkward and foolish about eating solo in the flickering candlelight, only the untouched steak sitting at the place across from me, I dug in. The fish was buttery and delicious. And the wine slid down my throat like a sudden rain through a dry riverbed, dampening my embarrassment at dining alone at a table clearly set for two.

Finally, my phone rang. Private caller. "Hello?"

"It's Detective Bransford. Nathan. Nate. I'm not going to make it," he said brusquely. "I'm really sorry."

"Rats! I'm sorry, too." The combination of feeling slightly tipsy and quite relieved made me babble. "The food has been wonderful so far. Can I wrap your steak and bring it to you?"

"Not necessary," he said. "I won't have time to eat it. I'll call the front desk and give them my credit card number."

"Don't worry about it. What's wrong?" I couldn't help adding, my curiosity kicking up a notch. In the distance, outside the restaurant, I could hear the shriek of sirens heading down Southard Street. Toward him?

"Looks like a silly prank gone bad," he growled. "Or if we're really unlucky, a suicide."

He never would have told me this much if he hadn't just stood me up at one of the nicest restaurants in town. "Where are you?" I asked.

"At the old harbor," he said. "Hang on another minute."

Then I heard another man's voice rumbling a question and Bransford's tense bark in return. "Find the owner of the boat. Now! And for god's sake, take a few pictures and then get the damn body down before the damn press gets here."

And then he came back on the line to me: "Sorry. I don't know when we'll get things wrapped up. Probably late. We've got a lousy situation. Why don't you finish eating and go ahead home and I'll phone you later if it's not too late."

"Fine," I said, at the same time I was signaling to the waiter for the check.

If there was a strange body on a vessel down at the harbor and Nate was in charge of the investigation, I wanted to find out what happened. Call me curious or just plain nosy, but I wasn't going to sit here alone and continue forking down the calories—though leaving the chocolate lava cake broke my heart. I hung up, and asked the waiter: "Could you box up the steak and the dessert and bring the bill? I'm kind of in a hurry."

I bungeed the aromatic package to the back of my bike and headed the few blocks over to the harbor. A quartet of blue lights flashed against the starlit sky, and beams of light probed the rigging of the moored boats. The water carried garbled gruff voices to the street corner where I'd stopped. The cops had gathered on one of the docks midharbor, and appeared to be peering through the forest of rigging to the darkness at the far end, where the mast of one of the smaller sailboats listed to the right. Squinting in the dim light, I was able to make out a bulky weight three-quarters of the way up the mast, which looked unlike any of the other boats' equipment.

Swallowing hard, not wanting to think too much about that lump, I parked my bike and circled around to the finger that led to the sailboat's dock, stopping at the chain with its rusty KEEP OUT sign hanging from the links. I peered at the weight again. Could it be a radar machine? An extra sail? A puff of wind gusted and the boat listed to a forty-five-degree angle, the dark lump swinging out toward the water, the mast groaning under the load.

I stepped over the chain and moved closer. To my

absolute horror, the heavy weight took the definite shape of a human figure. Dangling from the mast. White sneakered feet were illuminated by the beam of a flashlight. The wind picked up, pushing the person back and forth on the groaning rope like an oversized metronome. Two officers struggled to lower the figure to land.

I started up the dock, edging a few steps nearer.

"Go easy," said one voice to the other. "He hits the deck and we destroy evidence and our necks are on the block."

As the figure lurched and bounced down the mast toward the deck, a bright searchlight was switched on, lighting up the bizarre details: first the curly platinum-blond hair that had to be a wig and the red lipstick. Then the discolored features, the protruding tongue, the bulging eyes. And finally, a black cloak. The body landed on the deck with a resounding thud.

"Turtle?" The word came out before I could stop it and echoed over the water. I clapped my hand to my mouth.

"What are you doing here?" Bransford's voice boomed behind me, causing my pulse to gallop and my guilt-o-meter to surge.

I turned, met his angry eyes, and shrugged. "I was on my way back to houseboat row. I wanted to help. I brought your dinner over. I know I can't work worth a darn on an empty stomach, so I thought maybe you—"

"Go home," he said, and pushed past me toward the knot of cops and the body.

5

I would think a chef would look at me and kind of go, "Pfft, move on with your little fried self," he said.

—Katy Vine

When I arrived at our houseboat, Miss Gloria was watching a rerun of a cooking show on the Food Network while talking on the phone with my mother. They'd become fast friends after my mom stayed with us for a few days earlier this month. On the TV screen across the room, Emeril was hacking a chicken to pieces and then dredging the pieces in egg and flour.

"You're home early," said Miss Gloria, her face lighting up with a huge smile. Then the smile faded away. "Maybe home early from a big date isn't good news, though, is it?"

Mom's voice floated through the receiver. "How was her dinner with Nate?"

"I'll put you on speakerphone, so you can hear it first-hand," said Miss Gloria, even as I tried to wave her off.

I dropped the sack of leftovers on the coffee table and flopped onto the couch. Evinrude and Sparky hopped up to investigate the scent of grilled meat. After shooing the cats away, I gave my mother and Miss Gloria the short version of how I'd ended up eating alone, then a whitewashed version of seeing the hanged man down by the harbor.

"I'm scared to death it was Turtle, the homeless guy I bought coffee for this morning."

"Why would you think that?" Mom asked.

I explained about his cloak and Turtle's cape, but then had to agree with Miss Gloria's assessment—a hundred folks on this island might own a garment like that. Our island is rife with costume parties and pirate events and just plain kooky people. Besides, why in the world would a homeless man be wearing a wig and lipstick? Not that that helped me feel better in the grand scheme of things—a man was still horribly dead.

"So you never even saw Nate?" asked Mom.

"I ran into him at the dock," I said, and then admitted that he and I seemed to fit together like nails on a chalkboard.

"Even considering that he was called in to deal with an awful crime," I said, "he was pretty harsh when I tried to drop off the food."

"What were you wearing?" she asked.

"Mom! What does that have to do with anything?"

"I'm sorry, darling," said my mother. "You're completely right. Your Nate has such a stressful job. He probably doesn't always handle it as well as he might." She cleared her throat. "I liked him quite a bit when I met him. But maybe he really isn't ready to date again."

"Was it Maya Angelou who said 'when people show you who they are, believe them'?" asked Miss Gloria. Which seemed like deep wisdom from a tiny old lady in a sparkly pastel sweatsuit.

"On another subject," said my mother, "how are the plans for Connie's wedding coming?" Connie was my college roommate. She'd grown close to my mother after hers died of cancer during our freshman year.

"She's so busy," I said. "I haven't heard anything except they want it to be on the beach."

"But it's only two months away," said Mom. "What's she going to wear? Are there any attendants other than you? What are you going to wear? And what about the reception? What will they serve?"

I felt a rising surge of panic. If Connie was too overwhelmed to plan the occasion, the maid of honor should step up. Me. "I'll get on it," I said. "And keep you posted."

I had to drag myself out of bed the next morning. The caffeine in the chocolate lava cake that Miss Gloria and I had bolted down after hanging up with my mother, along with my alternating feelings of disappointment and humiliation over the interaction with Nate had kept me awake for hours. And worst of all, the sound of that body hitting the deck with a sickening thunk. Had it been Turtle?

One quick look in the mirror confirmed the crepey bags under my eyes: I had no business being on television. Besides that, I was wicked nervous about appearing on camera again. It would have been kinder for the show's theoretical audience—and me—if I went back to bed. Instead I showered, troweled on some miracle concealer that my mom had left behind on her recent visit, and spent a little extra time blow-drying my curls into submission. Then I donned the yellow *Key Zest* shirt again, layering it over a pair of snug black jeans. Finally, I swallowed a cup of coffee, laced up my favorite black sequined sneakers and headed downtown to the Studios of Key West.

I parked my scooter in between a Smart car and a motorcycle on Southard Street and walked through the alley behind the Armory building, which normally housed art receptions and artists' studios, to the courtyard in back. Chef Adam and Toby Davidson were already on the back porch of the little conch house; Sam Rizzoli was nowhere to be seen. Deena Smith was overseeing the application of makeup to the chef candidates in the other corner of the square.

"Morning, Deena!" I called out. She waved back and returned to her work.

I ducked through the sculpture garden to the porch and trudged up the steps. The lead cameraman muttered: "What do you people not understand about nine o'clock sharp?"

"Sorry," I said, and scuttled across the deck to take my place at the table. "Take a chill pill," I added under my breath. "I'm five minutes late. And it's Key West."

He began to suit us up with microphones, laying Sam's wires and power pack on the table in front of his empty chair. Through the mullions of the glass doors that led into the kitchen, I could see our producer/director, Peter Shapiro, on the phone—getting some crummy news from the look of dismay on his face. He punched a button on his phone, threw it onto the counter, and strode out onto the porch. His ruddy complexion had paled and his blue eyes watered. He gestured for all the TV personnel to move away from the set.

"I need to speak with the judges," he explained curtly. Then he approached us, leaned forward, his hands on our table, and spoke in a low voice. "We've had some unfortunate news," he said, lips thinning to a grim line. "Mr. Rizzoli is dead."

Toby gasped. "Oh my goodness, whatever happened? We can certainly reschedule. Or I for one, would understand completely if the show's taping is cancelled."

I raised a finger to indicate that I agreed.

Peter shook his head and smoothed a lock of white hair off his forehead. "I realize the news is horrifying," he said in a soothing voice. "I feel ill myself, but I beg you to understand that we must proceed with filming. We'll certainly be respectful of any services that are planned. But we've spent too much money and time on the show to risk letting it die—and even more importantly, these chefs have their careers riding on the outcome." He waved across the courtyard to the makeup area, where the three chefs whose food we'd chosen yesterday were being groomed for their first appearance.

"What in the world happened to him?" Toby asked. "He was much too young for a heart attack. Though in these stressful days I suppose men succumb younger and younger. Of all people, I should know that much." She frowned, her eyes sad.

Peter rubbed his chin, then said, "Mr. Rizzoli appears to have been murdered."

"Oh tell me no," I said, melting down in my chair, the horrible image of the dead man I'd seen on the rigging flashing to mind, oversized like the picture at a drive-in horror movie. "Tell me he wasn't found hanging from a sailboat's mast last night."

Peter looked shocked. "I certainly hope not! Where in the world did you hear that?"

I shrugged, wishing I could take my comment back. "There was a big brouhaha down at the harbor—something to do with a hanged man. They weren't letting anyone get too close. I imagine you can find the details in the paper."

"You were there?"

"Close enough to get a ghastly view that I wish I hadn't seen."

"I'm not privy to the details of how Sam died," Peter said. "We can only hope that wasn't him." He looked away from me to the other two judges and rapped his knuckles on the table. "Are we in agreement? We can continue?"

"Give us a minute," I said and turned my back on him to consult with Chef Adam and Toby. "We don't have to do this if it doesn't feel right." It didn't feel right to me, especially considering the way Rizzoli might have died. If in fact I'd seen his corpse last night.

"But I do worry about those young people who came to cook today," said Toby in a low voice, lifting her chin at the chef candidates.

They looked so excited. And after all, having written the memoir about her husband's death, wasn't she an expert on working through grief?

"More to the point," said Chef Adam, "yes, it's a

tragedy, but if the world stopped every time someone died, nothing would get accomplished. I don't mean to sound callous, but did either of you know him personally? I liked him fine and he seemed to know his way around a kitchen table . . . but yesterday was the first time I'd met him."

I most certainly wasn't going to mention my connection: how I'd trashed his restaurant in our magazine. "I've seen his name in the paper from time to time," I said. "He was a city commissioner, right? And kind of controversial."

I was pretty sure he'd stirred up some kind of trouble recently about widening the cruise ship channel. I remembered reading comments in the Citizen's Voice that suggested he voted for things that would advance his businesses, to hell with the town's needs.

"That doesn't mean he should have been murdered," Toby squeaked.

"Of course not," I said. Though if I were the police, I'd be asking questions about exactly this. Local politics on this island were anything but cozy.

"So you didn't know him either?" Chef Adam asked Toby. She shook her head no. "Then I'd suggest we go ahead and get this over with. I'm losing money every minute I sit here without getting anything accomplished. I told my kitchen staff I would be out two days, three at the most."

I reluctantly agreed. Wally was expecting an article on this chef competition for *Key Zest*. And my own scramble to get hired was recent enough that I could understand how fiercely the candidates on this show wanted to succeed. I could feel the buzz of their excited and nervous energy from twenty-five yards away. They'd be devastated to hear the show's taping had been canceled. Because canceling the taping would very likely mean the end of the opportunity. Peter Shapiro had warned us early on that he was operating with a gossamer-thin budget.

I threw my hands up in agreement and Chef Adam signaled to Peter that we were prepared to continue.

"Wonderful!" Peter clapped his hands together, flashing a relieved and grateful smile. "Here's how the morning will go. We'll introduce the candidates one at a time. You will want to ask them about the dish they prepared for you yesterday—their ingredients, their methods, their philosophy of cooking. Open-ended questions work best—sometimes these amateurs freeze in front of the camera. Try to understand their ambitions to host a cooking show—see how well they can explain themselves. And why do they think they would make a popular host? What do they bring to the table that's fresh? And always, look for a sense of humor—the audience will eat that up. At the end of the segment, I'll announce the challenge for tomorrow."

"I assume their personal lives should be off-limits?" I asked.

"Of course not," said Peter, rubbing his hands together and grinning. "The juicier the better. And remember, our job is to edit the whole mess into something viewable. In other words, don't worry too much about the blunders you make or dead ends you wander down. We expect all that. We'll fix it."

"But we'll try not to embarrass the candidates, correct?" asked Toby.

Peter all but rolled his eyes. "They've all signed releases giving us rights in perpetuity for their image and likeness. This is television, people, not grammar school. We take whatever they give us and exploit the bloody hell out of it!"

He flashed a big smile, adjusted his glasses, and snapped his fingers at the group hovering across the courtyard. Two men with cameras moved forward and began to film the chefs as they trooped from the courtyard to the TV set. Catching an oblique glimpse of myself in the monitor that had been set up in the kitchen, I tried to fluff up my helmet-flattened curls. Deena herded the first chef over to the porch; he looked like he felt as though he was the next chicken on the chopping block.

Peter took a few steps back and began to speak: "Ladies and gentlemen, meet our first contestant, Randy Thompson." He took the wrist of the slender man with green eyes and bleached blond hair gelled into points and pulled him forward. "Randy was born in Texas and raised near Houston. He moved here about ten years ago and has worked as a line cook in several of our Key West restaurants. He is also a singer who enjoys performing at local bars. Randy focuses on Keys-style cuisine and comfort food and says he loves highlighting local flavors in the meals he prepares."

Randy faked a curtsy and laughed, like a man who wasn't afraid of having a little fun once he relaxed, even at his own expense.

"You will remember enjoying his dish 'Homestyle Shrimp and Cheesy Grits,' which he says he based on a polenta recipe handed down from his grandmother,"

Peter continued. "Randy, please take a seat in front of our panel of distinguished judges."

Randy sat at the table, across from the three of us. Up close, he looked nervous and chalky under the makeup. The cameraman zoomed in and caught him licking his lips.

"Please tell us about your grandmother and her influence on your cooking style," I said before Adam could fire off a hardball that might cause Randy to crumble.

The skin around his eyes crinkled as he smiled at me. "Grandma loved company in the kitchen," he said. "But none of her other grandkids were much interested so I enjoyed the undivided benefit of her experience. She taught me about both Italian food and Southern-style recipes—like how to wrestle your vegetables into submission by boiling them for hours with salt pork, and how to tame your fear of butter. And Crisco."

"You've got to be kidding," said Chef Adam. "Crisco?"

Randy grinned again and patted his stomach, which was perfectly flat. "I don't believe in diet foods—they taste horrible and they trick people into thinking they are eating healthy and so can eat more. My theory is that diners should learn to eat fabulous food, only in smaller portions."

Chef Adam leaned forward, fingers knotted together. "So then, you are essentially repeating Grandmother's repertoire. But wouldn't you imagine that shrimp and grits might be found on fifty percent of the menus in America—at least in the southern half of the country? How would you stand out as the host of

Topped Chef? And how would your propensity toward fattening foods fit in with a world struggling with a full-blown obesity epidemic?" He sat back, looking satisfied.

By now I wished I couldn't see the monitor at all. I'd heard that the camera added ten pounds—on me it looked closer to twenty. And the slight time delay had the effect of repeating everything twice, making me feel as though I were moving in slow motion. Underwater. Bad enough to go through all this once.

Randy's face paled and he stumbled through an explanation of how he took solid cooking as his baseline and tweaked it with local flavors. "I'm not afraid of a deep-fat fryer," he insisted.

"Bravo," said Toby. "The restraint should come from the diner, not the chef."

"Fascinating stuff," said Peter Shapiro, "but we must move on to our second contestant." He hustled Randy out of the spotlight and had him sit on a high stool at the far end of the porch.

"Now, judges, what do you think about Randy's prospects?" he asked us.

No one said anything.

"You want us to talk about him now?" Toby asked, her pale eyebrows knitting together as she frowned. "Right here where everyone can hear us, including him?"

"That's the whole idea," Peter said. "It's reality television. No conflict, no ratings." He backed away, smiling a little stiffly, and signaled for us to continue the discussion.

More silence. We kept our eyes on the table, and

squirmed in our seats. Finally, I couldn't stand it. I had to say something.

"He clearly loves food," I said. "Seems like he'd be able to connect with home cooks. That's why my mom is nuts about Rachael Ray. Mom could sauté circles around her and yet she loves watching Rachael's show. She has a certain warmth that she's able to telegraph to her viewers. She makes us feel like we're friends at the table in her kitchen. I sense a similar possibility with Randy. I think his personality would really shine if he wasn't quite so nervous. His jitters would get worked out with a little more practice. And I'd love to meet his grandmother."

Chef Adam groaned. "You want to invite his granny? Sure death to our ratings. And don't we have enough low-brow shows on the air?" he asked. "If I want something fried, I'll go to the diner downtown, or even"—he shuddered—"a fast-food restaurant. How would this be different from what's out there already?"

"He's a man," Toby offered. "Maybe he'd appeal to gentlemen viewers?"

Through the glass doors into the kitchen, I could see that Peter Shapiro and Deena had begun to argue in heated whispers. He thrust his clipboard at her and strode back out onto the porch.

"Cut!" Peter swept his glasses off and clasped his free hand over his eyes. After heaving a great sigh, he replaced the glasses and then dropped his hands to his sides. "People, you have to speak your minds more bluntly here. This is reality television, not an edited sound bite on public radio. Viewers have the attention spans of gnats. You're losing them. You're losing me.

You're flat, you're forced, you're stiff." He wiggled his shoulders. "Let's loosen up, shall we?"

Chef Adam's face reddened and I imagined he was thinking what I was thinking: I quit.

"Honestly, Mr. Shapiro," said Toby, "it's hard to concentrate after getting that news about Mr. Rizzoli. It makes all this feel"—she gestured at the cameras, her lips trembling as she searched for the right words—"rather inconsequential."

Shapiro forced a smile but his voice softened. "Understood. We are all in shock over the news. But again, I must ask you to think about these young chefs. They have big dreams. Are you willing to quit on them because of this tragedy? I think not. You are our experts, handpicked. We brought you on board because we believe you can help us find the next star. Think outside the food here, people. Can you see the kernel of celebrity in one of our contestants?"

He made eye contact with each of us, his blue eyes intense, then waved forward a thin, tanned man with a long ponytail and settled him in the chair that Randy had vacated. With one hand on the man's shoulder, Peter turned to address the camera.

"Buddy Higgs has completed a number of internships in well-known kitchens, and dreams of opening his own restaurant. He takes the nouveau cuisine of Grant Achatz in Chicago and the former chef Ferran Adrià at El Bulli as his models. He would love to bring the sophistication of molecular gastronomy to the American public."

I fidgeted silently. Molecular gastronomy—replete with its foams, fumes, tubes of aspic, tubs of foie gras, and peculiar combinations and arrangements of spices—was something I felt the public could safely ignore. Higgs must have been the creator of yesterday's oddball lobster salad over which Chef Adam and the now-deceased Sam Rizzoli had swooned. I remembered tasting parsnip chips, caviar, jalapeños, saffron threads, mustard seeds, and god only knows what else in the lobster dish. I also remembered yearning for some simple steamed lobster meat and a ramekin of melted butter.

"I'm curious, Mr. Higgs," I said. "Why should the public take an interest in molecular gastronomy? My impression has been that the techniques are so complicated, and the results so, well, odd, that most folks—your TV viewers—will find this type of cuisine way over their heads. They cook with pots and stoves, not test tubes and Bunsen burners."

Buddy Higgs cleared his throat and touched a finger to his mustache, which undulated like a struggling caterpillar. "I believe you underestimate the public, Miss Snow." He leaned forward and tapped on the table in front of me. "Chef Ashatz," he said, "is purely a genius. What he has been able to do—and what I hope to expand upon—is to make his dining customers think."

"Example, please," said Chef Adam.

"Who says surf and turf has to be plain old lobster and steak? Why not a dish pairing foie gras with anchovies?" Buddy smiled slyly.

I could only think how grateful I was that he hadn't prepared this yesterday. First of all, anchovies remind me of hair-covered fish bait. Paired with foie gras? I would have struggled to choke it down.

"What would be the point of that?" asked Toby, her forehead furrowed.

"The point is not to present mounds of fatty food for already-overweight patrons to gobble," said Buddy. "The point is to challenge people as they eat. Food should be stimulating for the mind as well as the palate!"

For the first time, I saw the spark of creativity and joy that he hoped to convey in his cooking. But I still wasn't dying to try more of it, nor did I imagine him as a popular TV personality. Maybe a small cult audience would follow him.

Peter surged forward, clapped Buddy on the back, and directed him to take the stool next to Randy. "Thank you, Mr. Higgs. Panelists? Your impressions?"

"I may be too simpleminded," said Toby, "but I don't quite get why I should have to think this hard over dinner."

"He's an interesting fellow," I said, "and I can imagine the first few episodes making quite a splash. After that?" I shook my head. "I believe viewers would lose interest. Most Americans wouldn't have a single one of his ingredients in their larder."

"He's cutting-edge. He's brilliant," said Chef Adam grimly. "Can't you see the difference between choosing someone who cooks like his doddering grandmother and a host who is a brilliant professional?"

After a few more minutes, Peter cut off further discussion and brought forward Henrietta Stentzel, the third chef candidate. I sunk a little lower in my chair and avoided looking at her face.

"Please meet chef Henrietta Stentzel, Henri to her

friends," said Peter. "Ms. Stentzel owns and operates a burrito restaurant in Key West, and is the former owner of Hola on Miami Beach. Judges, you will remember her for her seafood fra diavolo presentation." He guided her to the hot seat and backed away. "Take it away, judges."

"I'm puzzled," said Chef Adam. "You chose to present an Italian dish and yet your background appears to be in Mexican food. Explain."

Henri grinned, looking everywhere but at me. "I love all kinds of food, but Mexican seafood dishes are not my favorite part of that ethnic tradition. On the other hand, when I'm in a restaurant that offers anything in a fra diavolo sauce, I leap to order it. If I were to land this show, I would love to share a variety of dishes with the viewers. My techniques are not overly complicated, but I like to spread the word about seasonal foods, along with spices that may not be common to the American palate."

"It sounds like such a show might appeal to a niche market, rather than the broader public," Toby said.

Henri leaned forward and spoke eagerly. "That's exactly the prejudice my show could fight. American food is not just steak and potatoes. It's cilantro, oregano, cumin, basil. I would love to introduce viewers to new things, to encourage them to try recipes they never dreamed they'd enjoy. And to show them how the foods from other countries have shaped our American way of eating."

"Your seafood dish was delightful," I said, unable to think of a single thing to say that wouldn't get her hackles up.

We stumbled through some other questions and then, as with the others, Peter instructed us to discuss her presentation and her personality while she looked on.

"There's nothing particularly wrong with her," said Chef Adam, "but where's the beef?"

"What do you mean by that?" Toby asked. "She's not a vegetarian chef."

His eyes rolled back in his head.

"I think it was a lame joke," I said. "He probably meant: where's the sparkle? She's got a lovely message, but maybe she's too nervous for it to come through clearly? Maybe that would improve with time?" I was starting to sound like a Key West–style Pollyanna.

My gaze darted over to Henri, who was glaring, laser-eyed, at me, right along with Chef Adam. I patted my hair and fiddled with my microphone. I could not have felt more uncomfortable and I was sure it showed.

"On reality TV," said Chef Adam, "there is no time to improve. Slooooooow-ly. Either you're scintillating off the blocks or the viewers punch their clickers and change channels."

"I didn't realize you were such an expert on reality TV," I said sweetly.

Peter was grinning madly on the sidelines. "Let's wrap things up for today," he said, striding to the middle of the porch. "Contestants, here is your challenge for tomorrow: Key West is the site for many destination weddings. Tell us about the themes you would exploit if you were hired to do a wedding. And bring a sample of a signature drink for the prospective bride and groom and a piece of your wedding cake."

The cameras panned the faces of the three contestants—Henri's expression pleasant and interested, Randy's excited, and Buddy's, disgusted.

Peter signaled for them to stay seated and then turned to address the judges. "Before I let you three go, let's buzz over where we are so far. If you had to choose today, do or die, for whom would you vote?"

"Ms. Stentzel, absolutely," said Toby. "Women have cooked meals for centuries and I'm sick to death of male chefs pushing forward to take the limelight when suddenly there's some money to be made of it."

My jaw nearly dropped open to my knees. I wouldn't have expected her to voice such a strong opinion. I said: "Point well taken, but are you saying we should choose a woman simply because she's female? If we go on just what we've seen so far, I'm liking Randy Thompson."

Chef Adam shook his head impatiently. "Buddy Higgs's food and his presentation as a chef are head and shoulders above the others." He pointed at the cameraman and said, "Cut!" and then turned to address Peter. "This is not for the camera. I think it was a mistake to continue without Sam Rizzoli. I'm not seeing how this panel has the necessary level of expertise to make an informed decision." He faced me again. "Are you aware of the details of Randy Thompson's so-called entertainment career?"

I shrugged and made a *who cares* face.

"He's a drag queen. How do you think that will play with the American TV viewing public?"

"Great stuff!" said Peter to us. And then "Cut!" to the cameraman. "Finally, we've got some conflict!"

6

Whatever I would have expected to feel at this moment, excitement, sadness, anger, frustration, exhilaration, is suddenly obscured by a sudden and almost uncontrollable urge for a bowl of escarole soup.
—Meredith Mileti, *Aftertaste*

A thick layer of gray clouds had dropped low during the time we were filming, bringing a spitting rain that matched my mood. I agreed with Chef Adam on one thing: It had been a mistake to continue. And clearly Peter Shapiro was uninterested in respecting anyone's boundaries. He had told us he would go for the jugular, and now I could see that he meant it.

I gathered up my backpack and sweater, wondering how to convince Wally that I had to bail out of the TV reality show assignment because one of the judges had been murdered and another was an idiot. Obviously a drag queen wasn't exactly corn-belt Americana, but this was Key West. Drag shows were obligatory fun on

Duval Street and some of the best entertainment in Florida came out of those clubs. Not that I completely understood the urge for a guy to dress up as a girl and dance around onstage, but if people loved to watch them and if it heated their skillets, why would anyone care? And if Peter Shapiro was looking for sparks— something livelier than your average "produce a homey casserole" cooking show—a chef in drag could be the answer.

I hurried across the courtyard—I couldn't wait to get out of here. But as I reached the alley that led out of the complex, I slammed into a City of Key West policeman who was emerging—officer Steve Torrence. And another cop was right behind him.

"Sorry," I said. "I wasn't watching." I extricated myself from the wall of blue and started around them, down the alley to the street.

Torrence touched my elbow as I passed, his brown eyes cool. "Could we have a moment of your time?" he asked. "We have a few questions about Sam Rizzoli."

Could we have a moment? in police vernacular really means *Get over here now.* And what were the chances that Nate wouldn't have told the other cops how I'd showed up at the harbor last night when Rizzoli was found? Practically nil.

So I followed them back into the courtyard and waited while Torrence announced in his booming voice to the milling crowd that they needed to talk to everyone on the set. Everyone.

Despite Peter's pro forma blustering about wasting everyone's time, the judges, chef contestants, and TV show personnel were herded into the main building of TSKW, seated in two rows of folding chairs, and then taken one by one to a far corner of the cavernous room. I sat between Randy Thompson and Toby Davidson, unable to think of any small talk that wouldn't cause problems. I'd said all I wanted to say about the TV show for today and I certainly didn't want to discuss Rizzoli. Compare recipes? Hardly appropriate. Toby looked small and scared. Randy, an odd mixture of impatient and anxious. And I felt nervous myself, for no good reason.

Finally, I was called over. I sat facing two cops, my heart racing and my thoughts racing even faster. A line of sweat broke out on my upper lip, though I had absolutely no connection with the dead man, other than spending one morning with him on the TV show set when he was still alive. And the bad review of his restaurant, of course. But what bearing would that have on his hideous hanging? These guys knew me—they would have to know I wasn't involved. And why would they need my opinion on that death when the harbor had been crawling with law enforcement officials who'd seen the same thing, only much closer?

After adjusting his glasses and smoothing his dark mustache, Torrence began the questions. "Miss Snow, as you are aware, we're investigating the death of Sam Rizzoli. We understand that you spent the morning here yesterday with him during the first day of the *Topped Chef* contest. Did he seem disturbed about anything?"

"Since I'd never met him before, I don't have a baseline for his behavior. We didn't agree on much so we argued a lot, but I have no idea what he's like normally. Was like," I added.

The second cop cleared his throat and uncrossed his legs.

"Argued?" asked Torrence, nodding at his partner and tapping his finger on the clipboard that lay on his lap.

Here we went. A familiar downward spiral—the cops leaping to conclusions because I used one wrong word or otherwise showed some small sign of acting guilty. I scrambled to repair the impression I might have given.

"Discussing, that's more like what I meant. We were only talking about food—nothing life and death. Yesterday was day one of the shooting." I waved my hand at the door, beyond which were the courtyard and the porch where the filming had taken place. "Four of us judges had to choose the three best dishes out of the six we were presented with. It was not easy; we all have strong opinions and different perspectives on cooking. Mr. Rizzoli seemed to have a preference for fancy recipes and haute cuisine. I don't think he and I voted the same way on any of them. And . . ." My words trailed off.

"And?" Torrence prompted.

I sighed. "You'll figure this out anyway. My review of his restaurant went live on the *Key Zest* Web site yesterday. It wasn't exactly complimentary."

I looked down at my fingers, twisted together on my lap, and then took a deep breath.

"But I sure wouldn't kill him or anyone else over a

difference of opinion on a recipe. And really, who would? And I didn't pick up on any particular tension with any of the other folks here, because I know that's going to be your next question." Feeling a little calmer, I squinted at Torrence, suddenly noticing that he looked bulkier. Almost buff. "Have you been going to the gym a lot? You look—different."

He puffed up a little and grinned like crazy but then his partner rolled his eyes and he gathered himself back into his stern-cop persona.

"You seem to believe Rizzoli was murdered," the other cop said.

"I guess I just assumed. From the way he was found. Wouldn't it have been enormously difficult for a man alone to hang himself from that rigging?" I rubbed my palm over my forehead. "And wouldn't that be a particularly harsh suicide? You would be making quite a statement, dressed up like that. Imagine how the people he left behind would feel. Though I suppose that would be true if someone killed him, too."

Then I remembered an article I'd read online last month. "Could it have been a case of autoerotic asphyxiation? Or maybe someone tried to make it look like that . . ." My words trailed off as Torrence and the other cop exchanged shuttered glances.

"Why did you show up at the harbor last night?" Torrence asked.

I pinched my eyes closed and tried to stay calm. Tried to tell myself he was only doing his job. "Not that my love life is any of your business, but I had a date with Detective Bransford. I was waiting at the restaurant and he kept texting to say he'd been delayed.

When he finally called with the news that he wasn't going to make it, he told me he was detained at the harbor. So I took a ride over that way on the way home."

"But why would you?" he asked. "Swing by the harbor, I mean, not go out with Bransford." His face softened, and he almost smiled again.

I snickered. "Though that's probably a good question, too, right?"

Seeing the other cop's face harden, I slumped forward, elbows to knees, wishing I had an easy answer. Old-fashioned curiosity—a Pavlovian urge to rubberneck—seemed like the wrong response. And I didn't very much like that about myself either.

"I packed up the steak the detective had asked me to order and the chocolate lava cake, thinking he'd be hungry later and glad to have the food." I wiped my eyes and heaved a great sigh before looking back up at Torrence. "I wish I hadn't gone. I wish I hadn't seen what I saw. It was gruesome. And if that was Sam Rizzoli, I'm sorry for him. It was an ugly way to go out—someone must have been really, really angry to leave him like that. Whoever it was," I added lamely.

Torrence turned his chin over his shoulder to the place where the rest of the cast and crew waited. "You're certain you didn't notice that one of the other folks here might have had a beef with Rizzoli?"

I shook my head. "I'll be glad to let you know if I remember anything different."

"We'll be in touch," he said, as he pointed across the room at Randy Thompson and gestured for him to approach.

I got up, feeling relieved to be off the hot seat, but a little battered.

"What was your relationship with the late Sam Rizzoli?" the second officer asked Randy as I walked away.

"Not good," I heard Randy say defiantly. "Lousy. But I didn't kill him."

7

*If Mom and I had one thing in common, it
was the urge to cook and eat during a crisis. Even the whiff of crisis brought a surge
of recipes to our minds.*

—Hayley Snow

If Eric had been in town instead of vacationing in Miami, I would have called him and invited him for lunch
and thereby scored an informal counseling session. He
had a way of jollying me out of the worst sort of funk,
and as a psychologist, he understood how to handle
people better than most anyone else I knew. He would
have known which parts of the last twenty-four hours
I really needed to vent about and which might simply
fade away with time. And he'd have tips about how to
get the picture of the hanged man out of my head.

My second best option was Lorenzo, the tarot card
reader. I almost always felt calmer after talking to him,
too, though the process was less easy to define. Raisin-
sized raindrops began to splat onto my face as I reached

my scooter. I pulled a crumpled blue windbreaker from my backpack and slipped it on. I doubted Lorenzo would be at his card table on Mallory Square if this weather kept up. But he'd given me his phone number back when I first moved to Key West so I dialed him up anyway.

"Lorenzo, it's Hayley Snow. What time will you be setting up shop?"

"Probably not happening today. I've got a meeting of the Mallory Square board later this afternoon. And the forecast is awful. Maybe tomorrow?"

My stomach rumbled, a familiar combination of hunger and disappointment. The idea of having him over for lunch popped into my mind and then out of my mouth before I could lose my nerve.

"How about lunch?" I asked brightly.

"Lunch?" He sounded surprised, yet pleased. "Why not?"

Now that I had an important guest, next came the problem of what to make. I craved something simple and warm—comfort food—to offset the gloomy weather and the deflating morning. The dish I would have prepared if I had been competing in the contest sprang to mind. "Do you like fish chowder?"

"Sure," he said.

"It's a red sauce base, not the creamy white New England kind," I added.

"Better and better," he said.

I gave him directions to Miss Gloria's houseboat, and then hung up and punched her number into my phone. "Hey, it's Hayley. Okay with you if I asked my friend Lorenzo to pop over for lunch?"

Gloria shrieked with excitement. "The tarot man? Oh what fun! What should I wear? What are you serving? Should I set the table inside or out?"

"Better make it inside," I said with a laugh. "It's raining. Could you fish the tub of chunky tomato basil sauce out of the freezer and defrost it? I have it labeled."

I fired up my scooter and drove four blocks south down Southard Street and then hooked a right over to the Eaton Street Seafood Market. In the market, I chose a pound of grouper, then continued up Eaton to Cole's Peace Bakery to buy a loaf of ciabatta bread to make croutons, along with a small assortment of cookies. I nibbled on a mango triangle on my way out the door. Flaky and not too sweet—pure heaven.

By the time I reached Tarpon Pier, it was almost noon and still drizzling. The damp weather brought out the aromas of the marina—the lingering fishy smell from the cleaning table, the fresh scent of someone's laundry drying in our mini-Laundromat, the sharp odors of marine oil and gasoline. I dashed up the dock to our boat and skidded across the deck, leaving my wet slicker on a hook outside the sliding glass door. Inside, the two cats were splayed on a paisley tablecloth that Miss Gloria had spread over her Formica table in front of the banquette in the galley. She emerged from her bedroom and let out a horrified yelp.

"Scat, you bad kitties!"

I scooped up Evinrude and dropped him to the floor with a thunk. He wound in between my legs purring, not the least bit chastened.

"Is this too much?" Miss Gloria asked, spinning in a circle to show me the sweat suit she'd chosen. The stretchy white pants had a line of blue rhinestones marching down each leg, and bejeweled blue manatees swam across the front of the shirt. "I can change . . ."

"It's so cute." I grinned, reminded of how lucky I'd gotten in the roommate department. "*You're* so cute. He's going to love you."

Once the half-frozen tomato sauce was warming in a pan, I began to dice zucchini, black olives, and onions while Miss Gloria cut the ciabatta into thick slices and brushed them with olive oil. Adding the vegetables to the pan with two-thirds cup of white wine and chicken broth, I brought the sauce to a simmer and cut the grouper into chunks. While the bread toasted, Miss Gloria finished setting the table.

"Do you think he'll read our cards?" she asked. "I've never had it done. I'm a little nervous."

I didn't tell her I was nervous, too. I'd never seen Lorenzo as a civilian. Or cooked for him. But more than that, the last time he'd read my cards, I'd almost lost my mother. I realized that somehow the two things had started to get twined up in my brain: tarot and danger.

We heard a ship's bell tinkle out on the dock—Miss Gloria's maritime doorbell. I went to the door and waved Lorenzo onto the boat. Dressed in black jeans and sneakers and wearing a yellow slicker, he looked completely different from the man I'd seen many times plying his trade at his card table on Mallory Square. No makeup, no jewels, no turban.

"This is adorable," he exclaimed, as he stripped off his dripping raincoat and hung it next to mine on a peg outside the door. "I was deathly afraid of boarding the wrong craft—I've heard stories about how protective boat captains are." He leaned over to kiss my cheek and we went inside.

"Well, this is Captain Gloria," I said, drawing Miss Gloria forward to meet him. "She's not very scary and we're thrilled you could come." Lorenzo took her tiny hand in his and kissed her palm. She shivered, speechless for a minute.

"Such a pleasure," he said with a small bow.

"But where's your eye makeup? And your turban?" asked Miss Gloria. "Hayley and her mom described you but you look nothing like what I imagined."

He touched both hands to his dark hair, looking sad. "Oh, I loved that turban. I felt like Lana Turner when I wore it. But all dressed up like that, I was being treated like a tourist attraction. People kept coming up and snapping photographs while I was reading my customers' cards. They didn't take me seriously—treated me like a fool. And it was so intrusive for the people waiting to hear what I had to say." He sighed dramatically. "There's a mass level of consciousness—or should I say unconsciousness—that turban tapped into, so I had to give it up."

"Why don't you show him around?" I suggested, "and I'll finish making lunch."

Miss Gloria beamed and led Lorenzo down the houseboat's short passageway, explaining as she went that her deceased husband had added many of the built-ins that took best advantage of the small space. "Not an inch is wasted," she said proudly, as she ushered him into her bedroom. "We have drawers everywhere. And it's all recycled Dade County pine. This wood will last long after I'm gone."

I could hear the smooth scrape of wood on polished wood as she opened the storage drawers under her bed. Hopefully she wouldn't spend too much time in my little room—I hadn't quite gotten her knack of keeping it pin neat.

"I'm not much of a cook." Miss Gloria's voice echoed out to the galley once they were back in the hall. "That's Hayley's specialty. You'll see. But I do have a green thumb." I heard the screen door open and then creak shut as she led him onto the back deck, which was chockablock with pots of herbs, a few tomato plants, and a jumble of palms and tropical flowers.

"This space is magical," I heard him tell her.

When they returned to the galley, a little damp from the misting rain, Miss Gloria directed Lorenzo to a seat at our table. Both cats jumped up on the bench beside him and began to nuzzle him and purr.

"Go away, kitties," Miss Gloria scolded.

"Never mind, I love cats," said Lorenzo, flashing a big grin. "How can you live on this island if you don't like cats and chickens?"

Miss Gloria beamed and settled a cup of hot tea in front of him, a plate of lemon slices and a jar of creamed honey on the side. "How did you end up here?" she asked.

He leaned forward, looking her in the eye. "There's a powerful current that runs from the Bermuda Triangle, right around Mallory Square. I guess it pulled me in, like a lot of folks. And then once you get here, the island either embraces you or chews you up and spits you out. I was embraced!"

I checked Miss Gloria's face to see how she was handling his "current" theory—she was mesmerized. I dished up bowls of steaming soup garnished with islands of crispy croutons and delivered them to the table. Sliding in next to Miss Gloria, I raised my water glass. *"Bon appetit!"*

"Delightful," said Lorenzo, after sipping the soup.

"Hayley, this is heavenly," said Miss Gloria. And to Lorenzo: "I told you she was a whiz in the kitchen."

I thanked them and tasted my broth—spicy and rich, with a hint of the sea—and had to agree. A perfect dish for a gloomy day. As we slurped our way through the first bowl of soup, and then on to seconds, Lorenzo told Miss Gloria stories about running for Queen Mother in the yearly charity drag contest at the La Te Da.

"I appeared as Marlene Dietrich—and I won."

"Congratulations! What did you wear?" asked Miss Gloria.

"A suit, of course. Women knew how to dress in those days." He took a deep breath and began to sing with a German accent: "I often stop and wonder, why I appeal to men . . ."

"Falling in love again," Miss Gloria warbled along with him in her reedy soprano.

Outside the boat, I could see our neighbor, Mr. Renhart, pausing on the dock in the rain, peering into our living room, looking puzzled. He never quite knew what to expect from us. I waved and smiled and he ducked his head and hurried on.

"Oh I bet you were marvelous, no wonder you won!" said Miss Gloria to Lorenzo, clapping her hands together.

"I can do Dietrich in my sleep," said Lorenzo modestly. "I was the right girl—I had what it took."

I hadn't realized that Lorenzo was a part-time drag queen, though with his dramatic flair, it didn't surprise me. But this turn in the conversation got me thinking about the *Topped Chef* candidate Randy Thompson—about his second career in entertainment and the TV show contest. And how nervous he seemed waiting for the cops. And what he'd blurted out about a lousy relationship with Rizzoli.

"Do you happen to know Randy Thompson?" I asked Lorenzo.

"Of course. He sings at the Aqua as Victoria. She's got a beautiful voice," said Lorenzo. "Why do you ask?"

"He's a 'cheftestant' for the contest I'm helping to judge." I sighed. "We've got problems over there—big ones." Not wanting to upset Miss Gloria, I told them the bare details about Sam Rizzoli's death, which was almost certainly a murder, and how the police had come around the Studios of Key West this morning and interviewed the contestants and judges.

"They wondered whether I'd noticed any conflict between Rizzoli and the other folks," I added.

"Was there?" asked Miss Gloria.

I sighed again. "There was some friction among us judges over the food, but that seemed more staged than real, I think. And of course Rizzoli would have been happy to wring my neck for that restaurant review." I heaved an even deeper sigh. "The three contestants we met this morning all seem really eager to win. Really eager."

Saying that made me a little queasy. Would winning have mattered enough to one of them that he or she resorted to murder? It did seem unlikely. In fact it seemed ridiculous. Because wouldn't a normal person assume that a murder would bring the whole contest to a screeching halt?

I turned to Lorenzo. "Why does a guy decide to become a drag queen?"

"That's a big question," said Miss Gloria, patting his hand. "He's going to need another cup of tea. Is there dessert?"

"I bought some cookies at Coles Peace," I said and got up to put the kettle back on. I filled a plate with the mango triangles, coconut almond macaroons, brownies, and oatmeal raisin cookies, and brought it to the table along with a fresh pot of tea.

"That looks like death to my waistline," said Lorenzo, as he stroked my rumbling Evinrude, who was now draped across his lap like a striped cummerbund.

He went on: "It is a big question. And probably as many answers as there are queens. Some of us just want to make a living. I've met some who had a terrible time as kids—they were bullied and harassed all through school. Performing fills an emptiness that was left in their lives by those negative experiences. And some of us feel pretty all dressed up and we love expressing our creativity that way." He smiled and nibbled on one of the macaroons. "Swoon." He patted his lips with a paper napkin. "Why do you ask?"

"Is it possible that a guy could feel trapped in that world? Desperate to rise out of it?"

Lorenzo shook his head, frowning. "I don't know anyone who feels like that, not consciously anyway."

I shrugged. Time to drop my improbable theory about Randy as killer. I really had not a shred of evidence to go on. One slip of someone's tongue and that unsubstantiated rumor would be all over town.

"Who is this Rizzoli?" asked Miss Gloria.

"He owned a lot of property on the island and he had a reputation for skewing his decisions toward his own interests," I said. "For weeks, the Citizen's Voice column has been full of comments from town residents who sounded like they'd have been delighted to see him dead."

"That's awful," said Miss Gloria. "Was he that bad?"

Lorenzo said nothing, but frowning again, he glanced at his watch. "This has been so lovely. You ladies have cheered up a perfectly gloomy day. I have to be off in a minute, but I brought my cards." He arched his carefully shaped eyebrows.

Miss Gloria's face lit up. "Oh would you? I've never had a reading. How does this work?"

"You shuffle the cards, and that sends your energy into the reading. I simply deal them out and talk about what I see." He touched a finger to his nose. "And trust me"—he shrugged as if she might not believe him—"what comes out of my mouth amazes me on my side of the table as much as it amazes you. Sometimes the universe is trying to get a message through to someone and they aren't getting it. But then the cards make it real."

We finished clearing the table. I clattered the dishes

into the sink, then shook out the paisley cloth, folded it up and put it in a drawer below the counter. Lorenzo had Miss Gloria shuffle his deck and then he dealt three cards out on the pink Formica—he turned over the Death card, the Wheel of Fortune, and the Four of Wands.

I couldn't help flinching when I saw the knight on a horse stepping over a dead body, but Miss Gloria didn't seem to realize that she'd drawn death. I took my friend's hand and squeezed. Lorenzo smiled reassuringly and then looked deep into Miss Gloria's eyes.

"The first card represents the conflicts in your past," he said to her, and placed one of his hands on hers. "People get frightened when they see that they've chosen the Death card, but it shouldn't be taken at face value. Probably you've had some conflict rooted in a time of intense change. And most people don't like change. But if we look at this card the way a child looks at death, it means change—and change can offer a time of positive transformation."

Miss Gloria pressed her palms together and blinked. "Last year my son began to insist I move to an old people's home near him in Michigan. I know he only wanted the best for me. He wanted to be near enough to help if I had medical problems—or needed anything. But he didn't understand that I would have dried up and died if I had to spend the last years of my life in a nursing home."

She glanced around the living area, eyes bright with tears. "All my treasured memories are here. Hayley saved the day on that one when she agreed to move in."

She flashed a brilliant, grateful smile, which made me feel unworthy. In truth, she had been the one to save my bacon, and she earned my gratitude every day with her warm hospitality.

Lorenzo nodded and patted her hand. "If you were able to accept that change, you will be able to move on to what's ahead." He tapped the second card, the Wheel of Fortune. "The card in your present position is saying that the things you set in motion are bearing fruit. And your future card is the Four of Wands, indicating the successful completion of some projects."

"Fascinating," said Miss Gloria. "I guess I'd better get busy thinking some up. You next, Hayley."

But I was stuck on Miss Gloria's Death card. She'd become part of my family. If something happened to her, I couldn't bear it. I shuffled the deck, and again Lorenzo dealt out three cards—the Judgment card, an angel blowing a horn above three nude figures; the Magician; and the Eight of Swords, showing a woman blindfolded and tied up, with eight swords stabbed into the earth around her.

Lorenzo began with the last one. "Hayley, you must look within yourself for answers—were you really as bound up by authority as you seem to feel? Are you waiting for someone else to rescue you? You have choices, even though you may need to let go of feelings to which you are attached."

Surely he was referring to how I was handling detective Nate Bransford, but I preferred not to hash that over. Not right now.

"The Magician tells us to watch what we bring into our lives as well as what we give to others. Walk your talk, Hayley," he said. Then he tapped the Judgment card with his forefinger. "Let go of the past and accept things as they are. There is no one to blame—not even you." He grinned. "Let me know how it goes?"

I took a great big breath—having my cards read stirred up such a weird combination of anxiety and relief. "I'll keep you posted," I said, pushing the cards across the table to him and getting to my feet. "We're so glad you could come today."

"The pleasure was all mine." Lorenzo put his cards away, and then stood and hugged Miss Gloria. I followed him out to the deck and walked with him to the end of the dock. He put his hands on my shoulders and looked me right in the eyes. "You may need to let go," he said. Then he mounted his scooter and drove away.

Let go of what, exactly? I watched him disappear over the hill toward Old Town, then trudged back to the boat. Several slips up the finger, I saw my former roommate from college, Connie, who lived a few boats up the dock. She'd taken me in after the debacle with Chad last fall, but my subsequent move down to Miss Gloria's place had taken the pressure off our friendship. Her place was simply too small for two women, one boyfriend who visited frequently and would soon be a husband, and one spoiled cat. I hurried down the dock to ask my mother's questions about the fast-approaching wedding.

Connie looked like she'd just gotten out of the shower, her short hair sticking up randomly like a well-used patch of catnip. My mother had been lobbying for her to grow it out for her wedding to better display a handmade headpiece and veil or even a ring of flow-ers—something "girly." But right now it was in that awkward in-between stage.

"Here comes the bride!" I warbled. "I have strict in-structions from Mom to pin you down about some de-tails." Connie made a face, as though she'd eaten something sour.

"What's the matter?"

She pressed her fists to her cheeks and blew out an exasperated puff of air. "Does Ray seem like a normal guy to you?"

I nodded. "Sure. Normal for an artist, creative nor-mal." I smiled but she didn't. "I think you've made an excellent choice—he'll be a great husband. He adores you."

"He's gotten it into his head that if we're getting married on the beach, it should be a pirate wedding."

"A pirate wedding?"

"The wedding party would be dressed in costume and we'd ask the guests to come dressed as deckhands. And then say our vows in pirate-ese."

I would have burst out laughing if she hadn't looked so near to tears.

"Would you mind going by this shop sometime in the next few days and snapping some pictures of the costumes? I'm up to my neck in cleaning jobs—and they don't have evening hours. I'm thinking if he could only see how silly we'd look, he'd drop this." She handed me a flyer with colorful pictures of full-breasted wenches in white lace corsets and their pirate grooms wearing feathered hats and eye patches. "They refer to getting married as *swallowing the anchor*. If that's how he really feels about it . . ." Tears shimmered the length of her eyelashes like crystals of sugar.

"Of course," I said, giving her a quick squeeze. "That's what maids of honor are for—heading off disaster in whatever form it takes."

8

The salt, the sweet, the brine, the crunch.
It was a culinary car crash of depravity.
　　　　　　　—Elissa Altman, *Poor Man's Feast*

All afternoon, I thought about Lorenzo's words: *Let go of feelings to which you are attached. Are you waiting for someone else to rescue you? Walk your talk.*

I finally drummed up the nerve to call Nate. Considering how our date failed to materialize, shouldn't he have called me first? But since he hadn't, Lorenzo's reading had convinced me that I had to take the lead, to be more direct. Whether we ended up in a relationship or whether we didn't, I shouldn't allow him to intimidate me. I punched his number into my phone. He answered on the first ring. I instantly considered hanging up. Foolish idea since everyone in the universe now has caller ID. Especially the cops.

"Oh hi. It's Hayley. I was wondering how you're doing? Did you get any sleep at all last night?"

Silence, but then he cleared his throat. "It was a long night."

That was all he could give me?

"Long night for me, too," I said. "Though your half of the lava cake helped cushion the pain."

He chuckled but fell silent again.

"I was hoping you might have more information about the murder. And hoping that you'd be willing to share." My voice sounded a little wobbly but I soldiered on. "I know you must think this is none of my business, but Rizzoli was a judge in the contest I'm involved with—as you know perfectly well. Since your guys were crawling all over the set this afternoon. Don't you at least think I deserve to know if that puts the rest of us in danger?"

"Nice to talk to you, too," he said, finally laughing. "And I am sorry about the dinner. In fact, I ended up eating a peanut butter sandwich last night, all the while thinking about that steak. And you. And the chocolate lava cake, though I suspect I wouldn't have gotten much more than a taste." He laughed again, a deep, charming laugh that loosened the knots of tension in my belly.

"You're saying I'm a glutton?"

"I've seen you eat—can we leave it at that? And I was planning to call you, but we've been flat-out crazy busy here."

"With Sam Rizzoli's hanging?" I asked. "Have you arrested anyone?"

I heard him sigh and close his door. "Right now we're narrowing suspects down, particularly considering the political opponents of the commissioner. Really, that's all I can say. But if we thought you were in any danger, I'd be the first to let you know. You have to trust me a little."

"You have to give me something to go on," I said back, keeping my tone light as a feather so he might imagine I was joking. Though I wasn't. Trust could not be a one-way street.

"Yes. It was Sam Rizzoli," he finally said. "And it was murder."

After I'd helped Miss Gloria clean up from lunch, I got dressed for the first event of this weekend's Key West Food and Wine Festival, the Mallory Square Stroll. This would be a quick and dirty way to develop material for my restaurant review column. Maybe I'd even be able to persuade Wally to swap out this story for my online review of Just Off Duval, considering that its owner had been murdered. Of course, plenty of people would have already seen it, but it seemed tacky to pile on to the man's already significant misfortunes.

I'd decided to skip the opening "Barefoot on the Beach" cocktail party and go directly to the first stop on the stroll: the Conch Shack on Duval Street. Right away that struck me as a good move as I watched a crowd of boisterous people tumble off a trolley car and hip-check bewildered tourists out of their way to reach the shack. I'd have to eat and drink quickly to catch up with these folks. A Food and Wine Festival volunteer handed out sheets of paper listing the restaurants we'd be visiting and the munchies and wine those establishments would serve.

The Conch Shack was an open-air restaurant with

no seating other than a single row of stools lined up outside the open windows. Menus had been painted on the bright blue and yellow walls, declaring "Home of the Best Ever Conch Fritters" and "Cheap Beer!" Inside the small kitchen, two men in straw hats and shorts manned the deep fryer. The heavy smell of seafood hitting hot oil hung in the alley alongside the shack. I fought through the rowdy crowd that had descended from the trolley, snagged a glass of Chardonnay, and then slid a small plastic cup off a passing waiter's tray. A fist-sized conch fritter drizzled with a pale green sauce filled the cup.

I moved away from the crowd and nibbled the fritter—hot and tender, not at all fishy, chewy, or heavy as I might have predicted. And the green sauce tasted like a rémoulade, with the faintest flavor of lime. I jotted a few notes, dumped my trash, and loosed myself into the stream of revelers headed toward our second stop. This was a crowd on a mission.

The next stop was Hot Tin Roof restaurant, two blocks away and tucked a stone's throw from Duval Street. We passed through an outdoor eating area on the porch upstairs and went into the bar overlooking the water. Bartenders poured red wine as servers passed shrimp skewers *al ajillo*, which seemed to translate to "load on the garlic."

I inhaled every spicy bite, set my empty plate and wineglass on the counter, and trotted downstairs toward Wall Street. Our next destination, El Meson de Pepe, a Cuban restaurant right off Mallory Square, had outdoor seating that ran the length of the alley leading from Mallory Square to Duval Street. Lively music, pitchers of margaritas, and inexpensive food catered to hungry tourists in their post-sunset celebration daze. I claimed my plantain cup filled with Cuban roast pork and had another glass of pinot noir thrust upon me, which I promptly poured into a potted palm. Any more alcohol and I'd have no business on my scooter. The pork was tasty, though also deep fried and rich.

By now I would have killed for a carrot stick, though what chef would choose salad or veggies as a showcase for his talents? I trailed the crowd to another upstairs venue, the Roof Top Café. With vaulted ceilings and twinkling lights, this restaurant appeared spacious and welcoming. I accepted another glass of white wine and ate half of a shrimp and crab cake; delicious, though drenched in butter. I could feel my cholesterol count shooting up as the evening progressed.

Feeling fat-saturated and close to exhausted, I marched off to our final and most exotic tour stop, dessert on a yacht. I checked my stroll cheat sheet to get the details: The Barefoot Yacht, docked at the Westin Key West Resort and Marina Pier, promised key lime–infused phyllo tartlets drizzled with a dark chocolate sauce. My mouth began to water.

I got in line to board the yacht, which looked to be about twice the height and length of Miss Gloria's houseboat. It was tethered a stone's throw from the Custom House Museum, at the slip near to the pier where the cruise ships docked. Why would anyone want to dock a boat here, even for a night or two? I would be embarrassed to sit out on the deck while tourists streamed by, ogling my indulgences and wondering why I deserved what most folks couldn't even dream of. When we reached the gangplank, bouncers in green golf shirts instructed us to remove our shoes. As the woman in front of me argued that her rubber flip-flops would not leave marks on the deck, I shucked off my sandals and was helped aboard. A young man in a pressed blue shirt passed out flutes of champagne as we entered the living area.

While waiting for the dessert to materialize, I explored the yacht for a few minutes, first checking out the upper deck—spacious enough for a dozen sunbathers—and then peeking into the berths on the lower level, which looked like actual hotel rooms. Definitely roomier and much more extravagant than Miss Gloria's tub, but not nearly so homey. There was still no sign of the key lime tartlets so I wandered down a passageway toward the bow.

A heavyset woman wearing thick makeup bustled out of the kitchen and blocked my way. "No admittance here, ma'am," she said. "This is a working galley."

I apologized and backpedaled quickly, but not before catching a glimpse of a man in chefs' whites squirting chocolate syrup from a plastic bottle onto a tray of desserts. He had thick eyebrows, a mustache, and a ponytail down his back. It took me a minute to connect the dots. This pastry chef was Buddy Higgs, one of the contestants from the *Topped Chef* contest. Buddy Higgs? Plastic chocolate? For a man enamored of molecular gastronomy, that struck me as sloppy and lazy. Astonishing. I returned to the living room and watched a few minutes of basketball on the flat-screen TV that covered most of one wall.

Finally, the woman I'd seen in the galley emerged from the hall with a platter of pastries and passed them around. I took one bite of the dessert, which should have puckered my mouth with the tart flavor of key limes. Instead the custard's sweetness made my fillings ache. Smothered in the saccharine corn syrup chocolate, the concoction was barely edible. I covered the rest with a paper napkin and slipped it into the trash. Then I abandoned my plastic flute of champagne on a shelf near the oversized television, and started for the exit. Enough was enough. I didn't even want to think about the conflict of interest involved in panning a dessert made by one of the contestants from the *Topped Chef* contest. If only I hadn't nosed into the galley, I scolded myself. Really, it was too late to worry.

Out on the deck, the same two beefy men grasped my elbows and lifted me off the boat and onto the gangplank. They weren't taking any chances with tipsy guests ending up in the harbor. I thanked them and began to poke through the pile of shoes left on the dock, looking for my sandals.

"Hayley, is that you?" a familiar voice asked. Toby Davidson, her voice sounding more reedy and anxious than this morning. I slid my feet into my shoes and turned to greet her.

"Did you enjoy the tasting?" she asked as I buckled my sandals.

"It was fun," I said. "Not something I'd want to do every night. There wasn't a vegetable to be seen, though I got acquainted with lots of butter and the excellent proceeds of a deep-fat fryer. And all that reminded me of our contestant Randy Thompson." I snickered. "He's cute, isn't he? Though I don't imagine we're supposed to be comparing notes off the set." I wondered whether to mention seeing Buddy Higgs in the yacht's galley. Probably best left unsaid.

Toby gave a weak smile while her gaze probed the surrounding darkness. "Do you have a minute?"

Though I was tired and my stomach had started to churn a little, she looked so worried that I nodded.

She motioned to me to follow her a little distance away from the yacht to a bench near a large cement trash barrel. The sounds of diners partying on the yacht caromed across the bight and strings of fairy lights outlining the handrails and portholes made it look more magical than it had felt onboard. On the far pier where the cruise ships docked, a row of lamps cast squiggles of light on the water, like the wavy lines on a Hostess cupcake.

"I don't know who else to talk with about this." A wisp of brown hair blew across Toby's forehead. She unclasped a barrette and recaptured the flyaway, then leaned forward to whisper. "I've been thinking. After the police talked with us earlier about Sam Rizzoli?"

The *rat-tat-tat* of firecrackers in the distance rattled through the air and Toby startled.

I nodded again. "It was a hard day. I'm not sure it was a good decision to go forward with the taping. We did the best we could, though, right? What are the chances this silly business will amount to anything anyway?"

"Oh no," she said, her eyes widening. "You're underestimating the situation. This type of show is very, very popular. With all the tourists who visit this island

and fall in love with it, I have no doubt that a Key West *Topped Chef* show could be a major winner. This could easily get picked up by the Food Network or even one of the majors on prime time." She squared her shoulders. "I have no doubt at all. That's why I'm so worried." She fell silent, her lips trembling. A gust of wind wafted over us, scented with the odors of old cigarettes and discarded food from the nearby trash can.

"Worried?" I prompted her after several moments.

"You'll think I sound like a nut." She glanced around, frowning. "Do you mind walking a bit? I'm not comfortable here."

I wasn't that comfortable either—we were no more than a stone's throw from my ex's apartment. It would only take one sighting to make him believe—again— that I was stalking him. We got up and wound our way through the happy residual crowds from the Food and Wine Festival, and headed toward Mallory Square.

Just outside the Westin's outdoor restaurant, the cat man was boxing up the paraphernalia from his nightly show. He looked drained, which made me think about how much energy he must expend to keep his cats in line while entertaining visiting tourists in his falsetto French accent. Several felines waited by the water's edge, silent and ghostly in their cages. Evinrude would have hated the confinement. And the whole business of leaping through fiery hoops, climbing rope steps, and walking tightropes as the show cats did? My cat was handsome and clever, but he liked to do what he wanted, when it suited him. No matter how many glistening entrails were offered as bribes. I had to admire the cat man's skills.

By the time we had crossed the wooden bridge behind the aquarium, the crowds had thinned to almost nothing, and we headed toward the water. The square was mostly deserted, streetlights casting a dim glow on the empty brick courtyard. Although the portable conch fritter stand had been rolled away for the night, I could smell the lingering odor of hot oil. A red plastic cup skittered by, causing us both to jump. Lorenzo had set his table up in the distance, not far from the bright yellow Ocean Key Resort. Two tall candles (more likely Coleman lanterns) framed his station. He was deep in conversation with a customer so I didn't bother to wave. In the opposite corner of the square, a small group of men drank and talked, too far away for us to make out their conversation, or for them to hear us. Probably my homeless friend, Tony, and some of his buddies.

"I wonder," said Toby, her voice so low I could barely catch the words, "whether Rizzoli was killed because he was a judge? What if it became clear that he favored one of the contestants over the others? And what if one of the other chefs noticed that and was desperate to win? If that's so, we also could be in danger."

She was right about sounding a little nutty—spoken out loud, her theory sounded paranoid and borderline ridiculous. Even though I'd had thoughts not so far from hers, Bransford had convinced me they were groundless. It simply made no sense to imagine that someone would have murdered one of the contest's judges, hoping to improve his chance of winning.

But Toby's anxiety was real and I thought I could help with that.

"I called my friend who's a detective at the police department. They aren't pursuing any *Topped Chef* connections."

"Why did they interview all of us?" she asked. "Why did they herd us all into the studio and scare us half to death?"

"Any one of us might have heard something about Rizzoli. I'm just guessing, but doesn't it make more sense if his death was related to town politics? That's where there's influence to be peddled and money to be made. Rizzoli owned bars, restaurants, and T-shirt shops on Duval Street."

"We know about one of his restaurants, for sure," said Toby, her eyes widening. "Everyone knows about it now. I salute you for speaking the truth. In spite of his politics and your position as a judge."

I winced. "I wish I'd never set foot in that place. And I can assure you I had no idea who he was when I wrote the review. The more I find out about him, the more I think his business dealings got him killed. Just think about how his fortune could increase or plateau depending on whether the town decided to widen the channel and let larger cruise ships in. He was not a disinterested observer when it came to Key West. And that makes some folks very, very angry."

But Toby didn't look convinced. "You haven't worked in a restaurant kitchen, have you?"

"No."

"Then you might not be able to imagine how much landing a TV show could change a chef's life," said Toby, her fingers curling into fists. "No more slaving long hours in a fiercely hot kitchen. No more worrying about the restaurant getting sold to a new owner who cares about profit instead of quality ingredients. No more relying on poorly trained sous-chefs who've moved to Key West because they can't manage life in the real world. Assistants who miss a third of their shifts because they were dead-dog drunk the night before and can't get out of bed, even by four in the afternoon."

"I believe what you're saying about it being a tough job," I said. "And I see your point about the cooking show being a big deal. But it's almost impossible to imagine that killing Rizzoli would fix anything. How would someone be sure which way he was leaning? And how could they be sure that he'd be persuasive enough to sway the rest of us? It all seems a little too circumstantial."

Toby frowned. "Nothing that Buddy Higgs does to win the contest would shock me."

My eyes bugged out in surprise at the vehemence in her voice. But before I could ask more, my phone rang. I slid it out of my back pocket. Connie.

"Girlfriend, a bunch of us are over here at the Green Parrot. The band is terrific. Are you finished working? Can you swing by for a drink?"

A half a beer with friends sounded like just the right nightcap after an unsettling day. And weren't hops vegetables? "On my way," I said and pressed OFF. "Let's stay in touch," I told Toby, and patted her thin shoulder. "I'll definitely let you know if I hear anything else about Rizzoli. Can I walk you back to Duval Street?"

"No thanks," she said. "I'm going to enjoy the peace and quiet for a few minutes. See you tomorrow."

9

*We live in an age when pizza gets to your
home before the police.*

—Jeff Marder

Wispy clouds fled across the moon, leaving striated
shadows on the brick courtyard. It hadn't rained since
this afternoon, but the air felt heavy and thick. I trotted
across the square, which stretched endless and enormous in the filtered moonlight without the buzz of
street performers and tourists. As I reached the opening of the alley that led past the Waterfront Playhouse
and out to the street, I heard another firecracker. Then
a muffled but high-pitched cry. And then a splash.

I spun around. Toby was not where I'd left her. My
cell phone in my hand, heart pounding, I hurried back
toward the edge of the pier where we'd talked. No sign
of her, but there was someone splashing frantically in
the water.

"Help!" a small voice cried.

I pressed 911. "Woman overboard at Mallory Square!"

I yelled, and then stuffed the phone in my sweater pocket.

I ran up to the edge of the water. "Toby, is that you?"

"Help!" she cried again. "I can't swim." She swatted at the water, sank briefly, then burst to the surface again, sputtering. The harder she struggled, the more quickly the current pulled her away from the dock.

I glanced around, shouting for assistance. But no one appeared. And there was no lifesaving ring, nor even a long stick that I might have used to drag her to safety.

"Lorenzo! Tony!" I screamed at the top of my lungs, my hands cupped into a megaphone, first in the direction of the tarot table, then toward the spot where I'd noticed the gathering of homeless men. "The cops are coming—tell them we're over here. My friend is in trouble!"

I couldn't wait to see whether either of them heard me. So I shucked off my sandals, dropped my cell phone and pack on top of them, and my sweater on top of that. I had no idea how deep the water was or what obstacles might lurk underneath. But I took a deep breath and pushed off the pier into a shallow dive.

If my mouth hadn't been full of salt water, I would have screamed out at the shock of cold. Not cold like the ocean in New Jersey in January, but still unpleasantly chilly. I surfaced, struggling to push away a disgusting, slimy hunk of seaweed, and dog-paddled in place, looking for Toby. Already the current was pulling me away from the pier.

Toby splashed frantically a few yards from me. I breaststroked over. She slapped at the water, gasping and choking, and grabbed onto my head.

I frog-kicked, trying to make a little space between us. She held on tighter, now with a death grip on my hair. Her weight pushed me under and I had to fight to get back to the surface and breathe.

"Toby," I sputtered, my adrenaline surging, mouth full of salt water, "I'm trying to help. But you have to let go."

"I can't swim," she shrieked, and floundered until she sank a second time, pulling me down with her. I bobbed to the surface, panicked at the idea of her fastened to me like a barnacle as the current swept us away. A fact from the lifeguarding class that I'd flunked flashed through my brain: To break the stranglehold of a panicked victim, drop down low into the water and then approach again from behind.

If I didn't try something, we would both drown. So I kicked hard and shot lower into the water. Flailing madly to stay at the surface, Toby let go of my hair. Then I surged up on her far side. Slinging one arm across her chest, I started an awkward sidestroke toward the extension of the pier that hosted cruise ships during the city's three-boat days. Toward the closest way out—a slippery-looking ladder attached to the concrete. She continued to flop and thrash like a hooked marlin as I kicked against the current. Finally, we reached the ladder; I grabbed her hand and wrapped it around the rusty metal. I was exhausted and breathless. And frightened and cold.

"You're okay," I said, shaking the water and some green glop out of my eyes. "The cops will be here soon."

She reached for the bottom rung with her other

hand, sucking in great gulps of air. Her hair, plastered
to her scalp, was covered with an oily sheen—something cruise-ship related I was sure—and some strands
of brown sea grass. And her eyes looked wild.

My friend Tony's worried, whiskered face appeared
thirty feet away, at the top of the ladder attached to the
main pier. "Lorenzo's gone to show the cops the way.
See if you can swim over here and grab my hand.
They've got the gates locked so I can't get over to you."
He dropped his battered cowboy hat on the cement,
wiggled prone, and reached out for us. But Toby
wouldn't let go of the rung she was gripping and I was
afraid to leave her there alone. In fact I was afraid to try
fighting the current again myself.

The welcome sound of a siren split the air. Once it
bleated to a stop, we could see the lights of emergency
vehicles flashing off the clouds. Then thin beams of
flashlights pierced the darkness.

"Over here!" Tony shouted. "Over here!"

When he'd gotten the attention of the officers, he
melted away into the shadows. He'd taken a forced
march to the police department last week on charges of
disturbing the peace—he would not be eager to be seen
by the cops, however positive the circumstances this
time.

After what felt like an hour, two policemen approached the edge of the pier, with Lorenzo in his
white shirt, black tie, and black vest decorated with the
moon and stars right behind them. All three struggled
over the fence and then ran across the dock to our ladder. The smaller cop, a wiry guy with thinning blond

hair, descended the ladder until he was wet to his knees.

"Take her first," I said, flutter-kicking out of the way and tipping my chin at Toby.

The cop grasped her arm and pulled her up so she could get a foothold on the ladder's lowest rung. Then she slipped her other foot on the ladder, too, this one still clad in a black leather sandal. The second policeman lay out flat on the concrete above us and reached for Toby's hand.

"Ma'am," said the first cop. "You're going to have to let go."

"You'll be okay," said Lorenzo, who hovered above him. "They've got you. You're safe." He squeezed his face between his hands and shook his head at me. "Good lord, woman, what were you thinking? I told you how strong the current is here."

"I couldn't let her die," I muttered, trying not to picture what might have happened if we'd gotten swept away. My teeth had begun to chatter as I realized how close I'd come to drowning, trying to save a woman I barely knew.

Finally, Toby was hoisted out, then the cops helped me. I flopped onto the concrete, my chest still heaving from fright and exertion.

"What happened?" I asked her, once I had scrambled to my knees and then to standing. "How in the world did you end up in the water?"

Toby crouched in a shivering heap, breathing hard, her eyes closed. Lorenzo took off his vest and wrapped it around her shoulders. She nodded her thanks. A town employee arrived to unlock the gate and we staggered over to the main pier.

Once I reached my pile of belongings, I wiped my face with my sweater, then pulled it on and slipped my feet into my sandals.

"Get a couple of blankets from the cruiser," said the wet cop to the dry one. Then he addressed Toby, repeating my question. "What happened here?"

But Toby was shaking too hard to speak.

"I was working across the square," Lorenzo offered, pointing to his table where the lanterns still flickered, carving out geodes of light in the darkness. "Unfortunately, I didn't see exactly how it happened. I heard a splash and then my friend Hayley yelled for help. And then there was another splash."

The cop looked at me. "And you are?"

"I'm Hayley Snow. This is Toby Davidson. We'd just walked over from the Westin," I said, "working off a few calories after the Mallory Square Stroll tasting event. As if walking a couple of blocks could make up for all that fried stuff." I smiled but got no reaction. "And then I left to meet up with some friends. I was halfway across the plaza when I heard a noise, like something hit the water." I gestured at Toby. "I was afraid she'd gone over because I didn't see her anywhere. Sure enough, she had."

The dry policeman returned with a shiny silver space blanket and wrapped it around Toby, over the top of Lorenzo's vest. "Why did you jump, miss?" he asked gently.

"I didn't plan on j-j-jumping," she stuttered. "A shot went off and I swear a bullet went right over my head."

One cop's eyes flickered up to meet his partner's gaze. They didn't believe her.

"I heard the cracking noises, too," I said.

"There was no place to hide—I was an easy target," Toby explained. "I was afraid for my life. I threw myself down to the ground but I misjudged how close I was to the water."

Another look exchanged between the cops. "Are you injured?" asked the dry man.

"No," Toby said, running her hands down her arms as if to check for wounds. But she winced when she came across an ugly scrape that reached from the inside of her elbow to her palm. And then I noticed the blood oozing from a shallow gash on her temple. I touched my own face.

"You're bleeding. Did you hit your head on something?"

Toby put her hand to her head and just stared at the blood that came away on her fingers.

The dry cop frowned, looking as though he still didn't buy her story. "You said you heard a shot. Did you see a shooter?"

She shook her head.

"Was there a flash of light?"

"I don't think so. I can't remember."

"Did you smell anything, like gunpowder? Or sulfur?"

She dropped her chin to her chest. "I only heard the noise."

He stared at her a little harder, then turned his attention back to me.

"So you heard a shot, too?"

"I did hear a cracking noise—that must have been what got my attention in the first place." Had it been a gunshot? My adrenaline had caromed off the charts as I tried to rescue her, shutting off my brain's usual whirl of curious questions. I touched my ears with my hands and shrugged.

"There have been firecrackers going off most of the night. I ran over after I heard the splash. When I saw it was Toby in the water and there was no one else around to help, I dove in. Once we got close to the ladder, one of the homeless guys tried to help us out."

"Where is he?"

I glanced around. Tony was gone.

"When we first got to the square, they were talking over there." I pointed to the now-empty bench where the men had been drinking.

"We've had a number of noise-related complaints tonight, especially from the folks over at the Truman Annex and the Westin hotel," said the cop. "We've tracked down two groups of kids who were shooting off illegal fireworks." He paused and squinted at Toby, shivering, wide-eyed in a wet heap. "Would you say this popping sounded similar to a firecracker, or different?"

"Like a gunshot—I thought that's what I heard." She crossed her arms over her chest and frowned. "I know what fireworks sound like. This was different."

While the cops went over Toby's story again, I put in a quick call to Connie. "I'm not coming after all. It's a long story but I'm soaking wet and absolutely freezing." Now that the adrenaline had ebbed away, I could feel how chilled I was.

"Wet T-shirt contest?" she yelled over the background noise of the bar. "I didn't think you had it in you."

"Ha-ha, so funny," I said. "One of the other TV show judges fell in the water off Mallory Square and I had to help her out."

"You went in *that* water? Do you need a ride home?" she asked, suddenly all business and concern. "We can swing up and get your scooter tomorrow. Where are you?"

"Behind the Waterfront Playhouse," I said, feeling suddenly relieved—the idea of a cold, wet scooter ride held zero appeal. "My former roommate is on the way over—she would be happy to give you a ride," I told Toby once I'd hung up.

"We're going to keep Ms. Davidson here until the paramedics can check her out," said the cop in a firm voice. "Then we'll take her home."

"I'll see you on the set tomorrow," Toby told me, as if none of this had happened. "Eleven, right? And thank you for coming in after me. I can't imagine what I would have done . . ." Her chin quivered and her lips trembled as her words trailed off.

The truth was, she probably would have been swept off to sea and drowned.

Four little judges, judging for TV. One swinging from the mast, and then there were three. Three little judges, tasting wine and roux. One couldn't swim, and then there were two. . . .

10

Mise en place *(meez en PLASS) comes
from restaurant kitchens, where a brigade
of helpers spends the day getting everything ready for the dinner rush. It comes
from a French phrase meaning "make the
new guy do it."*

—Pete Wells

I woke early in spite of my best intentions to sleep in,
troubled by the events of the previous evening. Had
Toby really heard a gunshot? Or had she ramped herself up so that she panicked and overreacted? Had I?

By the time Connie and Ray had arrived to take me
back to the houseboat, I was leaning toward the latter
explanation. And the police were definitely headed
that way, too, based on the "poor nervous biddy
thought she heard a gun" tone in their voices and the
matching skepticism in their eyes. Toby's injuries did
not resemble gunshot wounds, the paramedic who
cleaned and bandaged her up had reported. They more

resembled flesh scraping against the concrete dock, as it definitely had while we flopped around trying to reach the ladder and then climb out of the murky water.

And finally, a second phalanx of cops had searched the vegetation and the outbuildings around Mallory Square, and come up with zero evidence of a sharpshooter. No bullets, no bullet casings, no nothing. Which in the end was the good news we all preferred, even if it was embarrassing to Toby. What kept me awake more than anything was the visceral memory of Toby's arms, squeezing my neck and head in the cold, brackish water. And how easily my attempt at rescue could have ended with a double drowning.

There would be nothing gained by staying in bed. And Shapiro's comments yesterday about my plump-as-a-guinea-hen figure kept surfacing through the layers of my cortex, no matter how hard I tried to press them down. Exercising might calm those voices—all of them.

So I pulled on sweatpants and a T-shirt, fed the cats, and set off jogging in a slow chug toward the harbor. I motored up Palm and around the curve to Eaton and then over to the historic seaport harbor, thinking that once again, I would reward myself with a large café con leche on the way home.

A fog had settled in over the harbor, snugged up so tightly to the water that I could only make out a faint thicket of masts. But the clanking of rigging against wood and metal sounded an atonal cacophony, louder than I remembered hearing in sunny weather. Underneath all that, I heard the noises of hose beating against metal. My acquaintance Derek from the other day must be washing down the deck of the big Sebago catamaran—in case the weather cleared. Conditions could change on a dime on this island and the tourists would be clamoring for the sails to be set and the party to begin.

"Good morning!" I hollered once Derek's wiry frame and yellowing beard emerged through the mist. Then I noticed Turtle, the homeless man I'd seen fighting with Derek the other morning, was lounging against the hull, pointing out spots that hadn't been hit by the hose.

"Someday maybe you'll get your own damn job instead of standing around bothering me," Derek groused in return. Turtle spun around, swirling his cape like Dracula and growling like an angry bear.

It occurred to me again that the cape looked exactly like the one I'd glimpsed on Rizzoli the other night, as he dangled from the mast. No way it could be the same—that garment would be buried deep in the stacks of police evidence. But would these guys have heard news about the murder? Something more than what the detective had been willing to tell me? They appeared to spend a lot of time here—maybe they'd even been lurking in the shadows as Rizzoli was strung up.

"Turtle," I said, diving into the conversation without grace. "Where'd you get the cool cloak?" I imitated his swishing movements with the hem of my T-shirt.

"Fantasy Fest last October," he said, flashing a big snaggletoothed grin. "Damn tourists get so damn drunk they leave all kinds of good stuff right alongside the road."

"Terrible thing about the murder the other day," I said, trying to sound open-ended and conversational without coming off as shallow. "Wasn't Mr. Rizzoli wearing a cape like yours?"

Turtle slitted his eyes with suspicion.

"Nothing unusual about that. Anyone with a few bucks could pick one up at the pirate shop on Simonton Street," said Derek, bristling a little and sidling closer to Turtle. Making it clear that while they might have been fighting to the death the other day, I was still the outsider—a recent transplant from the northeast who had money and relatives and options. Who didn't have to worry about supper and a place to sleep in the visceral way that Turtle did.

"I didn't mean to suggest you had anything to do with it," I said. "Sorry if it came out that way."

"It was ugly, that hanging," Derek said finally, and Turtle nodded in agreement.

"Were you guys here before it happened?" Even if they'd seen the whole thing, I doubted they'd admit it. Not to me.

"I was in bed by nine," said Derek, waving toward a beat-up apartment building a couple blocks east of the harbor.

"My digs ain't quite as fancy as his," Turtle said.

"He likes the old Waterfront Market's Dumpster," Derek added, snickering. He pinched his nose. "He sleeps better surrounded by eau de garbage."

Turtle pointed an imaginary gun at him and pulled the invisible trigger. "I heard an awful ruckus," Turtle told me with a big guffaw of laughter, "loud enough to wake the dead. Or even those of us not dead, only slightly pickled."

"There had to be half a dozen police cars, and every

one with its damn siren blasting," said Derek. "Usually I would roll over and go back to sleep, but I could tell this was something big."

"And besides the fuzz, they called in the Navy scuba guys. Those dudes were in the water for hours. Glub, glub, glub, glub." Turtle chortled.

"How long did it take the cops to get him down?" I'd seen that part myself, but I wanted to hear about their experience.

"Cutting him down wasn't the problem," said Derek. "But they had to wait a damn lifetime for the photographer."

"Hey, show her the picture you got," said Turtle.

"She don't want to see that," Derek said with a scowl. But at the same time, he hitched up his faded blue jeans and pulled a smartphone out of his back pocket. With a few quick jabs of his finger, he found the photo in question and passed the phone to me.

The scene was worse than I even remembered. Sam Rizzoli had been laid out on the decking, the black cape spread out underneath him. The yellow wig was askew, revealing a fringe of thick, black curls. A rope was still tied around his neck. Even now, knowing exactly who it was, I could barely recognize his face under the makeup caking his swollen skin. No surprise that I hadn't been able to work out his identity when I'd seen him from a distance the other night.

"Killer would have to be some strong sonofabitch to haul him up that line," said Turtle.

"Those boats have electric winches, you moron," said Derek. "All you have to do is wind a rope around the poor bastard's neck and then press a button."

"Yeah, but you'd have to know what button to mash," Turtle said, adding a shrill cackle of laughter. "And how about wrestling him onto the boat deck to begin with?"

"Why do you suppose he was dressed that way?" I asked, handing the phone back to Derek.

"It's Key West, man," said Turtle.

"Yeah, but it's not Fantasy Fest or New Year's Eve," I said.

"That man liked to party," said Derek. "Ask any of the regulars at his bar." Then he squirted the deck near Turtle's feet with the hose, causing him to yelp and hop out of range. "I gotta get my work done here, fellas. You all go yak somewheres else."

I trotted off in search of my Cuban coffee, unable to get the hideous photograph out of my mind. Why was Rizzoli dressed in those clothes? What was up with the makeup and wig? Once I had my con leche in hand, I walked two blocks south to see if the pirate store might be open. If I was lucky, I could kill two birds with one stone: take some photos of the wedding garb for Connie, and talk to the staff about what I'd seen at the harbor. It was still none of my business, but the question nagged me. What if Toby was right? What if the contest was related to the murder?

A deeply tanned man with a shirt so tight I could see his washboard abs through the fabric unlocked the door to the shop as I arrived. I followed him inside, mesmerized by his bushy head of dreadlocks. My fingers twitched for scissors.

"We're not open yet," he said, looking pointedly at his watch. "I came in early to do some paperwork."

"I'll make it quick." I flashed a friendly grin. "My girlfriend's fiancé is interested in a pirate-themed wedding," I told him. "I told her I'd stop by and get some information."

He rustled through the shelves under the counter by the cash register and brought out a brochure listing options and packages.

"Usually the bride and groom wear pirate costumes, and they exchange vows in pirate lingo. The guests come dressed as scallywag crew members." He hooted out: "Ho, ho, ho . . ."

"No offense meant to your business, but why? Why would someone want a pirate wedding?"

"Often these are second marriages, or third." He grimaced and brushed a thick, snarled lock over his shoulder. "They want something different, something fun that reflects our island humor. Gallows humor, that's what's needed when you didn't get the memo after your first divorce. Or second."

I scribbled a few furious notes, hopeful that these details would deter Connie's boyfriend. Then I wandered around the shop snapping photos. A lace gown with a lace-up corset on top and a long train, a short red skirt with a black beaded top . . . Was that meant to be worn by the maid of honor? Then I noticed an outfit hanging on the far wall for the groom—a V-necked shirt, bloomer pants, boots, and a cloak similar to the one Rizzoli had worn.

I returned to the counter. "Thanks so much for your help. I think I've gotten what I needed—at least a start." How to segue into Rizzoli's costume? I couldn't think of an easy way so I blundered forward. "The cloak on the back wall . . . isn't that what the man who was murdered the other night was wearing?"

"Was he?" The man stared for a minute, his mouth set in an unfriendly line. "You can get a cape like that anywhere."

"I didn't mean your store was involved in any way," I said quickly. "It was so awful—I'm having trouble getting that image out of my mind. And it came back when I saw that costume."

"It was gruesome," he said, wagging his head somberly. "One of my customers told me the dead man's hands were tied in front. That's how they took care of criminals in the old days—hung the ones convicted of piracy and murder and then displayed their corpses to deter other miscreants from a life of crime. Though obviously Sam Rizzoli wasn't convicted of anything—except in the mind of his killer."

"So you knew him?"

"By reputation," he said. "Rizzoli first, Key West second. Even his own wife didn't like him much."

The clerk's phone rang. He answered, then pointed at the phone and shook his head. So I waved my thanks and headed home.

This information fit in with Bransford's theories about why Rizzoli was killed: Someone believed he was selling out the town to benefit his own businesses and chose to punish him for it. Which seemed like the simplest explanation, though awfully convenient and generic. Wouldn't committing a murder like this one take something more personal?

My phone began to buzz as I came aboard the house-boat and my mother's number flashed on the screen. "Hi, Mom," I said. "You're up early."

"It's almost nine thirty," she said. "I've been up for hours. You sound a little stuffy. Are your allergies kicking up? Sometimes it can be hard to get used to the vegetation in a new geography. Especially in the change of season."

"I'm fine," I said. Which was not true: Hearing her concerned voice made me realize I was more upset about the photograph I'd seen at the harbor than I'd let myself know. But I didn't want to discuss it with her or anyone, really. Seeing Rizzoli's tortured face was a nightmare I didn't want to share. Describing it would only burn it further into my brain. Not to mention worrying her sick.

"I went for a run and then to do an errand for Connie's wedding. Ray's come up with the silly idea of a pirate theme so Connie assigned me the job of figuring a way to talk him out of it."

"That shouldn't be hard." Mom laughed. "Sounds like he's just a little anxious about the wedding. Men get that way when they get close to the noose."

"The noose?"

"Oh heavens, on our wedding day, your father wondered whether we couldn't just be friends instead of getting married." She snorted with more laughter. "But Ray loves her so much. He'll get over it. How's the TV show?"

"Kinda crazy," I said. "As you'd expect. I have to get showered and dressed for today's taping." I needed to get off the phone before I spilled the beans about the near-drowning or the hanged man. Next thing I knew, she'd be threatening to fly down and act as my personal bodyguard.

I took a quick shower, swallowed a small helping of Special K, and dressed in an all-black outfit. The heck with the yellow *Key Zest* shirt today. Black matched my mood completely.

11

I think it is a sad reflection on our civilization that while we can and do measure the temperature in the atmosphere of Venus we do not know what goes on inside our soufflés.

—Nicholas Kurti

I arrived at the set twenty minutes early, and was surprised to find Peter Shapiro alone in the lovely little kitchen just inside the porch. He was studying something—a script?—a mug of coffee in one hand and a sheaf of papers in the other. I suddenly had a fierce urge to off-load some of my worries on him. He was the executive producer—shouldn't he know what was going on behind the scenes? But was it the right thing to talk to him about Toby's business?

"Morning," I said brightly, as I slid onto the bar stool next to him. "Looks like the weather's going to clear up by this afternoon." He grunted but continued to read.

I couldn't help it—I had to tell him. "So listen, can I speak to you in confidence about something?"

He glanced up, squinting, and put the coffee and the papers on the counter, his blue eyes focusing on my face. "Of course. I hope there isn't a problem with the show?"

"Sort of. Not really. This might sound a little silly, but I thought you should know . . . Toby could be a little shaky this morning." I described what had happened the night before at Mallory Square with Toby's near drowning, skipping past my part in her rescue. "She's worried about Sam Rizzoli's death."

"Of course she is. We're all concerned about that. It was very disturbing," said Peter, his dark brows drawing together, a sharp contrast against his mop of white hair and the closely cropped beard. "I would have stopped the filming altogether, if it hadn't been for those chefs. It didn't seem right to ruin their dreams. . . ."

"Understood." Though he'd used that line so many times—surely there was plenty for him to lose, too, if the show ground to a halt. "But here's the thing," I said. "Toby got the idea that someone shot at her last night. She actually wonders if one of the chef candidates could have killed Rizzoli in order to improve his or her chances in the contest."

"Oh my," said Peter, a small smile on his lips. "She is very worried."

I nodded. "Do you know anything about which of the chefs Rizzoli preferred? It seems like he agreed more with Chef Adam than with either of us women, right? And that would mean he probably would have voted for Buddy Higgs."

"That doesn't really make sense, does it? If two judges ended up dead, how would the contest even continue?"

"You're right. It sounds silly when you say it out loud."

Peter frowned and tapped the pages on the counter in front of him into a neat pile. Finally, he shook his head. "She's told all this to the police, I hope? We can speculate and make up stories until we're blue in the face, but really they are the professionals when it comes to a murder."

I nodded in agreement.

"I'm sure you've read the papers," he continued. "There was hardly a Key West controversy Rizzoli *wasn't* involved with. I hadn't realized that you and he had a little rhubarb recently." His eyebrows peaked, as though now he'd like to hear the dope from me.

I only sighed. "Honest to god, I'd never met the man before the other morning here. It was my job to review that restaurant. And once I'd eaten there—three times—I couldn't lie about it."

He nodded. "I appreciate that. The magazine has to have standards."

I tugged on one of my earrings, thinking again of Lorenzo's admonishment to speak up when I needed to. It might offend Peter, but on the other hand, he should understand that none of us was naïve about reality TV. Funny business was probably the norm.

"This isn't a contest where the outcome was determined before the show even begins, is it? You don't have a ringer who's bound to win no matter what we judges think?"

He laid his hand on my shoulder and gave a gentle

squeeze. "Now that would be an enormous waste of your time—and mine, wouldn't it? And what would be the point? My goal is to finish up the week with the chef who makes the most excellent food and is a terrific entertainer. That's it." He smiled. "Your job is to find her. Or him."

While we were chatting, the chef candidates and the TV assistants had begun to gather in the courtyard. The three chefs, wearing crisp white jackets and tall toques, were differentiated only by their size and shape and the pattern of their pants. Chili peppers for Henri, black checks for the two men. Peter whistled them over to the kitchen, and Deena rounded them up and led them over.

"Feel free to refrigerate what you need to," she said. "We don't want any of our esteemed judges contracting botulism."

The chefs snickered nervously.

"There's not a lot of room in here," Peter added, "so share the space, people."

Three of the show's staffers clattered in from the alley along the back of the Studios of Key West, followed by Chef Adam and Toby. Both Peter and I watched her cross the courtyard. She looked a little more pale than yesterday and wore long sleeves and a flesh-colored Band-Aid on her temple, but seemed otherwise unscathed.

"Don't mention this to her, okay?" I whispered. "She'd only feel embarrassed."

He swiped a finger across his lips, then stood and clapped his hands. "Let's go, people. We have a lot to accomplish today."

As soon as Toby and Chef Adam and I were seated and mic'd up at the judges' table, Peter left to organize the contestants, who were milling around the small kitchen, arranging ingredients, looking tense. I had to wonder again whether one of them could have shot at Toby last night. In the light of day after talking with Peter, this did seem like a preposterous theory. Where would they have been hiding? And I'd seen Buddy Higgs only fifteen minutes earlier squirting chocolate syrup on his tarts. No way he would have been finished in time to hustle over to Mallory Square. And none of them had looked surprised to see Toby alive and well this morning. All three had come prepared to proceed with the contest. They appeared nervous and determined, rather than guilty.

The makeup artist buzzed over to our table and squinted at Toby's face.

"Is the Band-Aid necessary?" she asked.

"Unless you want a close-up of ragged skin," Toby snapped. Chef Adam snickered and then returned to text messaging on his iPhone.

"May I see?" Without waiting for Toby to answer, the makeup girl ripped the bandage off Toby's forehead.

"Ow!" Toby yelped.

"I can work with this," said the young woman. "It will only sting a little."

"Whenever you're ready, people," yelled Peter from the kitchen. The makeup girl swabbed flesh-colored liquid on Toby's wound and ran a puff of powder over her face. Then she packed up her potions and utensils, and backed off the porch.

"Are you all right?" I whispered. "I felt bad leaving you there last night."

Toby shook me off with a fake smile. "I'm fine. We'll talk later."

The lights came on and Peter stepped forward. "As I mentioned yesterday, this morning's challenge is all about destination weddings. Today you'll have the opportunity to decide which of our chefs has the creativity and the talent to tally the most points for this round of *Topped Chef*!" He waved a hand for the theme music to begin—the song "Food Glorious Food" from the Broadway show *Oliver!* surged over the loudspeakers and then faded off, giving way to the Dixie Cups singing "The Chapel of Love."

"Our candidates will present their overnight brainstorms about a Key West wedding, and the judges will have the opportunity to sample their cakes and signature cocktails to determine whether they are or are not a Topped Chef. First up, chef Henri Stentzel." He stepped back and the cameras closed in on Henri. She forced a smile, smoothed a few tendrils of hair into her toque, and tucked her hands behind her back.

"In my mind," she said, "the bride and groom shouldn't allow themselves to be overly influenced by our island. Our tropical setting should enhance the classic nature of the wedding vows, not steal their thunder."

I snuck a look at the other two judges. Toby's expression was noncommittal, Chef Adam's, bored.

"I'm suggesting that the bridal couple should consider going for something classic and classy. And what is more classy than a historical museum? The sense of history grounds the couple in what's come before so they don't set out on their voyage feeling alone. One such venue in Key West is the Lighthouse and Keeper's Quarters Museum. A happy and successful marriage involves two people who look out for each other and remain committed through all the ups and downs of life. What better to symbolize the promise of a wedding than the searching beam of the lighthouse?"

Henri paused for a breath and seemed to assess her audience. Behind her, Peter pretended to fall asleep. Chef Adam looked positively catatonic. Henri smiled brightly and made eye contact with Toby.

"For the wedding cake, I've chosen to spotlight key lime cupcakes: They are light, they are lovely, they side-step the saccharine sweetness and staleness of so many wedding desserts."

Cupcakes. Now she'd caught my interest.

She opened a white bakery box, placed miniature cupcakes on three plates, and delivered them to us. I nibbled at mine—the cream cheese icing had flecks of lime zest in it, as did the pale green cake. Utterly delicious.

"Did you use food coloring in this?" Toby asked.

"Just a drop—to emphasize the lime. Wouldn't this look lovely with green hydrangeas in the bouquet and centerpieces?"

Since no one else was bothering to answer her, I nodded briskly.

"Often signature cocktails are heavy and sweet," Henri continued, "and they can result in drunken and boorish guests that night and queasiness the next morning." She popped the cork on a bottle of prosecco and poured the bubbly liquid into four flutes with raspberries nestled at the bottom. She brought each of us a glass, and clinked hers against ours as she talked.

"Classic setting, light and lovely cake, prosecco. That's my recipe for an elegant wedding."

I wished Connie had been here to listen to all this firsthand. She might not have loved the lighthouse idea, but she would have adored those pale green cupcakes. I'd have to try replicating them at home so she could sample. We hadn't discussed one thing about what kind of reception she wanted or what she wanted served.

Henri bowed and moved out of the kitchen so Buddy Higgs could take center stage. He nearly knocked her over as he pushed past her and leaned his hands on the counter.

"I couldn't disagree more," he said, staring in turn at each of us. "People choose to get married in Key West because it's Key West!" He straightened and threw his arms out wide. "To not take advantage of the magnificent setting is criminal! Let's be honest here: A wedding is a show—the most important party of your lifetime." He ticked off his points on his fingers. "You definitely want a spectacular, showy backdrop, like a glorious sunset on the Westin pier. And then you enhance that magic with the food and drink. The wedding planners should provide refreshments that haven't been done for a million other brides." He bared his teeth in Henri's direction and then leaned across the counter to look intently at Chef Adam.

"Cupcakes," he said in a scornful voice, "are so 2010."

He rummaged in the refrigerator and reappeared

with little chocolate cakes on plates decorated with a lighter-colored chocolate powder and tiny clear spheres that looked like bath beads.

"My presentation includes individual flourless chocolate-hazelnut cakes, garnished with Nutella powder and Frangelico caviar. Some chefs grind their hazelnuts finely and add them to the chocolate batter, but I find this distorts the texture. The secret"—he winked—"is hazelnut flour."

He brought us each a plate and continued to expound on his methods for making the Frangelico beads. I was too busy sinking into the decadence of the chocolate to pay close attention.

"As the signature cocktail, I recommend a mojito from the tradition of molecular gastronomy," he added. "The ingredients are simple enough—rum, mint, club soda, lime juice. But the presentation takes the drink from ordinary to spectacular." He delivered large spoons containing egg-sized gelatinous spheres with mint leaves suspended in them.

"What is this?" asked Toby. "What are we supposed to do with it?"

"Bottoms up," said Chef Adam, as he tipped the spoon to his mouth.

I followed suit, and felt a warm jolt, as though I'd just swallowed a shot of rum. Which I suppose I had.

"This is spectacular," said Chef Adam.

"Though perhaps a little gimmicky?" I asked, and Toby nodded.

Once Buddy Higgs had finished telling us which chemicals caused the drink to gel, and finally cleared out of the way, Randy Thompson moved into the kitchen. He stood behind the counter, his hands behind his back, and smiled.

"A wedding is about the people, not the show. And people connect on a more honest level when the setting is casual. Hence, I've designed a picnic at Fort Zachary Taylor Park."

He pulled a pitcher full of liquid and a small bag of mint from the refrigerator.

"I've got a mojito, too," he said ruefully. "But no gelatin involved." He turned to face Buddy Higgs. "By the way, Chef Buddy, on Duval Street, they'd call your concoction a Jell-O shot. And it's usually sucked off someone's belly. Hopefully not a beer gut." A titter of laughter swept through the crew, but Buddy looked grim.

We watched Randy crush his mint leaves in the bottoms of three pint-sized mason jars, which he then filled to the brim with ice and a clear liquid. He delivered them to us and we sipped—refreshing and powerful.

"Since I'm proposing a casual setting, and maybe even a barefoot bride, I envisioned the wedding dessert as casual, too." He pulled a tray from the freezer. "For the bride at the beach, what could be more fun than cake pops?"

He carried the tray over to us and we each took a ball of cake on a stick. Dark chocolate inside, a shell of white chocolate outside, studded with tiny silver beads of candy.

By now, I was feeling extremely light-headed, not to mention trembling from the sugar rush of the cumulative desserts. But the worst culprit had been the shimmery mojito. I reminded myself to watch for signs of

alliance, either between Toby and Chef Adam, or either
of them and the candidates. Pay attention to the sub-
text, I told myself. If something strange was going on
among the little factions, I didn't want to be caught un-
awares. I wanted the best candidate to land the show.
But more important: If one of these people had killed
Sam Rizzoli, the rest of us were also in danger. It was
that simple.

Henri had seemed less distant than she had the other
day. And Buddy had acted very confident. Either he
was doing a good job hiding things or he was sure he
had it nailed. Had he seen me last night on the yacht?
Did he realize what I'd seen?

But I was finding it harder and harder to concentrate
on the contest, my woozy mind wandering to the question of whether I'd ever get to plan a wedding. For me.
Hard to imagine when I couldn't even get through a
first date without ending up all prickly and out of sorts.

"Judges?" boomed Peter Shapiro, interrupting my
thoughts. "Your reactions to our contestants' presentations?"

"I have two words for you," said Chef Adam turning to face the camera. "Cake? Pops?"

"Yes, they were a little hokey, but you have to admit
they were delicious," I said, my words slurring just the
tiniest bit. "And fun. I'd like to be a guest at Randy's
wedding reception. On the other hand, that gelatin ball
might go over in Chicago or Los Angeles, but it doesn't
speak 'parrothead' to me. When I was a kid, I used to
love those bath beads—the ones that look like gelatin
until they dissolve in hot water. That's all I could think

about when he served us that Frangelico thing. Would it taste like soapsuds?"

Chef Adam glared at me as though I'd lost my marbles.

"The caterer has no business competing with the bride, in my opinion," said Toby. "And the molecular gastronomy products shout *look at me!* On the other hand, I found the key lime cupcakes to be delightful."

When we'd said all we had to say, and more, Peter signaled that the taping was over. "You people did well today. You kicked it up a notch. And you look good, too. The black is a big improvement," he said to me. Then he touched his hand to his forehead and looked at Toby. "Everything all right with you?"

"I'm fine," she answered with a forced smile. "Are we finished here?"

When Peter nodded, she leaped up and hurried across the courtyard.

12

That would be enough for him. To find her plums in season, and perfect nectarines, velvet apricots, dark succulent duck. To bring her all these things and watch her eat.

—Allegra Goodman, *The Cookbook Collector*

On the way out of the studio, I had the happy realization that the police station was exactly on my route home. Before I returned to the boat to take a nap, I'd swing by to talk to Nate in person. I was feeling just this side of euphoric, happy and generous enough to realize that I'd been brusque with him lately. Maybe I'd overread his comments and his reaction to me the other night—he was only trying to do his job. And a brutal job it was. Just seeing the photo of the hanged man up close was devastating—how must it feel to be sifting through every detail of that murder?

I decided I would tell him everything I'd learned about the case so far, and then see if he might like to come over for dinner. But what to fix? I could try re-creating the seafood diavolo that Henri Stentzel had prepared for the first leg of the contest. But without the squid. I was off them after watching an Animal Planet rerun about their intelligence—how they watched humans with as much curiosity as the humans watched them.

What had the detective eaten the one time we'd been out to dinner? Nothing too unusual. But the spicy red sauce—no man could resist that. It would warm him from the inside out. I felt a small tremor of excitement, thinking about what might follow.

Maybe Miss Gloria could be persuaded to spend the evening with her friend Mrs. Dubisson, especially if I sprang for takeout. Or two tickets to the Tropic Cinema. And a cab to get them there. Or all of the above.

I parked my scooter in a visitor's spot outside the station. Luckily another civilian had just been buzzed in through the locked front door, so I tripped in behind her, and was saved the awkwardness of calling and explaining myself to the clerk on duty. And I'd never, not once, had an easy phone conversation with the detective. In person was definitely preferable.

I followed the hallway around to the back of the first floor, and took the elevator to Nate's second-floor space. Outside his office, I fluffed my hair and applied a quick layer of lip gloss. The thought flitted through my mind: Would he kiss me right now? Then I remembered the video camera hidden in his wall clock and had to laugh. He wouldn't want the first stirrings of romance caught on videotape, fodder for the other cops' teasing. I took a deep breath, arranged a sweet but flirty smile, and tapped on his closed door.

My heart galloped as I waited, then the door swung open. "Yes?"

Surprised didn't begin to describe Nate's expression when he saw me in the hallway. But he recovered quickly, smiled back and reached out to shake my hand. Behind him, in the chair beside his desk, sat a woman—a beautiful woman with enormous brown eyes, black hair, and radiant skin. The kind of gorgeous but slightly foreign-looking woman who tended to take first runner-up in the Miss America pageant, back when I was a girl watching the TV show with my mother. Stunning, but a little too ethnic to represent the US of A.

"Hayley. Did we have an appointment?"

Of course we didn't have an appointment. "N-n-n-no," I stammered. "I was driving by and just thought I'd stop in."

The beautiful woman lifted one dark eyebrow, her perfectly shaped lips pursing like a resting bow. Yes, stunning.

After an excruciating pause he said, "Hayley Snow, meet Trudy Bransford, my wife."

"Ex-wife," she said to him, but added a smile that would have melted a softer man to a helpless puddle. In the running for Miss Congeniality, too.

She rose to her feet, crossed the room in two quick steps, and placed a slender hand in mine, which was still outstretched after the shock of the detective's handshake, and then his announcement. I looked down. Her nails were capped with perfect pale half-moons. No chips in the polish. No ragged cuticles either. She wore an eye-popping diamond engagement ring on her right hand.

"Your island is so lovely," she said in her contralto voice. She barely reached his shoulder. Looked like she would fit perfectly tucked under his arm. "Have you lived here all your life?"

"Uh, no," I said, finally meeting her eyes. "New Jersey. Recent transplant. My boyfriend—ex-boyfriend— invited me down here. The truth is we didn't know each other well enough to weather that much intimacy—"

Nate cut in: "Can I help you with something?"

But other than this incessant babbling about my story of moving to Key West, my brain was firing blanks. "Just checking in about the murder. Any news?"

"Still following leads." He bared his teeth into a feral grin.

Trudy grinned, too, a wide, generous smile that reached all the way to her eyes, lighting her face up along the way. She tipped her head and tapped two fingers on his chest. "He was never too good at sharing information. I can see that hasn't changed. He doesn't like to talk about his feelings either."

"No problem." I held up a hand and began to shuffle backward from the door out into the hall. "Nice to meet you, Trudy. Catch you later."

Then I wheeled around and burst the length of the hallway, listening for his following footsteps but not surprised to hear nothing. I vaulted down the stairway to the first floor, thinking I couldn't bear to be trapped in the elevator with anyone else where I'd have to act normal and unruffled.

At least I hadn't rushed into his office announcing my intention to cook him dinner, nattering on about the level of heat in the pasta sauce. That would have been too mortifying for words.

Very near tears, I pushed the heavy door from the stairwell into the hallway and nearly slammed into Officer Torrence. His expression of surprise, followed quickly by sympathy, cracked my dam.

"Oh my," he said, glancing up the stairs and frowning. "You've come from the detective's office. I'm sorry. How did you get in? I would have warned you she was here if I'd known you were coming."

I started to sniffle in earnest. He circled an arm around my shoulders and shuffled me around the corner to his office. He handed over a box of generic brand tissues and shut the door, waiting for me to pull myself together.

A million questions surged through my mind. How long had Trudy been here? I remembered from an article I'd read about their home invasion a couple of years ago that she lived in Miami. Had he asked her to come down? Had they been talking all along? Where was she staying? Were they reuniting? Was that hair color real? And why the hell hadn't he said something, like warned me that his wife was back in the picture? His *wife*.

But Torrence shouldn't be put in the position of feeding me information about his boss. And to preserve the tiny shreds of dignity I still had intact, it felt important to act as though those details couldn't have made the slightest difference. So I blew my nose and wiped my eyes and tried to smile. "You do have a way of finding me in shaky condition."

"Don't be silly," he said. "Not to worry. Can I help you with something? Besides him?" He jerked his thumb over his shoulder.

I laughed. "I had some thoughts about the murder, that's all. That's what I came to tell him." I shuddered and squared my shoulders.

"You might as well tell me," he said. "I can pass it on."

"It will sound silly."

"Okay." He nodded.

"You know that Sam Rizzoli was a judge for the cooking contest I'm involved with?"

He nodded again.

And then I told him about my conversation with Toby Davidson. "She's afraid that someone might be targeting us three other judges. I spoke with our executive producer this morning—he swears that none of the candidates have been preselected to win. That was one idea Toby had about a possible motive—that one of the candidates believed that Rizzoli would gum up the machine."

"That's a big leap," said Torrence.

"As Toby pointed out," I argued, "there's an awful lot riding on the outcome. It's not only a local fundraiser. Winning could mean a huge game change in someone's career. And we're definitely not all in agreement. Chef Adam really loves this guy Buddy Higgs. Toby seems to like Henri Stentzel. And so far I'm leaning toward Randy Thompson. Except for the cake pops. Randy suggested *cake pops* for a wedding." I hated to agree with Chef Adam on much of anything, but in this case, after thinking it over, I had to admit he was right.

"At first, I thought it was a fun idea. But when he described how they're made, I realized he'd lost his mind. He actually admitted that his ingredients were a boxed cake mix and a can of Betty Crocker icing."

Torrence's eyes had begun to glaze over like the chocolate frosting on one of Randy's treats. Torrence was clearly no chef. He wouldn't have a clue about how using a cake mix would be anathema to a culinary professional.

"All I'm saying is no one's a lock. But I keep wondering who's got the biggest stake in winning the contest. And how far would he or she go to be sure he or she won?"

Torrence squinted and shook his head. "To be honest, your theory, while interesting, feels like quite a stretch. How would killing off another judge garner a win? More likely it would end the contest."

"Point taken." The same thing Peter had said. But then I reminded him about last night, how Toby dove into the water off Mallory Square when she thought someone was shooting at her. "Doesn't that mean something?"

"I heard about the incident in this morning's report," Torrence said. "Good thing you were there to pull her out. I think her body would be floating toward the Bermuda Triangle about now if you hadn't. Shark bait." He rubbed a finger over his mustache. "I shouldn't say much, but we have examined the footage from the Mallory Square webcam before and after the time your friend went overboard. We didn't find much—only a fuzzy sequence of her ducking, and then leaping over the concrete lip into the water. And then you followed soon after. One man came up to the edge but he appeared to be talking to you, not shooting."

"That was Tony," I said. "He's not a threat. Except to himself. He's homeless and I don't think he really wants to change that. I'm sure he didn't care to stick around and get harassed by Key West's finest." I grinned to take the edge off my words.

"These are all excellent observations." Torrence's voice was gentle. "You're a real student of human behavior." He paused and lapped his lower lip over the upper.

"But—"

"But there isn't any real evidence to substantiate your theories. To be honest? I think your friend is nervous." He drummed his fingers on the desk, thinking. "Don't you find it odd that a woman who can't swim and says she's terrified of the water dives into the harbor right at the point with the worst current?"

"Unless she really heard a gunshot. Unless she panicked because of that and tripped and fell in."

"Yes, but no one else heard it. You yourself said you didn't hear it."

"I thought it was firecrackers."

"Does it occur to you that she's lying about something? I even wonder if she's suicidal. Is it possible that she intended to drown herself but then panicked when the reality of what she was about to do hit her? Did you get the sense she was feeling down last evening? Do you know her well? What has she been like the past few days?"

"I only just met her," I admitted, hating to think how much sense his questions made. "So I don't have any idea of what she's like normally. She did seem nervous right off the blocks and it's gotten worse each day. A few times she's told us what she really thinks about the *Topped Chef* contestants, but speaking out seems to set her back. She worries about what other people think of her opinions. And whether we'll disagree." I balled up the tissue in my fingers and fired it at his trash can. "I never considered whether she might be depressed. That would explain some things."

"Such as?"

"She's quite well known for a memoir about food and grief. It wasn't that long ago that she lost her husband. Then she wrote a book about the experience, which was a huge bestseller."

My friend Eric would probably have said she might have been better off letting herself feel her sadness, instead of writing about it for the general public. That way she would have had a better chance at putting it behind her instead of having her face rubbed into it everywhere she turned.

"But I do wonder how she'll follow up on a success like that."

He adjusted his glasses. "Hmm. I'll pass your information along." Then he stood up, a signal that our impromptu counseling session was over. "Anything else?"

"One more thing." I described the idea that sprang from my pirate wedding research—how maybe Rizzoli had been strung up to teach someone a lesson. I did not mention the photo on Derek the dockhand's iPhone because he'd never forgive me if his cell got impounded as evidence. How many early mornings had he rolled

out of bed to clean spilled beer and puke off that catamaran to afford the darn thing?

Torrence walked me to the door. "You feel free to
feed me any information you come across." He read off
his cell phone number and I punched it into my con-
tacts list. "I may look old-fashioned but I do accept text
messages. I am not putting you 'on the case.' Understand? You don't have a deputy star pinned to your
chest. You're not to go rushing around like a junior detective. Don't *do* anything, other than keep your eyes
and ears open. Got that?"

"Roger that," I said.

He grinned, and then chucked my chin. We walked
down the hallway and he held the door to the outside.
I stood blinking in the sudden sunlight, feeling as
though all the ground had shifted subtly beneath me. I
seemed to have lost a boyfriend, but gained a friend.
Which left me feeling a little hollow, but not as bad as I
might have if I hadn't run into Torrence. Boyfriends, in
my limited experience, were dust in the wind. Friends,
my rocks and anchors.

I no longer felt like napping. Instead, I hopped on
my scooter and headed south to the *Key Zest* office,
where I could start my article on the Mallory Square
Stroll and enjoy the camaraderie of my coworkers. And
avoid thinking about what I'd just seen in detective Nathan Bransford's office.

13

The cult of celebrity associated with the postmodern chef is kept alive by armies of publicists, but it is rooted in the chef's psychological yearning to be loved by thousands.

—Scott Haas

Danielle jumped all over me the minute I emerged from the stairwell into our office reception area. "Hayley, you're on the front page of the *Citizen*. I'm so proud of you!" She held up the newspaper.

LOCAL FOOD CRITIC MAKES HEROIC RESCUE, the headline blared. I skimmed the brief report, which named me but, thank goodness, not Toby. She would have been mortified by the publicity. Although below the story was an unfortunate photo of her draped in a police blanket, me standing alongside her in my white blouse that when wet, showed the lace of my bra right through it. Completely embarrassing.

"Anyone would have done the same thing," I said. "But maybe dressed a little better."

Danielle snickered.

Wally stuck his head out of his office. "Good work, you. Too bad we don't write straight news—we'd have the inside scoop. How did this happen?"

I explained about Toby's worries over the contest and her reaction to the subsequent, perhaps imaginary, gunshot.

"Good Lord, Hayley," said Danielle. "You're jinxed! Have you told the cops?"

"Thanks for the confidence," I said. "I just got back from the police station. Officer Torrence doesn't think there's much basis for Toby's concerns. A group of officers came through and interviewed every one of us judges and the staffers and the chefs themselves yesterday, and the upshot is that they don't seem to think the TV show has any bearing on the murder."

"Sounds like you're not convinced," said Wally, leaning against the doorjamb.

"Peter Shapiro, the executive producer, keeps saying how important it is to keep taping. Because winning this contest would mean so much for each of the candidates. Toby said the same thing—big bucks, fame, escape from drudgery. In other words, there's an awful lot at stake for these three chefs."

Wally's eyes widened. "Whether it has anything to do with the murder or not, this could be a fascinating story—who wants to win this TV spot and why. This is one hell of a great feature for *Key Zest*."

"Who's writing that angle?" I asked.

"You are, of course." He grinned. "You'll have to do some digging to get the background on all of them. We'll help you do the research. And if you're worried about a conflict of interest, I'll take the byline."

"I'll do the work and you'll take the byline?" I asked. "Are you kidding?"

"Of course," Wally said with a laugh.

"Road trip!" said Danielle. "It's four o'clock—maybe the boss will let us knock off a little early." She winked at Wally. "Where do we start?"

"Officer Torrence did tell me to keep my eyes peeled for anything related to the murder," I said and described what Bransford had said about Sam Rizzoli's connections to Key West politics. Then I told them about the conversation I'd had with the men at the harbor regarding Rizzoli's bar. "Maybe we'd learn something there. And then I'd love to see Randy Thompson perform. He's our drag-queen contestant who cooks like his grandmother. Maybe even talk with him, if we get the chance."

"I think he's doing dueling bartenders tonight at the Aqua," said Danielle.

Aqua was a well-known drag bar on Duval Street. Miss Gloria had been there several times with her bridge group, but I'd not yet drummed up the nerve to go in. Miss Gloria—bridge group—drag bar. I had to mentally shake my head every time I thought of that combination.

"It's probably too late to get a reservation," I said. "But maybe we could get a bite to eat later at Chef Adam's restaurant on Simonton Street." I looked over at Wally. "It's not exactly in my budget. Is this *Key Zest* business?"

"Definitely," Wally said. "I'll deal with Ava Faulkner when the time comes."

Ava Faulkner, Wally's copublisher who managed the finances of *Key Zest*. An antifan of mine. The name spoken aloud made me quiver.

Danielle patted my hand reassuringly. "Chef Adam isn't a candidate for the show, is he?"

"No. A judge. And the one I know least well of all the players. The one who doesn't seem to have anything riding on the contest outcome. Which makes me suspicious of course." I grinned. "Give me a minute to put some things away."

"No offense Wally," Danielle said, "but I think I'll change out of this shirt. We look a little too much like fast-food employees, don't you think?" She plucked at the sleeve of her yellow shirt.

"Traitor," he said.

"Hayley doesn't have hers on," said Danielle, pulling out the bottom desk drawer where she kept her makeup and an extra blouse.

Half an hour later we had found a table at Rizzoli's outdoor bar, down the alley from his restaurant. We were early enough to snag a position near the bar, but at the same time overlooking Duval. I made sure to sit facing the street so I didn't have to look at the restaurant I'd shredded in my review not forty-eight hours ago.

A bustling happy-hour crowd began to trickle in— sunburned tourists, mostly. The prices were on the high side, and I saw no signs proclaiming a locals discount, which some of the bars and restaurants in town embraced to encourage the patronage of real Key Westers.

Rock-and-roll tunes from the sixties and seventies pounded out from the loudspeakers. We waited for about five minutes, watching the people around us and hoping a waitress would materialize.

"Weren't you scared last night jumping into the harbor?" Danielle asked. "I can barely swim. If I tried to rescue someone, it could only end up with two of us drowning."

"Honestly, I didn't spend one nanosecond thinking it through," I said. "I just reacted. It scares me now, though, thinking about it." I shivered. "Especially if someone really does have it in for Toby. Which I know is not likely, but still . . ."

"You can quit the show," Wally said, a worried look crossing his face. "If you're that concerned."

But by now I was way too invested to quit. I wanted to see which contestant won the contest, and then whether and how his or her career got launched with Peter Shapiro's TV show. If one of these guys made it big—became the next Bobby Flay or Paula Deen or Jacques Pépin—I wanted to have been part of the process.

And I wanted to make sure Toby was okay. Wasn't there a Chinese proverb that said once you'd saved someone's life they were your responsibility forever?

"You don't really mean that," I said with a big grin. "And I swear I won't do anything else that reckless. And honestly, I do think she overreacted."

Wally finally gave up on the waitress and threaded through the crowd to the bar, squeezing in between an overweight man sipping an icy white drink topped with a paper umbrella and a skinny woman covered in blurry tattoos of birds and links of chains, drinking Coke.

"I'll have three Key West pale ales," we heard him tell the bartender. "Awful shame about Sam Rizzoli."

"He's smooth, isn't he?" Danielle laughed.

"And he's kinda cute in that silly shirt," I said, squinting at the back of his neck, which had a sunburn that stopped just short of his new haircut. He probably wasn't five inches taller than me, but there wasn't a pinch of flab on him.

"I tried to talk him out of the company-shirt idea before he hired you," said Danielle, "but it's grown on me. At least during business hours."

"You don't look like a fresh case of hepatitis when you're wearing yellow," I said. "The way some others of us do."

Wally came back to the table with our drinks. "I got a few snippets," he said. "Rizzoli's funeral is tomorrow. Private service for the family at Saint Mary Star of the Sea. But they're having a memorial open to the public around lunchtime on the White Street Pier."

"Any more word on who killed him?" I asked.

"I overheard the guy at the end of the bar say Rizzoli had some troubles with his wife recently." Wally pointed through the crowd to a tall man with a faded Fast Buck Freddies ball cap and a dappled white and gray beard. "But I couldn't hang around to hear what kind of troubles. And it's hard to imagine his own wife hoisting him up the rigging, no matter how mad she was at him."

"Somebody hated him," said Danielle, and then turned to me. "Say, what's happening with you and that adorable detective?"

Tears pricked my eyes, surprising me and bringing expressions of concern from both Wally and Danielle. I'd hoped I was over it—wishful thinking. Even I— champion of denial—wasn't that good at sweeping disappointment under the rug. I ducked my head and took a big slug of beer. "His ex-wife is in town. I don't know what that means, except I'm sure it's curtains for me and him. They looked very cozy. And she's a stunner."

"You deserve better," said Wally softly. He held my gaze for a minute and then changed the subject to a feature he wanted to write about literary Key West.

"*Travel and Leisure* did a nice piece about our town in 2009, but a lot's changed. Not the history, of course—everyone knows about Hemingway and Tennessee Williams. But this place is rife with artists and writers. Do they come because they sense they can be a big fish in our small town? Would a painter who's a big deal in Key West be a nothing in New York City? Or is there something about the atmosphere that nurtures creativity and brings out the best in artists and writers? We're the insiders—we know this stuff better than anyone."

"The same questions work for restaurants, too," I pointed out. "Would a place we rate four stars get one in New York? Or do we really have top chefs working here?"

Once we'd finished our drinks, we left a couple of bucks on the table and went out onto the sidewalk. A herd of motorcyclists without helmets or mufflers roared by, drowning out the conversation until they were several blocks down Duval.

"There's something I don't get," said Wally, shaking his head. "Why is that allowed? Do you think our commissioners and police are afraid to take them on? This is what I don't like about our town. We should make reasonable guidelines and rules and then stick to them—not bend them according to whoever's pressuring the commissioners. Or paying them off."

"Sam Rizzoli, for example," I added.

A couple of minutes later, we reached the Aqua nightclub. I'd passed this bar by scooter or on foot a hundred times since I'd hit town, but I'd never found the right opportunity to go in. The doors and shuttered windows had been folded open to the street so passersby could see in. A cloud of cigarette smoke wafted outside, along with a blast of music. Wally looked a little nervous, as I must have, but Danielle pushed us through it.

We stepped into the semidarkness and stopped a minute to let our eyes adjust. A bar stretched along the left side of the room, "AQUA" written in turquoise neon script above the bottles of liquor on shelves against the wall. A second U-shaped bar was set up to the right of the entry, glasses hanging from the ceiling. At the back of the hall stretched an empty stage, and empty tables and chairs were clustered around a deserted dance floor. Right now, all the action was at the two bars.

Behind the bar on the left, a lovely young woman with sculpted arms, a sparkly sequined top, and narrow hips poured glasses of wine and draft beer for two customers. And standing outside the other bar was an enormous person with a behind shaped like a divan, wearing a wig, high heels, and thick, thick makeup.

She crooned a scratchy rendition of Donna Summer's "Last Dance" into a portable microphone.

"That's Gassy Winds," whispered Danielle. "But I assume you want to get served by Randy Thompson, right?"

I stopped stock-still. "Where's Randy?"

"Behind the other bar. Well, Victoria at the moment," said Danielle as she herded us over to take seats at the bar.

"How do you know all this?" I asked, trying not to stare at Randy/Victoria, who had better muscle definition in his/her arms than I ever dreamed of.

"I come here for karaoke as often as I can," she said with a shrug. "I love this place." She slapped a twenty on the bar. "Looking good, Victoria!" she called out. "Three Coronas with lime. And can you sing some Patsy Cline?"

The bartender—Randy? Victoria?—winked at her, thumbed through a notebook on the back counter, and then called out a number to the DJ who sat in a glassed-in cubicle at the back of the room. After serving us the beers, Victoria began to sing "She's Got You" in a mournful, vibrant baritone. She looked straight into Danielle's eyes as she crooned "I've got your memory . . . ," then turned to wash out a few glasses left in the small sink behind the bar. "Or has it got me . . ."

"Wow, some voice," said Wally. "So how do you address a drag queen? Is it he or she?"

"She, when she's dressed up, like Victoria is now," said Danielle. "And he, when he's Randy. It's that simple."

When the song wound down, Victoria stopped by

our end of the bar to deliver the drinks. "Slumming tonight?" she asked Danielle, still making no eye contact with me.

"I think you know Hayley," said Danielle, placing a hand on my forearm. "And the cute guy is Wally."

"Hey, big fella," said Victoria. "Are you a three-woman kind of man?" She winked and Wally flushed absolutely crimson.

"Oh stop," said Danielle, giggling. "He's our boss. How's the TV show going?"

"It would be a lot better if the judges hadn't decided ahead of time who was going to win," said Victoria, an edge in her voice. "And better if they weren't in the executive producer's pocket."

"That's not fair," I said. "Nobody's approached me about how to vote. And I'm certainly not getting paid. Everything's been real and aboveboard so far." I turned to Wally. "You tell her, I sure didn't ask for this job."

"She's right," Wally said. "Deena Smith called and asked if we could send someone because we cover a lot of local food events in our magazine. Hayley's the real deal."

"There's nothing real about this business—it's television. And as fake as they can make it," Victoria said and grimaced. "The TV people don't care about the best local food. They care about ratings because ratings sell advertising." She flounced down to the other end of the bar and then came back to lean in closer to Wally. "Just like a lot of people give lip service to supporting local performers—and that includes drag queens. But underneath the surface, life is not all champagne and cake pops. It's downright ugly. Why do you think Rizzoli was hung in a wig and makeup? Trying to point a finger at one of us, that's why."

She sashayed away to take another customer's money. I chugged my beer a little faster than I should have, feeling chastised and chagrined. If I was completely honest, as much as I liked Randy's cooking and personality, I did have trouble imagining a drag queen winning the contest and going on to host a cooking show. Maybe our biases were showing through more clearly than I'd ever imagined.

We slunk out of Aqua and walked a couple of blocks north to Chef Adam's restaurant, which he'd named "Boyd's Nest."

"Why not 'Boyd in the Hand'?" Danielle asked, snickering.

Wally secured us a table in the back of the dining room near the side window, which looked out on a small garden. Once we'd confirmed that we wanted Miami's finest tap water, rather than bottled, the hostess dropped off some menus. My eyes practically bugged out of my head when I saw the prices. I was glad Wally was here to pick up the check, courtesy of *Key Zest*.

"We do have one special on the menu tonight. But Chef doesn't like us to call them specials because everything he makes is special," said the waiter with only the smallest hint of a smile.

"Sounds like him, all right," I muttered under my breath.

"The dish is a sautéed, blackened grouper, served with crashed new potatoes, and steamed squash. The fish is on the spicy side," he warned us.

"What are crashed new potatoes?" I asked.

"They're steamed, and then smashed and broiled with kosher salt and herbs until crispy. Out of this world."

Once we'd ordered, Wally asked the waiter to ask the chef if he was free to visit for a minute or two. "I'll ask," said the waiter. "He's pretty busy in there, bossing people around." He smirked and hurried off to place our orders.

Halfway through the meal, Chef Adam barreled through the dining room to our table. "Oh, it's you," he said when he arrived and recognized me. "I thought one of our customers had lodged a complaint."

"Not about this dinner," I said graciously. "The fish is magnificent—fresh and zingy. Your waiter described it exactly."

"And the potatoes are even better," said Danielle with a melting smile.

"None of us have eaten here before," said Wally. "I don't think Hayley can do a review with both of you serving as *Topped Chef* judges, but we did want to tell you how much we're enjoying the food."

"How about you, Chef?" asked Danielle, tossing her hair off her shoulder so her cleavage showed more clearly. "How are you enjoying being a judge?"

"Not so much," he said, scowling. "It's an amateurish production rife with amateur cooks."

"You miss Mr. Rizzoli," I said.

He looked at me with surprise, and then nodded. "No offense, but he knew food."

"I'd say Hayley's pretty darned good at that, too," said Wally.

No comment from Chef Adam.

"If you don't mind me asking," I said, "when were you tapped to be one of the judges?"

"Maybe a couple weeks ago?" He shrugged. "Why?"

I couldn't very well come out and say I was trying to rule him out as a suspect in Rizzoli's murder. Or rule out a setup in the judging process. "I wondered why you agreed. You seem to think the whole enterprise is foolishness."

He stiffened and straightened his toque. "It is. But I like to do my bit for the town. And besides, having a panel of rank amateurs as judges would only serve to sink the show to an even lower level. Excuse me," he added with a small bow. "They'll be looking for me in the kitchen." He bustled away.

"More like relieved for the respite," said Danielle, once he was out of earshot. "Is that what he's like all the time?"

"That's pretty much him," I said.

"Seemed as though he really liked Rizzoli," Wally said.

Back at the office after dinner, I said my good nights and got on my scooter. Still feeling revved up by the evening, I decided to swing back around Mallory Square to find Tony. I wanted to know in person what he'd seen and heard the night before when Toby Davidson ended up in the drink.

I parked my bike on the street outside the Waterfront Playhouse and hurried back through the alley to Mallory Square, a little spooked by the darkness. As I'd expected, Tony and his buddies were hanging out on the same corner where I'd seen them a night earlier, talking loudly. A pile of empty beer cans and cigarette butts littered the ground at their feet.

"Hayley!" Tony called out as soon as he saw me. "Hope you're all right. That was some scary crap yesterday."

"Yes, yes, it was. Thanks for helping out."

"I couldn't stick around." He shrugged an apology. "I stayed until the cops got here."

"Watch out for five-oh!" another of the men razzed him.

Tony elbowed him in the ribs.

"I understand," I said. "I was wondering, did you guys happen to hear a gunshot last night before my friend went into the water?"

"I knew that's what them cops were lookin' for," said one of Tony's pals. "That's why we took off. Once they mistake us for a shooter, we're goin' to jail and never getting out."

"I'm playing your sad story on my violin," said the first man, making a sawing motion with his hand. He turned back to me. "We heard firecrackers all night. That's considered big fun for those idiot college kids— drink too much beer and then wake up the whole island."

"We definitely heard fireworks," Tony agreed. "We heard that whistling noise. Wouldn't a gunshot be flatter?" For a few minutes they argued about the difference in the two sounds, but came to no conclusions.

"You didn't happen to notice anyone running away after Toby dove in?"

"Just us chickens," the first man said, and laughed.

"It was quiet here," said Tony. "Course, we were minding our business, shooting the shit. Not looking for trouble." He rubbed the stubble on his chin. "We didn't have a good view out that way." He pointed toward the Westin, toward the bridge in front of the aquarium that Toby and I had crossed last night.

As I left the men, I glanced across the square. Lorenzo was at his table again. A thin woman was just getting up from the chair facing him. She shook his hand and walked away, sniffling into a tissue. I wondered what news he'd given her. Since no one was waiting to take her place, I hurried over and slid into the seat.

"Just wanted to say hi," I told him.

"I've been thinking about you," he said, "holding you in the light. No bad effects from your dip last night?"

"We're both okay," I said. "Toby a little more shaken than me. You were right about speaking up and cutting things loose." I pulled my hair back into a loose ponytail and then let it go. "My detective friend's wife showed up in town."

"I'm sorry. But it's hard to argue with the cards." He placed his hand over mine and squeezed. "What are you doing here this late?"

"I wondered whether Tony and his friends had seen anything unusual last night. Besides Toby in the water, I mean."

His forehead wrinkled in concentration. "I did see her on the square earlier. Chatting with another woman. That doesn't help much, does it?"

"Not really. Not like if you'd read her cards and there was a secret in them you could share with me."

He laughed. "Can't help with that. And couldn't share anyway—wouldn't be ethical."

I was exhausted by the time I fell into my berth on the houseboat. But not tired enough to keep the image of Bransford's wife out of my mind. To keep from wondering why she'd come to Key West. I'd checked the answering machine just in case he might have left word. Though why would he call home when other times we connected we'd talked on my cell? Even so, I checked the pad attached to the refrigerator with a magnet where Miss Gloria left me important messages.

"Sleep tight!" was all she'd written.

When pigs fly, I thought grimly.

I went back to bed, listening for hours to the clank of ropes and winches against the mast of our neighbor's boat, two slots up the finger. And wondering just how different it might have sounded with a body tangled up in the rigging.

14

A crust eaten in peace is better than a banquet partaken in anxiety.

—Aesop

I woke up late and logy. I went straight to the galley, looking for a decent breakfast—do not pass Go, do not pass Anything Edible. Unfortunately, our cupboard space was jammed with three boxes of dietetic, cardboard-tasting cereal that I'd bought earlier this week when I was thinking Diet with a capital *D*. Not acceptable in my current frame of mind. Miss Gloria's leftover bran muffins from the local Publix supermarket had been moldering in a plastic container on the counter all week—I ruled them out, too.

Visions of the rolled oats, pecans, coconut, and slivered almonds I'd bought at the Sugar Apple Natural Foods last week flashed through my mind; I started to salivate with possibilities. Pulling those ingredients out of the freezer and the cupboard, I began to measure and mix a batch of my favorite granola. I stirred maple syrup, brown sugar, and canola oil into the bowl of nuts and grains, poured it into two big cookie pans, and slid the pans into Miss Gloria's oven.

I retreated to the back deck of the houseboat with a big mug of coffee and my laptop, intending to write up my notes for the Mallory Square Stroll. It was not easy to develop a flow when I had to get up every fifteen minutes to stir the granola so it would roast to a consistently lovely golden crunch.

Besides, every time I put fingers to keyboard, the image of Nate's wife popped into my mind—excruciating. Even though I'd purposely left my phone in the bedroom to avoid distraction, each time the oven timer went off, I cadged the Wi-Fi signal from one of the neighbors to check my e-mail. I found the usual junk mail to sort through and a couple interesting updates from old college friends on Facebook, but not a word from the detective.

When the granola had turned a gorgeous caramel color, I scraped it into a large glass bowl and added dried cherries to the mixture. After pouring myself a sample of the toasted oats and dousing it with milk, I left the rest to cool on the counter. Back outside, I sat basting in the sun and nibbling, still thinking about Nate. I tried to convince myself that I should be happy for him. I really, really wanted to feel that way. Really. In truth, it hadn't ever sounded like his marriage had ended because he and his wife didn't love each other. It ended because they had experienced a horrible crisis and they hadn't known how to handle the emotional fallout. And they needed to gnaw down to the marrow of their matrimonial boneyard before either of them would be ready to move on.

I set my bowl down on the deck so Evinrude and Sparky could lap up the dregs of sweetened milk. Who was I kidding? If I were really honest, I would ask myself why in god's name he'd even want to move on from that gorgeous woman. I was strictly Miss Congeniality to her Miss America. After I'd spent forty-five minutes crafting two lifeless sentences about the thrill of the *Topped Chef* competition, I gave up and went back inside the boat.

"Your granola is to die for. Need another cup of java?" called Miss Gloria from her comfortable spot in front of the television. The Food Network, of course. She was watching an episode of *Restaurant: Impossible* in which host Robert Irvine pronounced the kitchen of the restaurant he was visiting the most disgusting he'd ever seen. The show always made us feel better about our own housekeeping.

She tore her gaze away from televised close-ups of a grimy stove and a sink full of dirty pots and pans. "I can make a new pot." The cats had migrated from the back deck to curling up on either side of her. Lounging with the three of them watching foodie blunders from a comfortable distance looked oh-so-tempting.

"I think I'm going to run over to Sam Rizzoli's memorial service," I told her. Speaking of a bone that needed gnawing. That death drove me crazy. Why had he been killed? And why had he been left in such a publicly gruesome position? I felt torn between wanting to go and wanting to mind my own business, but in the end, I was too antsy not to attend.

I dressed in my nicest black jeans and a clean white shirt for the occasion, pulling on the jeweled sandals

my mother had given me earlier this month instead of
my favorite, more comfortable red sneakers. Then I
motored across town to the White Street Pier and
parked a couple of blocks away.

The concrete square at the end of the pier was
jammed with people, the crowd obliterating the faded
compass that was painted on the surface of the cement.
A man standing with his back to the ocean called for
quiet, and a hush rippled across the gathering. Before
the speaker began, a large brown pelican plummeted
through the air behind him and stabbed his beak into
the water. As the bird floated peacefully on the surface
with his freshly caught dinner, a gull landed on his
head and began to peck at his gullet. A metaphor for
Rizzoli's life? Maybe even the big guys are vulnerable
when they are hoarding something valuable. Maybe
two birds in action provided a message more powerful
than anything his friends and colleagues might say.

While several of Key West's politicians held forth on
the contributions Rizzoli had made to the town, I circu-
lated around the outer perimeter of the crowd, listening for any undercurrents to the dead man's story.

"Sam Rizzoli always put his hometown first," said
one of the city commissioners through the microphone.

"Yeah right. Assuming his hometown is ME ME
ME," muttered a man several rows back from the podium. "He never made a vote without first consulting
his own interests. And the tie always went to Rizzoli."
From the rear, the man looked vaguely familiar, like
someone whose picture I'd seen more than once in the
local paper.

I edged around the pier until I had worked into a

position where I could observe Rizzoli's wife. Not that you could always tell what was going on by looking at the deceased's closest relations. Sometimes a great show of mourning covered rage or revenge or even relief. But Mrs. Rizzoli looked pale and sad, swathed in a black dress that accentuated her slender figure, leaving bare her sculpted arms—impressive for what I estimated as her forty-something years. Enormous sunglasses covered much of her fine-boned face.

I felt a tap on my shoulder and, startled, I whirled around to face detective Nate Bransford. My already fast pulse hitched up another level. I mouthed "good morning" and turned back to the speaker, who was droning on about Rizzoli's love for and support of the arts in Key West. If Nate hadn't been feeling bad about the awkward incident with his ex yesterday, he might have demanded to know what the hell I was doing there.

But instead, he said: "Sorry to surprise you like that yesterday. It all came up kind of suddenly."

I fluttered my fingers behind my back like his ex-wife's appearance was no problem, no problem at all. And by the way, didn't he have more important things to do here than make excuses to me? I refused to turn around to look at him a second time, because I could feel the heat in my face—I was sure it would not match that message.

He sighed heavily. Out of the corner of my eye, I watched him move off through the crowd. He wore a dark navy blazer and a white-collared shirt and a narrow tie that he must have thought would help him blend in with the mourners. Instead all he needed was an earpiece to resemble the Secret Service. People parted to give him space as he headed toward the podium. He stopped about five paces away from the man I'd heard heckling the eulogist, scanning the crowd. I wondered if I was the only one from *Topped Chef* who'd come to the service.

After five speakers and a thank-you from Rizzoli's brother on behalf of the entire family, an informal receiving line formed and I felt myself getting pushed forward to join it. I considered cutting away, but the crowd was too thick to make an easy escape without drawing the notice of the mourners.

The woman in front of me seized Mrs. Rizzoli's hand and clutched it to her chest. "So sorry about your loss. I hope you got my phone message?" Both women burst into tears and hugged each other. There was a long pause as they disentangled themselves. Mrs. Rizzoli's friend patted her cheek dry. "Can I do anything for you? Bring dinner? Call We Be Fit and let them know you won't be in tomorrow?"

Mrs. Rizzoli adjusted the sunglasses that had been knocked askew in the big embrace and smiled. "We really have as much food as we can manage. As you can imagine, I have no appetite anyway. But thank you for the offer. And I do plan to go to the gym." She chuckled grimly. "After all, Sam's the one who died. I'm not dead yet."

"We'll talk tomorrow at ten?"

Mrs. Rizzoli nodded. "I'll look forward to that." She lowered her voice so I could barely catch the words. "I'm ready to burst here."

When my turn came, I mumbled my condolences

without mentioning how I knew her husband and bolted as quickly as I could. I hadn't meant to get that close in the first place. Nate Bransford stepped in front of me while I was waiting to cross through the traffic streaming along Atlantic Boulevard to reach my scooter.

"Find any clues?" he asked with a hint of a smile.

"You're the detective. What do you think?" I snipped back. I didn't mean to sound quite so thorny, but a protective barrier of prickliness had slid into place as soon as I saw him. I didn't want to show him how disappointed I'd felt, seeing his wife in his office and noticing the sparks that snapped between them.

"Officer Torrence told me he spoke to you at length yesterday," he said, sidestepping my question.

I tried to read his expression, but the only thing I could see in the dark lenses of his sunglasses was my reflection. Had Torrence told him how I'd wept? How humiliating that would be . . .

"I want to underscore his advice—you're not on the case, Hayley. You need to leave the police work to the professionals. Rizzoli's death was brutal and personal. Whoever killed him is a dangerous criminal who would not hesitate to kill again to protect his secrets. Do you understand?"

If he was trying to frighten me, it worked. I stared back, speechless, and then darted across the street. I heard brakes squeal and a horn blasting from the car that almost hit me.

"I mean it, Hayley," the detective yelled. "Watch out."

My hands shook badly, as I registered the cold steel of his warning. And the near miss with the car. Perched on my scooter, I breathed deeply for a few minutes until I could fit the key into the ignition. Apparently he thought I was an idiot who would bumble into risky situations without considering the possible cost. And he wasn't completely wrong. I wasn't thinking straight—I had to be more careful.

Though it never hurt to listen if presented with the right opportunity—like dropping by Mrs. Rizzoli's gym.

I fired up the scooter and headed for the small We Be Fit gym a couple of blocks north of the pier on First Street. A tall blond woman, dressed in sweats, but graceful like a dancer, greeted me as I came in.

"I'm wondering whether you have any small-group weight-lifting classes for women?" I asked. I raised my arm and jiggled my tricep. "I'm a runner and I thought some weight training might be a good complement to my exercise program." Which was all quite an exaggeration—I'd only been out running three times, and that hardly constituted a "program."

"I'd love to start tomorrow morning if that's possible," I added. "Sometime around nine thirty or ten?"

After Leigh, the trainer, had ascertained that I had no experience in a gym, she was less than enthusiastic about having me work out with a group. "I recommend a few personal training sessions so we can assess where you are in terms of physical fitness and get you acquainted with the machines."

"I may need personal attention," I said with a smile, "but my budget is definitely group-oriented."

"Let's try a one-on-one session and then if it's going well, we'll try to find you a workout buddy," she suggested.

Then she rattled off a list of embarrassing questions about my goals, my current workout schedule, and my eating, about which I was only partially honest. I had to think most people lied rather than expose their miserable habits at the first meeting. I signed a raft of permissions and disclaimers and she faxed a medical release off to my doctor in New Jersey. I hadn't visited a medical professional since coming to Key West last fall—other than after my car accident, for which I had been treated in the ER; there had been no need for it. I cleaned out the last two twenties in my wallet to pay for tomorrow's session.

"See you at ten," she said when we were finished. "Or better still come fifteen minutes early and you can warm up on the treadmill."

15

I always tell people, "Just put it in your mouth," she said. "What's the worst that can happen? You're not going to die. Either you're going to like it or you're not."
—Emma Hearst, chef at Sorella

I puttered around at my *Key Zest* desk until four o'clock, when Peter had told us to show up at the Westin Resort and Marina Pier on Mallory Square for the next *Topped Chef* challenge. The usual gaggle of tourists was snapping pictures of the oversized Seward Johnson statues dancing behind the Custom House Museum, a few silly man-boys posing beneath the statues of the naked women.

Behind the museum, alongside the Westin, three cooking stations had been set up under an enormous white tent. Stainless steel six-burner Wolf stoves with grills and ovens had been installed at each station—the equipment had me absolutely drooling. Peter must have spent a fortune to get it here. Each station was designed so the chefs would face the onlookers, with the food supply counter behind them. Although the advertising flyers said the show would begin at five, a large crowd had already begun to mill around outside the ropes. The central island counter space was piled high with the secret food supplies that had been promised, all covered by a white sheet. Deena waved me right over so I could get set up with my microphone.

"We're doing things a little differently today," she said. "You're going to have an earpiece as well as a mic so Peter and I can give you instructions during the cook-off."

"What kind of instructions?" I asked, suspicious. Hoping this wasn't the point in the contest where they told us who we had to vote for.

"We might want you all to circle around and watch someone's sauté technique or their knife skills. Or if something's going terribly wrong, we'll definitely want your reactions, live." She grinned. I hadn't seen her look this lighthearted since I'd met her last fall.

"How in the world did you get involved with all this?" I asked.

"I worked in reality TV in my previous life. I didn't realize how much I missed it until I got hired for this gig," she said as she clipped the microphone to my shirt and slithered the wire down the back of my shirt.

"Did you know Peter Shapiro before this week? Is that how you got hired?"

"No, I'd never met him. But I jumped at the chance when I saw his listing on RealityStaff.com," she said. "And he's not the worst I've worked for, by a long shot.

Besides, how many reality TV shows are filmed in Key West, right?"

"Right." I knew the Weather Channel had provided fake snow for Christmas at a home just up the Keys. And there had been an episode of *House Hunters* that my real-estate friend Cory Held had appeared in. And a local key lime pie taste-off a while back, but nothing major and national. "So you're not working for Chad anymore?" My ex-boyfriend didn't really deserve her—she was smart, organized, gorgeous, and *kind*. I found myself sort of hoping she'd dumped him.

"I took the whole week off," she said with a grin. "When I explained to Mr. tight-fisted Chad Lutz that he could let me have paid leave or he could find a new secretary and start from scratch, he didn't have much trouble deciding."

"He's not stupid," I admitted. "He knows no one else would put up with him."

I was just about to ask her whether she'd heard anything new about Rizzoli's murder, when Peter Shapiro beckoned her over. I wandered around the impromptu set, watching the cameramen set up their equipment and the makeup people work their magic. One of the girls whisked a layer of foundation and blush onto my face, and shellacked my curls with hairspray until not one follicle could move or even breathe. Ugh. I couldn't help making a face as she sprayed on one last layer.

"You don't want hair dropping into the food on television, though, right?" She winked and hurried off to nail Chef Adam, who enjoyed getting buffed up for the camera even less than I did.

Volunteers had begun to admit the folks who'd paid

big bucks for up-close insider tickets into the area marked off by the ropes, close to the action. Here a waiter passed around glasses of champagne. Cheap champagne, I suspected, given Peter's concerns about the budget, which, between the fabulous cooking equipment and the rather extensive staff, had to be shot already. At five o'clock the theme song from *Oliver!* piped out over a loudspeaker and Peter announced that the festivities would be starting shortly. Then my earpiece buzzed and he instructed the three judges to report to the front of the tent.

"Welcome to *Topped Chef* Key West–style," he bellowed to the onlookers, which caused our earpieces to shriek painfully. "Please meet our panel of distinguished judges." He went on to describe our resumes, which sounded better than the facts as I knew them. Toby was a bestselling author, I was a world-respected food critic, and Chef Adam sounded like Jacques Pépin's bosom buddy.

"And we are so pleased to present our *Topped Chef* contestants, Ms. Henri Stentzel, Mr. Buddy Higgs, and Mr. Randy Thompson." They smiled nervously and bowed, their every rustle amplified through the microphones clipped to their starched white chef jackets.

"So far, our guest contestants seem to be in a dead heat in the opinions of our judges," Peter continued. "As you may be aware, the assessment of their performances by our judges is cumulative. And so, tonight's event will weigh heavily in the outcome. You will see this up close and personal." He paused to allow the onlookers to cheer, with a couple of the staff urging them to yell louder.

"Our chefs' task for today is to prepare the best meal

possible with the secret ingredients we have provided, in a short one-hour time span. Some of the ingredients are ordinary or local, while others will be, shall we say, challenging. They may also choose to use any of the common ingredients that we've provided." Peter smiled, an impish look on his face. "You should be assured that none of these chefs has had access to our preparations so they will all be cooking by the seat of their checkered chef pants—without consulting either their own recipes or any outside parties. They will be expected to use as many ingredients as possible from the surprise baskets, and the resulting dishes will be judged on taste, originality, and appearance."

Behind Peter, Deena motioned for the crowd to applaud as the cameras panned over the audience and then zoomed in for close-ups of us three judges. Underneath the makeup, my face felt frozen into a false conviviality that I definitely wasn't feeling.

"Our three judges will be circulating through the stations, commenting on the chefs' choices and techniques," Peter continued. "When the hour is up, they will sample the resulting dishes, as will our gold-level ticket holders."

Gold level, meaning they'd paid a fortune to watch from inside the ropes. I was beginning to sweat under the pressure of the contest; I couldn't even imagine how hard it would feel to cook with strange ingredients—and no recipes—in public.

"Chefs, please man your positions!" said Peter.

Henri, Buddy, and Randy walked over to take their places in front of the cooking stations.

"Ready, set, cook!" Peter shouted.

Two of Peter's assistants snapped off the sheet that

had covered the central island. The cameras zeroed in on the chefs' faces as they studied the array of ingredients. I could see limes, mangoes, avocado, leeks, and carambola or star fruit, an odd-looking tropical fruit that I'd never tried to cook with. Buddy Higgs's expression remained flat, and Henri's grim, but Randy broke into a delighted smile.

"I do adore star fruit," he said, "though it doesn't really 'go' with anything else on the table." He hummed tunelessly for a moment, tapping one bicep with his fingers. "When in doubt, start with a mirepoix, as they say in France," he said, reaching for a large yellow onion. "Or *sofrito*, as the Spaniards might say. In any language, that's often chopped onion, celery, and pepper." He slid open a drawer underneath his cooktop, pulled out a chef's knife, and began to chop. "Wasn't it Julia Child who said the best way to execute French cuisine is to get loaded and whack the hell out of a chicken?"

He broke into a peal of laughter that rippled through the crowd, and they began to abandon the spaces in front of Henri and Buddy and push over to Randy's station. "In this case I'll choose the yellowtail snapper as my main dish because it's an icon of Keys cuisine."

"Do we have to listen to this idiot natter on for the whole hour?" Buddy muttered. He snatched four chicken breasts from the supplies, along with a variety of spices, orange juice, and the required fruits. The distinctive smell of toasting cumin soon wafted from his stovetop.

"When unexpected guests are on the menu, I choose grilling as my go-to option. It's fast and furious, yet always seems special—it sends the message that you were hoping they'd drop by all along." He grimaced and began to mash garlic into the toasted cumin and then spread it onto the chicken.

I couldn't imagine dropping in on Buddy with or without an invitation.

Peter gestured for more camera close-ups on Buddy and Randy. "See if you can fan the flames of their competition," he said for our ears only. "So far this is falling flatter than a pancake. I need you to take some action, people. Get them arguing if you can."

I moved around the U-shaped cooking stations so I could get a better look at the food on the island, with Toby trailing behind me. Chef Adam marched off in the other direction.

"Looks like they have a choice of chicken, shrimp, and yellowtail snapper," I reported, feeling self-conscious about talking to myself. And producing such trivial drivel. But Deena signaled for more.

"Looks like Randy Thompson is reaching for the heavy cream and optional jalapeños," I said.

"Of course," said Chef Adam from the other side of the central island, with an exaggerated roll of his eyes. "Everything's a cream sauce for Chef Thompson." He circled around to join us from the far side of the tent, and watched as Randy finished dicing his onion and then dumped the chunks into a sizzling pan of butter. "His knife skills are barely more than basic," he added. "Do you see how ragged and misshapen his chunks are? Chef Buddy Higgs, on the other hand, could offer a class at Le Cordon Bleu."

"But would anyone take it?" piped up Toby. "Boring, as our producer would say. I'd go for taste over uniformity any day of the week!"

She looked as though she wished she could take the words back as soon as she'd said them, but Deena flashed her a quick thumbs-up. I trotted around to the other side of the tent so I could watch Henri sauté bites of snapper and shrimp.

"I like to marinate the seafood in tequila to give it that extra splash of bold taste," she told the audience. "But then be sure to pat dry before cooking in order to get the full benefit of flash frying." While the seafood sizzled, she chopped up an avocado and a mango and added them to a bowl with minced jalapeño and torn mint leaves. She squeezed a lime over the top of the salsa just as the six p.m. buzzer sounded.

"Chefs, it's time to plate your meals," said Peter.

After a flurry of last-minute frying and stirring, the contestants arranged their dinners on three heavy white stoneware dinner plates. Two assistants brought out a small table covered in a crisp white cloth and Peter motioned for the judges to come forward. As we prepared to taste the first dish, Peter came around the edge of the tent and thrust his microphone to Henri's lips.

"Chef Henri, describe your contribution please!"

"I've chosen to make a Mexican seafood sauté," she said, hands held out to the plate like a priest offering communion. "It gives an impressive appearance to guests, but even inexperienced home cooks are capable of producing such a dish. And I've chosen to use the mango, avocado, and star fruit in a salsa to complement the seafood."

"Judges?" asked Peter, swinging around to face us again.

I was the first to take a nibble of Henri Stentzel's

Mexican seafood sauté. "Honestly, on the plate the dish does not look that appealing," I said without meeting her eyes. She might never speak to me again—unfortunate when we both lived on an island—but I felt I had to tell the truth or I'd be called out for it later. I understood that this event was made for television; it was not reality. But my reputation rode on a frank assessment of what was put on the table in front of me.

"The final product's a little runny. Though she did warn us to blot the seafood dry, it appears that she hurried that step herself. But I will say it tastes better than it looks. It's fresh and tropical—really quite good." I stepped away from the plate to signal that it was someone else's turn to comment.

"It looks like the chef panicked and threw every ingredient she was obligated to use into the pan without considering the outcome," said Chef Adam, wrinkling his nose as he nibbled on a second bite. "It's an unattractive mishmash, which might be fine if it was wrapped up in a burrito skin. And of course that is Ms. Stentzel's most recent culinary background." He swallowed the last of his sample. "One more thing—there is something bitter in the aftertaste as well."

"Oh, this is truly ridiculous," Henri huffed, undoing the top button of her jacket and fanning her face with a spatula. "Sometimes you run that risk using older citrus. If I had ordered the ingredients from my own suppliers, and they delivered those miserable limes, I would have sent them back as soon as I opened the box."

"Thank you, Chef Stentzel!" said Peter, and pointed at Toby. "We want to hear from the judges now, not the chefs."

"I'm not a fan of liquor in food," Toby said. "I have to say I prefer my tequila in shots." The audience snickered while I looked at her with astonishment.

We moved on to Chef Buddy's station to sample his grilled Cuban-style chicken—a relief from the other overly fancy things he'd produced this week. This time around he didn't have access to the chemicals that would turn a perfectly good dinner into gelatin spheres. The chicken had been marinated briefly in a cumin and garlic paste, grilled, and then sliced over an arugula, mango, and avocado salad.

"If this had been prepared in my restaurant, we would have allowed the chicken to marinate for a longer period of time," he said, before Peter could shut him down.

"It's tasty," I said. "Certainly a home cook could manage this."

"Now there's damning him with faint praise," said Chef Adam. "It's a gorgeous presentation of a classic summer supper salad."

"The garlic is somewhat overpowering," said Toby. "Not something you'd want to consume on a first date." I looked at her with astonishment and she winked.

Finally, the plates were shuffled away and replaced with Chef Randy's dish. He'd steamed white rice and topped it with a sautéed yellowtail snapper bathed in a jalapeño-scented cream sauce, which was based on the finely chopped vegetables he'd been so pleased to transform into mirepoix. My mouth watered just looking at it.

"If I were making this dish for a dinner party,"

Randy said, "I would serve okra beignets with a sour cream and cilantro dipping sauce as starters. And finish up with key lime marscapone cannoli served in a pool of mango sauce, with star fruit as garnish."

"None of those things were provided to us," Buddy protested. "He's just making things up."

"A chef should have a good imagination, don't you think?" Randy replied. "It should never be a drag to entertain." He executed a few dance steps behind his stove, ending with a twirl, one hand posed overhead.

Buddy turned away, frowning. "Ridiculous," he muttered, and stumped over to join Henri.

While we three judges dissected Randy's contribution—delicious to my mind, odoriferous and heavy to Chef Adam's, and overly spicy to Toby's—the *Topped Chef* assistants began to cut the remainder of the food into bite-sized portions and set small plates out on our table for the big-spender gold-level audience members to enjoy. The crowd pushed forward to get dibs on the samples, nearly trampling the rest of us in the rush. A cacophony of clanking silver on plates and the chatter of the diners began to rise.

Right in front of me, a large woman with a florid face suddenly crumpled to the ground, moaning and grabbing at her stomach. She flailed on the concrete, foaming at the mouth.

"Stand back!" I called, my voice weak with fear, and then crouched down to speak to her. "Are you all right?" Of course she wasn't all right—she was writhing in pain, her eyes rolling back in her head, unable to answer at all.

"Call 911," I yelled into my microphone, and this

time the words echoed out over the crowd. I smoothed down her purple-flowered muumuu to cover her thighs, murmuring platitudes about how help was on the way.

More people pushed forward, grabbing for plates and asking how they could help and what was wrong. . . . I began to feel light-headed and queasy myself and sat cross-legged on the ground, patting the woman's sweaty forehead with a paper napkin.

Finally, Peter Shapiro and Deena pushed through the onlookers, forcing them aside to leave space in front of the stricken guest. I heard the whine of the approaching sirens and then the clatter of a stretcher being pushed across the bricks.

A gaggle of paramedics appeared and two of them knelt to attend to the woman. One slipped an oxygen mask over her nose and mouth, while the other attached a blood pressure cuff and took her pulse. Then he started an IV while the first medic attached what looked like an EKG machine to her chest.

"What happened here?" the lead medic asked as he worked.

"I have no idea," I said. "One minute she was eating and the next she just crumpled."

"Eating what?" he asked. "Does she have food allergies?"

I shrugged helplessly and Peter elbowed me aside.

"It's a cooking reality show," he explained at the same time that one of the cops assigned to crowd control on Mallory Square arrived. "Our top chefs have prepared meals from the ingredients we provided. They all had access to the same things, with varying degrees of success in the outcome. But it looks to me as though she may have been stricken with a heart attack."

Ignoring Peter's explanation, the policeman consulted with the paramedics and then addressed the crowd. "Does anyone else feel ill?"

No one came forward.

"Is anyone here related to this woman?"

A tiny woman wearing a pantsuit that resembled pajamas pushed up from the back of the crowd, looking shaky and scared. "We're traveling together. We came off the cruise ship this morning." She pointed over at the hulking boat tethered to the pier and then glanced at her watch. "Oh my gosh, I told her we should have stayed on board. We're due back in an hour. Do you think she'll be okay?"

The paramedics did not answer, hoisting her large friend onto the gurney and strapping her down. They raised the stretcher waist high and pushed the woman and all the equipment back toward Front Street, clattering across the brick and concrete, the distressed woman's companion in tow.

A policeman I recognized from the near-drowning incident on Mallory Square came over to me. "Miss Snow, yes?"

I nodded.

"Please tell me what you noticed before and after this woman took ill."

"As Mr. Shapiro said, this is one of the legs of a contest that will determine a new reality cooking show host. Once the food was set out on this table, there was a mad crush for people to grab plates and taste it. She was one of the first to get a plate. And then she simply buckled to the concrete."

"What was she eating?" he asked.

"The food that our contestants had prepared. All three of our chefs had access to the same ingredients," I explained. "Some were used by all three and some were only chosen by one. But she would have had a little of everything on her plate." I paused to re-create the dishes in my mind's eye and identify anything that seemed off. "Henri Stentzel did not use the jalapeño, if I remember right. Which is a little odd, considering her background. And her salsa tasted a bit salty, which I don't think she intended. I think she intended for it to mirror the sweetness of the mango."

The cop wrote all that down and glanced back up. "Anything else?"

"The cream sauce tasted a little curdled," Chef Adam broke in. "And remember that I thought there was a bitter aftertaste to Henri Stentzel's dish?"

Though that was all true, I hated to say anything else that would implicate one of the chefs in a poisoning when it was more likely the woman had arrived with a medical condition. She had appeared heavyset and red-faced—a walking medical time bomb.

"Chef Stentzel did complain about the citrus tasting old," I said, and then continued. "Randy Thompson used a ton of butter and cream. Is it possible that the woman had a severe case of lactose intolerance? All of us judges ate the same things she had on her plate, and none of us are sick. Although I do feel a little woozy."

The cop squinted at me, pen hovering over the small

pad, looking as though my theory was so absurd that he could hardly bear to write it down.

"I'm only saying . . . there were so many variables. How would you possibly sort them out?"

When all the questions had been asked and answered, and the crowd had been cleared away and all traces of the sick woman removed, Peter pounced on the remaining cops.

"Someone is absolutely sabotaging my show," he said, his voice furious and hoarse from shrieking at the onlookers to clear the way. "This is not acceptable. First my A-team judge is murdered, now this. I'll be completely ruined. Is there one law enforcement official on this godforsaken island who has the slightest clue what they're doing?"

16

But as a whole, the thing is gout on a plate.
—Julian Sancton

I staggered back down the dock to our houseboat, homing in on the cheerful white lights that twinkled along the roofline and the magical tones of Miss Gloria's wind chimes. As I got closer, the fine, pungent odors of barbecued spareribs and sweet-and-sour soup scented the air. I felt immediately ravenous. We'd hardly had a chance to eat anything before the flowered muumuu woman took sick and all taste-testing ground to a halt. On the way home, I'd decided the queasiness was a sympathetic reaction, all in my mind.

I hung my jacket on the peg outside the door and went inside. Miss Gloria, Connie, and Ray were eating Chinese takeout at the kitchen table.

"Oh my, you're home early. We didn't wait for you to order," said Miss Gloria. "We figured you'd be stuffed after tonight's event. Your mom's here, too," she added, and pointed to the computer.

They had Skyped my mother, so she could join in the feast. On the computer screen, I could see that she also had cartons of Chinese takeout arrayed in front of her on her table at home in New Jersey.

"Hi, Mom," I said, waving at the screen. "Actually, I'm starving." I dropped my backpack in my room, washed my hands, then stopped in the galley to grab a plate and a pair of chopsticks. As I took a seat and began to scoop food onto my plate, I noticed the man sitting next to Mom, eating an eggroll. I froze, put the green beans down, and gawked.

"Oh, Hayley darling," Mom said, blushing, "where are my manners? You haven't met Sam Cooper. My boyfriend." She grinned and put a hand on his forearm.

My friends stopped eating and fell silent, trying not to stare at me.

"I wanted to introduce you two first before the gang met him, but then Miss Gloria called and suggested I join them for Chinese. And I figured we could chat about wedding stuff, too, since Connie and Ray would be there. But then Sam called for an impromptu dinner—" She took a deep breath and smiled again. "So here we all are."

Sam the boyfriend smiled, too, leaning toward the computer screen to make eye contact with me. He had a full head of salt-and-pepper hair and wore a pair of black-rimmed glasses and a white button-down shirt with the sleeves rolled up. Cute in a middle-aged, professorial kind of way. Not the free spirit, artsy kind of man I imagined my mother would fall for. Not like that at all.

"I've heard so much about you," Sam said. "And

you look so much like Janet. Two beautiful ladies. I look forward to getting to know you at the wedding."

Mom had invited him to Connie's wedding? Things had moved a lot faster than she'd bothered to tell me. I forced a smile. "Same here."

"Speaking of the wedding," Mom said, "Connie's agreed to let us throw her a shower early in the week of the wedding. It makes more sense to do it then when everyone's already in town. It's not that easy to get to your little island paradise."

"That's part of the point," I said, feeling grumpy. Wasn't the shower supposed to be the maid of honor's territory? That would be me. I forked a big helping of General Tso's chicken onto my plate, along with lo mein and spicy fried green beans.

Connie poured me a big glass of white wine and patted my hand. "Eat. We've all been so busy here, we haven't had a chance to hammer out some of these details. Thank goodness Janet's willing to goose us along a bit."

"I knew you girls would get around to it," Mom said. "But I have more time on my hands than you do."

I slumped down and began to shovel in the food. Who could argue with her logic?

"We worked out three dates when I could fly to Miami to shop for the dress," Mom continued. "You and Connie can decide when it's convenient to drive up and meet me. It's less than two months away now— way too late for a special order. But Connie's so tiny, I'm sure we'll find something lovely. And a dress for the maid of honor, too." She winked at me.

Ray moaned and stood up, heading to the galley. He

clattered his dish into the sink. "Speaking of which, I need to get to work or we'll never be able to afford all these wedding gewgaws." He stopped to ruffle Connie's hair. "Are you sure we can't just be friends?"

Mom giggled. Had she told him the story about my father's panic?

Connie slapped his hand away and gave him a little push. "Sit down, you silly man. Getting married was all your idea. We're almost finished here."

"Whatever happened to the taste-off?" Mom asked me. "We never thought you'd get here so soon. And we certainly never thought you'd show up hungry."

"Most of the food ended up getting packed up in trash bags to be taken to the police department. One of the guests took ill after eating what the chefs prepared. You can't imagine what a disaster that was—an ambulance, angry chefs, and hordes and hordes of hysterical tourists watching the whole event come unraveled."

"Good lord, Hayley," said Miss Gloria. "Was it some kind of allergic reaction?"

I shrugged and finished chewing a mouthful of vegetable lo mein. "The medical people looked worried, for what that's worth. They whisked this woman and her friend off in an ambulance." I explained how she had been among the first to score a small plate that contained samples of each of the contestants' dishes. "Obviously, you think about nuts first, since some people have such a deadly reaction."

"I bet I took your father to the ER ten times over the ten years we were married," said Mom. "If you're a grown man and terribly allergic, wouldn't you think you'd ask about peanuts before you ate a strange dish? Even a nice restaurant can make a mistake."

"But there were no nuts on the ingredients table," I said, trying to divert my mother from a rant about Dad's flaws. Especially in front of Sam. "Shapiro and company would never take a risk like that."

"But you don't think there was something wrong with the food?" asked Miss Gloria. She discarded a barbecued rib on her plate that had been gnawed down to bare bone.

"I can't imagine that there was," I said, scraping the last bite of General Tso's chicken onto my plate. "We three judges sampled everything before this spectator took sick. But I'm positive the police will be testing for poison, just in case."

"Certainly the reality show staff wouldn't have tainted the food—that would totally ruin the show," my mother said.

"And the legal repercussions would be staggering," added her boyfriend. He shrugged and added: "Sorry. I can't help myself. I'm a lawyer."

"And a good one, too," said Mom, picking up one of their white cartons. "More fried rice?"

"Thank you. Just a soupçon." Sam patted his stomach and beamed.

Lordy, lord. I'd encouraged my mother to date but I hadn't thought through what it might feel like to watch her in a blossoming romance.

"Peter Shapiro, the director, was livid," I said. "He suspects sabotage, but then he's been kind of paranoid all week."

"Well," said Connie, "if you wanted to knock out a

certain rival, one sure way would be to poison the food they'd prepared and make their fans ill. Though you might run the risk that they'd earn a certain sympathy vote."

"And how would you know who was going to eat the doctored plate?" asked Mom.

"Maybe you wouldn't care," said her boyfriend. "Maybe that's not the point."

Mom frowned. She had a hard time thinking the worst of people, except occasionally my father. "Tell us about the contestants again."

I started with Henri. "It seems like she's been antsy ever since she had to sell her restaurant in Miami Beach. Not that I've talked to her at all this week—she's still pissed at me because I suspected her of murdering Kristin Faulkner." I bit into the lone remaining egg roll, not that I needed more calories. But eating helped me think. I corralled the snippets of information I'd noticed over the past few days and tried to piece them together in my mind. "She badly wants to win, even though she's not saying that directly as much as the other two. Her career is stalled—you can see it in her eyes."

"How's her cooking?" Connie asked.

"Her food was okay," I said. "Nothing that would win a prize today." I thought for another minute. "Buddy Higgs is into molecular gastronomy." Sam looked puzzled. "It's complicated," I told him. "Nothing ordinary people want to eat." I frowned. "But I don't know enough about Buddy personally to be able to say whether he'd sabotage someone else to get ahead. And Randy seems sweet, but he wants to win as much as anyone."

Not as much as anyone, I thought, remembering our conversation in Aqua. More.

"I always wondered who'd be willing to go on reality television," said Mom's beau. "You have to be prepared to make a complete fool of yourself in public."

"Tell me about it," I groaned, reaching for the fried rice.

After I'd polished off every bite of the Chinese food and we'd signed off with my mother, I whipped out my smartphone to show the pirate wedding photos to Connie and Ray. "Of course this is totally your call," I said, "and as the maid of honor, I will do anything you ask of me. But I think these people look a little silly." Not a little silly, a lot.

Ray took the phone and flashed through the pictures. "Ahoy, matey," he boomed to Connie in a resonant pirate voice, "wilt thou be my wench for life?"

She did not laugh.

"Okay, okay, I bow to the wishes of my bride. Buy a gown and whatever you want me to wear—I won't complain."

She threw her arms around him and kissed him on the lips. "Thank you! I swear you won't look like a monkey. And I'll stick to the budget."

"I got some great ideas for the reception, too," I said. "I'll make the key lime cupcakes tomorrow and see what you think."

"I hope you don't mind that your mom got involved," Connie said, talking fast. "She started asking me about the plans and I panicked a little about how much there is to do. And it makes me feel less bereft to have her interested." She paused. "I miss my mother so much."

"It's fine," I said. "She loves a project. And she's so thrilled about you and Ray. And there's certainly enough of her to go around—I'm happy to share." We hugged, both a little teary-eyed, and they headed up the dock.

"I'll clean up," I said to Miss Gloria, who looked worn out.

"I love your family," she said. "Doesn't Sam seem like a perfect match for your mother?" She sighed a big happy sigh and went off to bed. It was hard to stay annoyed with a mother whom everyone adored.

Once I'd cleaned up the dishes and cleared away the trash, I stretched out on Miss Gloria's living room floor to rest my back. Between the memorial service and my phony visit to the gym and the stress of the tasting disaster, every disk and nerve in my spinal cord was crying for mercy. Imagine how I'd be feeling if I'd actually exercised. I eased the phone out of my back pocket and put a call into Deena.

"No real news here," she said as soon as she answered. "The woman is in fair condition in the ICU, getting flooded with IV fluids. The police packed up every bit of food we had on the set to run tests, but it could be days before we have an answer." She sighed. "And as you well know, the hundred-fifty-a-plate fundraiser is set for tomorrow. We've already had calls from people wanting refunds or wondering if the event will be cancelled."

"What's Peter saying?" I asked.

"A lot of words that wouldn't be fit to print. Basically, he's crazed. That's the only way to describe it. As long as no one dies, he thinks we can edit the tape we've got and save the episode. If we don't go forward with the final leg, he loses three-quarters of his camera crew because they are committed to other shows next week. Plus I have to go back to the office on Monday. Chad has a big, ugly divorce trial coming up and there's no way he can spare me longer than that."

"We have to finish then," I said. "Do you think anyone checked the trash cans around the Westin? Is it possible that someone subbed a tainted ingredient into the mix on the counter—and then when the woman fell ill, switched the bad stuff for the good?"

"You could come up with a thousand scenarios," Deena said. "But why? Why ruin the show?"

I hung up and texted Torrence, asking him to call me tomorrow. Then I considered getting back on my scooter to buzz over and check the trash cans around Mallory Square. That idea lasted about ten seconds as I pictured myself sorting through all the nasty garbage from tonight's sunset celebration, in the company of one or more hungry homeless folks. Instead I went off to bed.

17

*"I love you," Elizabeth said, and I started
to cry all over again.*

*In the oven, the chocolate soufflé began
to burn.*

—Vanessa Diffenbaugh,
The Language of Flowers

My heart was beating like a kettledrum as I parked my
scooter in front of the We Be Fit gym the next morning.
Couldn't I have thought of an easier way to squeeze
information from Mrs. Rizzoli? Like follow her to a coffee shop? A bakery? A diner? Anywhere but here.

Leigh, the trainer, was waiting for me inside the
door, looking hungry as a German shepherd in front of
his food bowl. She showed me where to store my helmet and backpack in the ladies room lockers at the back
of the gym. Next she pointed out the cooler containing
stainless steel bottles of water and had me choose a colored band to identify my bottle.

Nothing I couldn't handle, so far.

I asked questions about the workings of several of the machines, but then I could tell from the steely flint of her blue eyes that I'd procrastinated a whisker too long. She herded me through a series of what were supposed to be regular warm-up moves that I'd never remember and then led me toward what she called a "TRX machine" at the back of the small gym.

"The rack," I muttered. "I'll be lucky if I don't hang myself on this thing."

"Let's start with some push-ups," she said, in a pleasant voice.

All she needed was a black hood and a mace.

"Isn't that old-fashioned? I haven't done a push-up since high school."

Leigh just laughed and showed me where to place my hands on a bar eighteen inches from the floor. After eight repetitions, every muscle fiber in my arms was trembling.

"Two more," said Leigh with an inscrutable smile.

As I finished the final grueling couplet, Mrs. Rizzoli and the friend I'd seen hugging her at the memorial yesterday bounced into the gym wearing tight, bright spandex. They went right to a nearby rowing machine where they were greeted by a male trainer with bulging muscles who looked like he'd just come from a photo shoot for *Muscle & Fitness*.

"Morning, ladies," Leigh called.

I tried to follow their conversation but Leigh was killing me by placing ten-pound weights in my hand and forcing me through a series of squats, and then a return visit to the scene of the push-ups. When she finally granted me a short rest, I sank gasping to a nearby bench, gulped a stream of water, and mopped my sweating face. Ten feet away, the two friends were zipping through a routine of weights and planks that would have brought me to my knees.

"We've got perfect weather today," said Mrs. Rizzoli's friend. "Even our old dog felt frisky this morning."

"Nice," Mrs. Rizzoli agreed, but without much enthusiasm.

"You had a fabulous turnout at the memorial service yesterday. How are you feeling?" the friend asked her.

"Honestly?"

The friend nodded.

"I would have liked to have killed that bastard myself," Mrs. Rizzoli said. "But someone got to him first."

The other woman looked at her like she didn't believe the bravado. "You sound so angry. And sad."

Mrs. Rizzoli's lower lip quivered. For a moment, only the *click clack* of their weight machines broke the silence. "We'd been having trouble for a long time. You know that. But . . ." She choked back a sob. "The morning of the day he died . . ."

A tear leaked down the side of her face and splashed onto her bosom, darkening the purple stripe on her fashionable yoga top. Lucy brand. Expensive, I thought, my mind pushing away from her obvious pain.

The friend reached over to smooth a wisp of hair off Mrs. Rizzoli's face. She tucked it behind her ear and nodded with encouragement. "Something happened the day he died?"

"Let's try a plank on the exercise ball," Leigh suggested to me. "Forearms on the ball and then straighten your knees and draw your navel in tight. We'll start with thirty seconds." I stretched into the position, my arms quivering. It hardly seemed fair to say "we" when one of us was doing the work while the other held the stopwatch.

"He admitted that he'd been having an affair." Mrs. Rizzoli barked out a harsh laugh. "Not that *that* was breaking news. Him being faithful—now that would have been worth a special marital conversation. But he admitted this new relationship had gotten more serious than he ever intended. It wasn't his fault, of course. It crept up on him. He actually cried about not knowing what to do."

"You're joking," said her friend.

"I wish," said Mrs. Rizzoli. She picked up a couple of heavy-looking free weights and began to execute bicep curls, her muscles bulging gracefully with each rotation. "And then he told me how torn he felt and how he couldn't bear to lose either one of us. Really, it was as though I should comfort him for getting in too deep with his girlfriend."

"That fat bastard," said Mrs. Rizzoli's friend.

"I don't think I can do any more," I whispered to Leigh.

"Almost there," she said. "Ten seconds."

"And the worst thing is, I did comfort him," said Mrs. Rizzoli to her friend. "He's off screwing another woman and I'm patting his hand." She thumped the weights down to the floor. "And then I threw him out. Told him to go stay on his boat a few days—I needed some space."

"You'd feel a lot worse if you'd acted angry and

mean and then he went and got himself killed," said the other woman. "Do the police have any news?"

"Nothing," said Mrs. Rizzoli with a shrug of indifference I knew she couldn't feel. "I believe they've cleared me of suspicion because they can't imagine I could have hoisted him up onto the rigging."

Her friend grinned. "They haven't seen what you can do in this gym. I have to run—I'll call you tomorrow, sweetie." She bussed Mrs. Rizzoli's cheek and hurried off toward the locker room.

"That's it for today," said Leigh, snapping my mind away from eavesdropping and my own agony. "We'll meet the same time next week? Or we can step things up and make it twice a week?"

"Same time next week. If I don't die from lactic acid poisoning after this session," I said, only half-joking.

Leigh chuckled and pointed to the aerobic machines, lined up to the right of the desk where I'd checked in. "You should stop on the way out and put in fifteen minutes on the treadmill. When you come next week, get here early and you can warm up the same way." She patted her own flat stomach. "Good for the heart, lungs, and waistline."

I was about to tell her I'd put in more time working out when my mother served Thanksgiving gravy from a can, when I noticed that Mrs. Rizzoli had moved over to the machines. She was pumping the pedals of a stairstepper, her tanned shoulders and chest glistening.

"Great idea, coach," I said with a smart salute. Then I headed to the stationary bike, thinking that sitting down might feel like heaven. But I could barely lift my leg over the center bar of the bike.

"It gets easier," said Mrs. Rizzoli, smiling as she watched me struggle. "I promise."

"I sure hope so," I said, smiling back. I punched in fifteen minutes on the bike's computer, at an easy level, the lowest. When asked for my weight by the computer, I shaved seven pounds off and began to pedal. "I'm awfully sorry about your husband."

She startled, as though she suspected I'd been listening in on her private conversation. Which I had. I began to pedal the bicycle.

"Mr. Rizzoli and I were serving together as judges in the *Topped Chef* Key West competition," I added quickly, hoping to correct the impression that I was a snoop for no good reason. "I'm Hayley Snow. I was hoping I'd get the chance to talk to you because some weird things are happening with the contest. It's hard not to worry that they're connected with his murder."

She took a long drink from her stainless steel bottle and increased her speed on the stair-stepping machine. She was barely breathing hard, but perspiration poured off her body and soaked her lavender top until it turned deep violet.

"I know he made some political enemies. You can't help but do that working in the public sector," I blundered on. "If you take a strong stand, you won't please everyone. But it does seem possible that there's a connection to the TV show. For instance, Randy Thompson said something about having a bad relationship with your husband."

"Oh, Randy was a pain in his patootie," she said, her fingers flicking the idea of him away like a mosquito. "Half the time Sam told me he didn't pay the rent on his apartment and the other half he paid late. My husband finally had enough and gave him notice. I think he was supposed to get out by the end of the month." She squinted and stared at me, her legs still churning on the stair-stepper. "You're not suggesting he was angry enough to murder my husband? That seems a little extreme."

"I'm not saying that, only wondering about the possibilities," I said, sucking for air as my machine's workout leaped up to a higher level.

"Who are you? Are you working with the police?" she asked.

"No, no. I work for *Key Zest*. Like I said, just gathering information. We all felt awful about what happened to your husband. And to be honest, we're pretty scared, too. Could one of us be next? We have no idea."

Her eyes narrowed as she studied my face. I tried to look open and trustworthy, at the same time I was panting. "Not Randy," she said finally. "I don't think so." She shook the loose hair off her face and reset her headband. "Whoever did this was ruthless and powerful and very, very angry. To leave him like that?" She blinked away a sudden rush of tears and swabbed at her face with a towel.

This was exactly the warning that Torrence had given me about the killer. "What kind of man is he?" I asked. "Your husband, I mean."

"Was he," she corrected. She began to tick his characteristics off on her fingers. "He was a strong personality, brilliant in business and tireless in bed. Unfortunately, as you probably overheard, I was not the only recipient of those gifts. He wanted what he wanted and he didn't mind lying or cheating to get it."

"I'm so sorry. I had a boyfriend like that," I added. Those few months with Chad were of course nothing compared to a long-term marriage where you'd promised in front of God and all your relatives to hold each other gently for life. And then gotten drop-kicked from heaven to hell when the rat bastard let you down. I'd felt shocked and outraged and embarrassed and furious—hard to imagine how she was coping. Hard to figure what was real in the façade she was showing, and what wasn't.

"Does the name Buddy Higgs mean anything to you? He's another one of the TV show contestants."

I could have sworn her lips twitched, but she pulled them tight and answered: "Don't know him." She shook her head and gulped another swig of water. "Thinking back, I can't imagine why that producer even asked Sam to judge food. Sure he owned restaurants and he loved hanging out at the bar and feeling like the big cheese, but he was no foodie. If I served him something new, he poked at it like I was trying to poison him. So you see he wasn't altogether crazy." She grinned. "More than once he asked to order off the kids' menu—that's what he was like when it came to food."

Then her eyes widened until they looked like two dinner plates—like my mother's Burleigh china, with all its shifting shades of blue. "Hayley Snow. You're the one who slammed Just Off Duval. He was soooooo angry. The food isn't that bad, is it?"

I lifted one shoulder and faked a smile. "I felt like I

had to be honest about my experience. And I swear I gave it three tries . . . because I hate writing negative things about someone's restaurant. I go in hoping I can give a good report. That's the fun part of the job, spreading the word about great meals." I was babbling and she wasn't even cracking a smile.

My bicycle beeped, signaling that the fifteen minutes I'd programmed were up. According to the computerized display, I'd consumed fifty-six calories in this aerobic segment of my workout. Not even enough to counter a single café con leche.

"He was gunning for you, dear. You should be grateful that he's dead."

Mrs. Rizzoli tipped her chin and stepped off her machine, leaving me in a pool of guilt-ridden sweat. I knew writing negative reviews would hurt people's feelings, but I didn't expect they'd make someone want to kill me.

She banged into the TRX machine on the way out, leaving its pulleys and levers swinging like the rigging of a sailboat.

18

You're better off peeling potatoes at a great kitchen than working saucier at a really mediocre place.

—David Chang

As I struggled off the scooter at Tarpon Pier, every muscle screaming, a text message came in from Peter Shapiro instructing the staff, chefs, and judges to gather at the Studios of Key West at two p.m. He planned to tape pick-up interviews to fill in slow spots in the show, which were many, according to Peter. Apparently he had no intention of closing the show down just because of one gut-sick fan.

Then I scrolled through my e-mail. I was reading a note from Mom about a new catering gig she'd landed and how much she wished I was there to act as souschef, when my psychologist pal Eric called.

"Just checking in," he said. "How are things going?"

"I've been dying to talk to you, but I didn't want to interrupt the flow of your vacation," I said, feeling ridiculously relieved to hear his voice. I took a seat on the bench outside the laundry room at the head of the dock.

I needed to hash things over with someone, but I refused to worry Miss Gloria with every gory detail. And Connie's life was so hectic these days, between her business and the wedding. Mom would have been happy to listen, but I try not to tell her everything. Not because she wouldn't take my side, but more because she'd take it so definitely. And once my side was taken by my mother, there was no room for going back. Chad, for example, was doomed for life once Mom found out I'd discovered him in bed with another woman. She was a mother hen and I will still be her chick fifty years from now when we're sharing a suite in an assisted living facility.

"We're finding vacation to be a little boring." Eric laughed. "We may even come home early. What's new down there?"

"What isn't new?" I hated to dump everything on him at once—he didn't know about the *Topped Chef* contest, Rizzoli's hanging, or all the events that had unfolded after. I'd have to ease him into it. "You'll never guess where I just came from."

"The police department? The county jail? Detective Bransford's yacht?"

"Very funny," I said. "None of the above. The gym. My first personal training session."

After he'd squawked in disbelief and feigned admiration, I admitted how I'd really made the appointment hoping to learn something about Rizzoli's murder. And then I summarized the hanging, Toby's near-drowning, and the disaster at the Mallory Square cook-off. Eric was pretty much speechless by the time I finished.

"So someone strung him up wearing pirate drag?" he asked. "Why in the world was he left like that?"

"Torrence asked the same thing. And Bransford, too. Randy Thompson thinks the killer was pointing to the drag queen community." I sighed. "Whoever did this was ruthless, and maybe crazy."

"And terribly angry," Eric said. "You need to keep your distance."

I sighed again and stretched out on the wooden bench, breathing a mixture of salty harbor air and dryer vent odors. "I'm in the thick of it, ready or not."

"What did Mrs. Rizzoli say?"

"She's a funny person. She was telling her friend how her husband cheated on her, yet at the same time he seemed to want her sympathy. And she says she gave it to him."

"You don't believe her?"

A couple of seagulls landed near the trash can and began to squabble over a partially eaten sandwich. "Maybe. But why would any woman be solicitous after her husband tells her he's having an affair? Why wasn't she furious?"

"Makes a good story though, doesn't it?" Eric mused. "Especially when the cops are nosing around looking for murder motives. Gets her off the hook, right? Speaking of cops, what's happening with Bransford?"

I covered my eyes with one hand and groaned, then drew my knees up to my chest to ease the strain in my back. There had been a lot going on over the past few days and I was feeling it settle hard in my sacrum. "We've ground to a halt. His ex has arrived in town and they looked very cozy."

"Sorry about that," he said, not even asking for the gory details.

"You never did like him much, did you?"

"I tried," said Eric, "because you liked him. From a friend's point of view, I couldn't help finding him standoffish and condescending. Hang on, I'll be right there," he said to someone talking to him. "Listen, Bill's calling me to get moving. I think we'll be back day after tomorrow. But call me if you need me. For anything, okay?"

I hung up feeling slightly less lonely, but utterly disappointed in Bransford. I knew Eric wasn't crazy about him, but it still stung to hear the unvarnished truth. Shoving that thought away, I turned back to mulling over what I'd heard from Rizzoli's wife. Just how angry was she at her husband?

I had plenty of time before I had to shower and dress to return to the Studios of Key West, so I decided to run back over to the old harbor. The more I thought about it, the more I wondered how in the world Rizzoli had been hoisted up into the rigging without anyone noticing. And who'd finally seen him and called it in? I hadn't heard anything about that. Two days after the murder and there were still no leads? That was hard to believe.

Quite possibly the two guys I'd talked with at the harbor—Turtle and Derek—had not told me their whole story. And if they hadn't told me, they certainly wouldn't have told the cops. Derek just on principle, because the cops were authorities and he'd come to this island to shed as much big-brother baggage as possible. And Turtle because he hadn't had a good interaction with the police the whole six months he'd lived on the island. And probably a long time before that.

What else might they have noticed—and held back?

Muscles complaining, I struggled back onto my scooter, buzzed across town, and parked it at the rear of the Schooner Wharf Bar. My body was starting to scream for caffeine and calories, so I trotted over to what used to be called the European Village Cafe, now Key West Munchies, next to Kermit's Key Lime Shop. A cute young man with a Russian accent took my order for a café con leche, extra sugar. While the milk steamed and the TV chattered in Russian, my stomach began a serious rumble. Telling myself I'd been planning to review this place anyway, I added two Cuban sandwiches to my order, one for me and one for Turtle in case I found him.

"That was an awful tragedy the other night," I said, when the young man delivered my coffee to the shelf separating his little kitchen from the outdoors.

"Terrible," he said, as he began to pile ham, roast pork, Swiss cheese, and pickles on loaves of Cuban-style bread. "I'm glad I wasn't here to see it." He slathered mustard over the top of the bread, closed up the sandwiches, and weighted them down on his grill. The cheese melted down the sides and sizzled on the hot metal. I tried not to drool on the counter.

"Any word on who did it?" I asked, thinking he must see and hear a lot from his little window on the seaport.

He rubbed his chin and looked out across the horizon, over my head. "They've gone door to door interviewing at the shops and restaurants that were open that evening. They even had Navy Seal scuba divers come in to search the harbor bottom around the boat. There's so much garbage down there, I doubt they could tell what might have been new." He pulled a rag from a sink full of soapy water and wiped his counters down. "That was a low trick to hang a man on his own boat."

"The boat definitely belonged to Rizzoli?"

He nodded and threw the rag back into the sink. After drying his hands on his apron, he flipped the sandwiches. "Can't say how often he actually sailed, but the guy who does my deliveries said he stayed aboard fairly often." He grinned. "Probably the nights his wife was mad at him. Or when he planned to party harder than she approved."

As I started to cross the street with my loot, an orange and green trolley rattled around the corner. A man dressed in chef's hat and clothing burst out of Kermit's Key Lime Shop and pretended to throw the pie at the tourists on the bus. I estimated that he performed this stunt ten times a day, but he acted as if this was the first time he'd thought of it. I detoured around the back of the trolley and settled on a bench overlooking the bight, thinking about a slice of key lime pie for dessert. Or frozen pie on a stick, dipped in chocolate. How many push-ups would it take to counteract those calories?

I sat with my face tipped to the sun until I couldn't wait another second to dive into the lunch. Maybe Turtle would smell the roasted pork and come out of hiding. But I made it all the way through my sandwich, washed it down with the sweet, thick coffee, and there was no sign of him.

I strolled past the bar at the Conch Republic Seafood Market, passing the slips that held charter fishing boats, most of which were empty for the day. Then I came to the sign that read TARPON FEEDING 4 P.M., which reminded me that I needed to take more advantage of the quirky things that made this island so endearing. In front of the A & B Lobster House, I finally had a decent view of Sam Rizzoli's sailboat. A piece of yellow crime-scene tape was still strung across the stern; a loose end fluttered in the breeze. Standing on the dock and looking up at the restaurant, I tried to imagine whether diners would have been able to see Rizzoli's body as it was hoisted up the rigging. Maybe not, if it was dark outside and light in the restaurant. The death had been all over the front page of the *Key West Citizen* for several days running. Wouldn't someone have come forward?

A little farther, around the corner, at the end of Front Street, a homeless woman named Elsa was sitting in the dappled shade of a royal poinciana tree. I'd seen her many mornings as she wandered the island on a three-wheeler bike, with its rusty wire baskets stuffed with her belongings. A gray tiger kitten with muted stripes that reminded me of Evinrude ribboned through her legs, batting at the ragged hem of her blue skirt. She had laid out a tiny bowl of kibbles and another of water in the shade beside her.

"Morning," I said. "That kitty is so cute! What's his name?"

"I was thinkin' of Cloudy. Or Stormy. Or Foggy. Or Whisper," she answered, her weathered face creasing into a wide smile. "I'm havin' some trouble deciding."

She hooted out a peal of laughter and I laughed along with her. "You need a whole litter of kittens to use up all those good names."

"Yep. Right now, I'm calling him Cat."

"That works." I crouched down to their level and wiggled my fingers until the kitten pounced. After wrestling with him for a few minutes, his sharp white teeth pricking my hand, I smiled again at Elsa. "Are you okay on cat food?" She wasn't the kind who'd take a handout easily, but I figured showing concern about the cat was something else.

"For now," she said.

I left it at that, not wanting to push about whether he'd had his shots or flea medicine. Maybe next time I saw them, I'd tell her there was a program that paid for veterinary care. Me:

"I was looking for Turtle. I bought an extra sandwich, thinking he might enjoy it."

Her smile in return flickered and then dimmed to a worried frown. "Haven't seen him since early this morning," she said. "He was across the harbor real early." She waved a hand in the direction of the dock where the Sebago party boats were tied up each night. "Seemed like he was having a fight with another man. Shouting and going on the way he does when he stops takin' his meds. That's the last I saw of him. Honest to god, I'm a little worried."

"What did the man look like? Could you hear what they were fighting about?"

"Whitish beard maybe, blue jeans? It was still this side of dark and I was too far away to catch much of the conversation."

I sighed and got to my feet. It sounded as though Turtle's truce with Derek had ended. I hope he hadn't ended up in serious trouble, like a trip to the county jail for disturbing the peace. "Would you like the sandwich?" I didn't want to insult her, but on the other hand, I hated to see it go to waste. And chances were, she was hungry, too. "I inhaled one just like it—it was amazing."

She grinned, a little shy now. "I'll share it with Cat. And Turtle if I see him."

19

While cooking shows can inspire, you can only learn to cook at the stove. The grand-mother is the ultimate cooking teacher in the world.

—Mona Talbott, *Zuppe*

On the way back to my scooter, I stopped at the dock where Derek washed the Sebago party boat every morning, but neither he nor the boat was in evidence. If I wasn't too stiff to jog in the morning, and if Turtle hadn't made an appearance before then, I'd come back tomorrow and talk to him then.

After showering, dressing, and slapping on some mascara and blush, I drove over to the filming session at the Studios of Key West. Peter was working with the camera crew to set up lights for the interviews in a corner of the big gallery. I joined the judges and chefs clustered by the coffee and snacks that had been set up on a table near the entrance. Randy Thompson and Buddy

Higgs were arguing about what had happened at yesterday's tasting.

"You were the only one who used cream in your
dish," said Buddy. "It wouldn't have been hard to slip
a little something into that container before whipping
up your disgusting sauce."

"What sense would there be in poisoning my own
food?" Randy asked. He ran a hand through his buzz
cut; it looked like he'd bleached the tips again overnight. "I'm trying to win the contest, not kill it."

"You're suggesting someone else messed with our
ingredients, right in front of you and in front of that
mob of people?" Buddy perched a cheek on the table,
his free foot swinging, his neck flushing pink.

"How are you so sure it was my food that caused
the problem?" Randy asked. "I wouldn't put it past
you to make your rivals' customers sick." The forced
smile on his face disappeared and he looked fierce and
intense.

Why didn't Peter put a stop to this? I turned to wave
him down and signal for help. But as I tried to get his
attention, I noticed that one of the crew, who carried a
camera on his shoulder, was filming the back-and-forth
not five feet away from where we stood. They were
getting this whole argument on film. Which meant Peter had instructed the cameras to roll.

Deena walked by and I tapped her on the shoulder
and motioned her aside. "What have you heard about
the woman who got sick at the tasting yesterday?"

"She's in stable condition," Deena answered. "I
haven't had time to get over to the hospital, but we did
hear that."

How to phrase my concerns without making her mad and shutting her down? I couldn't think of a way so I smiled as I asked: "Surely the incident last night wasn't planned all along? Surely you wouldn't have risked people's lives to add drama to the show?"

"Oh, Hayley," she said, and pretended to chuck my chin. "Don't be naïve. This is reality television, remember? Conflict makes for good ratings. If everything was to go smoothly, there's not a viewer in the country who would watch the show." She winked and walked away. "But no, we didn't plan it." The words floated over her shoulder.

Did I believe her? I hated the way I'd started finding everyone suspicious, even Deena, who'd stuck with me after Chad did his best to poison her opinion of me. And I really hated the idea that the producers would risk the health of the spectators to spice up the program. Or even the contestants. Would one of them have slipped something into the food? I tried to remember how each of the chefs had reacted when the woman took ill yesterday. Angry? Scared? Worried?

Then Peter called all of us over to begin the filming. "I'd like for Chef Stentzel to be interviewed first," he said, pointing to a metal folding chair at the center of the lights and cameras.

Henri ducked out of the crowd and took the seat. She wore a light-pink collared shirt with her hair braided down her back; she looked younger than she had yesterday in her chef's garb. The expression on her face flickered between nervous and resigned.

"Chef Stentzel. It's a pleasure to have you here with us this week." Peter flashed a phony crocodile smile.

"How do you think things are going for you so far?" he asked. "How do you rate your chances?"

"Everything's going fine," she said, squaring her shoulders with a confidence I didn't think she felt. "In spite of the chaos last night, I think my seafood dish turned out well. The thing is"—she bit her lip and paused, maybe searching for the right words—"we can all cook. You narrowed the field down to the best the island had to offer. Of the folks who were crazy enough to audition." She smiled and tweaked her braid. "The thing is, I can only be me. If you're looking for an excellent cook who can relate to home cooks on an honest, natural level, you're looking at her." She frowned a little. "I can't be Randy or Buddy. If that's what the judges are looking for, so be it." She folded her arms across her chest and glared at us judges.

Which I didn't think would help her case one bit.

"Thank you, Ms. Stentzel," said Peter, who then beckoned for Buddy.

Buddy took the hot seat.

"How does the contest look from your perspective?" Peter asked.

"She's right," Buddy said, tipping his head at Henri. "We can all cook. But there's a difference between a cook and a chef. A chef has his own point of view and he doesn't cut corners or lean on someone else's recipes. If you want some guy telling you about what his grandmother cooked for Sunday supper, or some lady who's good only for a late-night slot because her presentation and her food are a snooze, your choices are clear. If you want a chef who can dazzle your viewers, there's only one choice." He stood up and thunked his chest. "Me."

"Bravo," said Chef Adam softly, clapping his hands.

Randy glared at him as he was escorted, bristling with energy, to the metal interview chair. He began to speak without waiting for Peter's question. "First of all, admit it, people, I look good on the camera." Several of the crew members chuckled and one flashed him a thumbs-up. "I know how to dress. I know not to kill everyone's appetite by wearing an unwashed ponytail down my back that looks like a dead animal." He bared his teeth in Buddy's direction, whose hair, now that Randy mentioned it, did bear a resemblance to roadkill. More laughter from the crew. "The camera loves me and I love sharing my Southern-style we-may-be-old-fashioned-but-we-ain't-old-fogeys food with my fans."

He skipped back to join the audience and Peter instructed the three judges to come forward. We settled into a semicircle of those same uncomfortable metal chairs, the lights bearing down on us.

"Let's talk about what we've seen so far this week," Peter said. "We have one event left and then we will be choosing our Topped Chef of Key West. What have you loved so far? What have you hated? Don't hold back, folks. Now's the time to tell us what you're really thinking. There's a lot riding on your decision."

Chef Adam cleared his throat and leaned forward. As Peter had advised the first day, he'd left his chef's whites at home and donned a pale green polo shirt that made him look a little sickly. "The stakes couldn't be much higher, could they? Buddy Higgs stands out in my opinion. He's a master of his ingredients. He doesn't just give you recipes, he gives you a philosophy of cooking. Something to live by."

I tried not to snort with laughter. "I think our decision has got to be about who looks ready to be on camera," I said. "Certainly yesterday opened a window onto how these three chefs work when circumstances are challenging, how they deal with the unexpected. Mr. Higgs is fine as long as everything is going his way. I'm afraid both he and Ms. Stentzel wilted a bit under the pressure."

"Ms. Stentzel doesn't seem natural," said Chef Adam. "She's too earnest. She's not having a good time."

"Who is?" I muttered under my breath.

"I think you're right for once," said Toby. "Ms. Stentzel is a little awkward on camera, not comfortable in her skin. With Randy, you can look at him bounce around the kitchen and you know what you're going to get. He may stumble, but he's back on his feet before a single viewer is lost. They are going to want to root for him. They are going to watch him one week and come back the next week just to hear about what he ate over the weekend."

"But what's his point of view?" asked Chef Adam. "If he's going to star in a network show, I need to know not only who he is but what to expect from his food. Not just his granny's recipes, but something unique and focused."

"I don't know what you mean by that," I said, feeling irritated by his pompous posturing. He and Buddy actually made a perfectly matched, annoying pair. "How does a chef have a point of view?"

"I don't know how to say it any plainer. His philosophy. It can't just be 'I love my grandma and I love food.'"

"You keep saying that same darned thing, but why

not?" I asked. "That's pretty damn straightforward if you ask me." The whole conversation had begun to feel like listening in on one of Eric's troubled families in therapy. Tense and awkward, but without his calm presence to sooth the waters and coax a sense of unity from the family. Instead we had Deena and Peter asking pointed questions and fanning the flames of any friction they spotted. I couldn't wait for this to be over.

"Before we wrap up," said Peter, "remember we will be filming the final challenge at 484 Johnson Street at ten a.m. tomorrow. Judges should wear cocktail attire. Chefs—no street clothes. Please come dressed as professionals. You will be preparing your signature dishes. Before you leave, we need your list of ingredients— Deena will be doing all the shopping so we have some quality control. That's it, people. Be on time tomorrow."

Quality control—huh. Meaning no one would get sick from eating the food? I unclipped the microphone from my collar, extricated the wire from my shirt, and handed the battery pack over to Deena at the same time Buddy Higgs gave her his scribbled list.

"See you guys tomorrow!" Deena called cheerfully as we headed out the back door of the studio into what was left of the cool January afternoon.

Buddy stumped ahead of me so we wouldn't have to converse, which only made me certain I should talk to him now while I had the chance. As I hurried to catch up, I decided I would ask him point-blank what kind of relationship he had with Mrs. Rizzoli, because I doubted she'd told me the truth. Maybe it had a bearing on Rizzoli's murder and maybe it didn't, but I wouldn't feel satisfied until I knew.

And maybe I would mention the incident with the chocolate syrup, too. This had weighed on my mind ever since I saw him squirt it on those desserts the other night on the yacht. It wasn't the fact that he'd used fabricated chocolate whose first listed ingredient was probably corn syrup—the demon of the American obesity epidemic. I understood that not everyone who cooked was a purist (read: food snob) like my mother and me. Lots of normal, hardworking people needed to take shortcuts in their cooking—they didn't have time to make every dish from scratch. That was okay—better than sacks of greasy fast food or fake food from a box.

What bothered me about the chocolate syrup was the fact that Buddy had pretended he was serving something else. I worried about choosing him as the Top Chef of Key West. I worried about siccing him on the public, to whom he was liable to flat-out lie about how easy a dish was to make and how good it might taste. He turned the corner out of the alley and started down Southard Street.

"Buddy, wait up!" I hollered after him.

He kept going.

"Buddy! Wait!"

He wheeled around, scowling. "I have to get to work."

I jogged up behind him. "I need just a minute. I didn't want to ask you in front of the others, but I do have a question. What is your relationship with Mrs. Rizzoli?" Smooth, Hayley, I thought. It would be a miracle if he answered.

Stopping beside him, I smelled the sour odor of old alcohol and garlic, underneath a topcoat of breath mints and sweat. The kind of odor that seeped from your pores after a long night of drinking, that couldn't be washed off no matter how long the morning shower.

"Why is this any of your business?" he asked. "It isn't."

Which hit home. But why was he so defensive? I sidestepped the question of why I was asking and pushed a little harder. "Her husband was killed this week, as you know perfectly well. And then one of us judges was attacked. And then a lady was sickened by food from our contest. If you have some kind of relationship with the dead man's wife, you need to come clean." I paused, hands on my hips. "Unless you killed him."

"Did she put you up to this?" he said, practically hissing.

I shook my head slowly, keeping my gaze pinned on him.

"I screwed her once or twice," he finally said, almost spitting the ugly words. "That's it. Her husband was off with another woman. She told me all about it at the bar. She felt devastated, so she said. Like she wasn't a real woman. So I did her a favor and took her home. A pity poke, that was it." He wiped his upper lip, where a sheen of sweat had appeared. "There was no relationship. And there sure won't be now."

He stomped down the sidewalk, steaming.

Which left me wondering: Who was the liar?

20

*After reading a lot of overheated puffery
about your new cook, you know what I'm
craving? A little perspective.*

—*Ratatouille*

I returned to my scooter, thinking it was definitely time
to call the police and report on what I'd learned. But
the idea of talking to Detective Bransford made me feel
sick to my stomach. So I punched in Torrence's number
instead.

"It's Hayley here," I said when he answered. "I said
I'd call if I heard anything and well, I have a few tid-
bits." I told him how I'd run into Mrs. Rizzoli and how
angry she seemed. And then how I'd discovered that
she and Buddy Higgs had had an affair while her husband was busy with someone else.

"You just ran into Mrs. Rizzoli and she spilled out
this story?" Torrence asked, a note of disbelief in his
voice.

"At the gym," I replied, all breezy. "People talk

about all kinds of personal things to get their minds off sweating and suffering."

"Is that right?" he asked after a moment of silence. "And the television show? Anything new there?"

"They're pretty much all at each other's throats," I said. "This afternoon the contestants were accusing each other of spiking the food yesterday to eliminate their rivals."

"Interesting," said Torrence, "if a little far-fetched."

"Just passing it on. For what it's worth." I had the feeling I was losing my credibility as a finder of useful tips. "Did you guys happen to bring in a homeless guy named Turtle today? I'm a little worried about him. He gets kind of crazy when he's off his meds."

"I know Turtle well," said Torrence. "He hasn't turned up on our radar—he hasn't been arrested and he isn't in the drunk tank. I would have heard about it. I'll call you if I hear anything. And thanks."

Since it was getting near the time for the sunset celebration, I decided to buzz down to Mallory Square and see if Tony was around. Maybe he'd run into Turtle over the course of the day. If so, I'd have one less thing on my mind.

When I reached the square, the crowd was still light, but beginning to build. As I emerged from the alley that runs along the Waterfront Playhouse, Lorenzo waved me down. I wove around the ropes marking off the fire-eater's territory and stuffed a dollar into a pail beside a woman with long gray hair playing guitar and singing her heart out. She deserved a buck just for having that much nerve.

"You're okay?" Lorenzo asked when I reached his

table. His eyebrows arched almost to his turban. "I had a bad feeling today."

"I'm fine," I said. "What kind of bad feeling?" Not sure I wanted to hear.

He tapped his chest with his fist. "Heavy. Something ugly," he said. "You be careful."

If he wasn't about the fourth man who had warned me this week, I could have laughed at his melodrama. "I will." I ceded my place by his table to a thin woman in a tank top and short shorts. With the sun about to set and the temperature dropping, I felt cold just looking at her.

"I need to know about my boyfriend," she said, and started to cry.

I slipped away, leaving him to his work, and skirted the edge of the square until I found Tony and his buddies.

"Good evening," I said. "Has anyone seen Turtle since this morning?" I explained what I'd heard from Elsa about Turtle's argument and how she hadn't seen him since. "I checked in with the cops—they haven't picked him up."

"She checked in with the friggin' cops? Who is she, Nancy friggin' Drew?" muttered one of men seated along the ledge.

"Shut up, man," Tony told him, and kicked at his sneaker with a worn cowboy boot. To me: "No, haven't seen him."

"Do you have any idea where he stays? Where he keeps his stuff?"

Tony rasped a hand over the stubble on his cheek

and resettled his cowboy hat. "I think he's got a little hidey-hole over at the end of Duval."

"Thanks," I said, and turned to go. Though how in the world I'd find him with those directions wasn't at all clear.

He dropped his smoldering cigarette butt to the cement and ground it out. "Let me run over with you." He doffed his hat at his friends. "Later, you sorry dudes."

Tony shambled along ahead, me muttering "Sorry to bother you" and "he's probably fine" in his wake. We passed the Ocean Key Resort and then the Pier House and finally reached the tiny beach at the very tip of Duval Street. Where would someone find a place to hide here? But Tony crashed through a row of palmetto bushes along the side of a building. I pushed in behind him, stung by the snap of a few sharp leaves, until we came to a makeshift lean-to made of cardboard and pieces of castoff wood. Tony got down on hands and knees and crawled into the opening, its dirt floor layered with newspaper. The headline about Toby Davidson's rescue from the harbor was on top.

"Holy mother!" said Tony.

I crouched down and crawled into the tiny space behind him. Inside, the hut smelled like unwashed clothes, sweat, urine, and the coppery scent of fresh blood. Tony kneeled beside what appeared to be a pile of rags. Only bloody. As I looked more closely, I recognized Turtle's battered face. And shreds of the black cape he'd been wearing that first morning at the harbor.

"Oh my god, is he alive?"

Tony brushed a strand of red hair off Turtle's face, and then took his hand and felt for a pulse. "No idea. You better get help."

My heart sank and I backpedaled, whipping out my cell phone to call 911 for an ambulance. And then I called Torrence.

"We found him. Turtle," I said, feeling a surge of anger and then hopelessness. "Someone beat the crap out of him. And he crawled off to die like a wounded dog."

21

Plumes of white, pink, and purple blos-
soms offset the one hundred shades of
green our little city is known for this time
of year: lime, celery, and avocado, butter
lettuce and kale, Granny Smith apple and
broccoli and sage.

—Jennie Shortridge, *Eating Heaven*

By the time I got home it was close to six. I felt jittery
and sick to my stomach about Turtle, and definitely
blue. He'd only looked worse the longer I stayed—
barely breathing and sticky with old blood. At least I
knew he was alive because he produced a groan like
pain itself when the EMTs arrived and loaded him, almost tenderly, onto a gurney.

Torrence had arrived on the scene with another cop
shortly before the EMTs. Even he had a horrified expression when he emerged from the bushes—and I
imagined he'd seen the worst of the worst. After Turtle
was packed up and carried off, Torrence poked around

looking for evidence to explain the beating. I told him everything I could think of—about the fight I'd broken up between Derek and Turtle a couple days ago, and Elsa's report about another argument early this morning.

Then I motored on home, feeling washed out and impotent. I couldn't do anything for Turtle—either he'd make it or he wouldn't. Even though it sounded a little shallow and silly, the only thing I could think of that might drive those hideous images out of my head was cooking.

Ever since the wedding challenge the other day, I'd been thinking about Connie's wedding cake. If I was going to bake for her wedding, I wanted to make something that would reflect her best qualities, the things Ray had seen shining in her. A cake that was solid, yet light. Sweet but not treacle-y, with just the right dash of tart. If I could tweak those lime cupcakes into a version that would be lighter and less sweet, they could be the answer.

I paged through several cookbooks, looking for a recipe that might come close to the lime cupcakes that Chef Stentzel had made. Without green food coloring. And with half the frosting. And a third less sugar. But nothing popped out. I booted up my computer and did a search. Mystery Lovers Kitchen, a Web site created by a gang of culinary mystery writers, provided the closest approximation—at least a place to start.

While one stick of butter softened in Miss Gloria's microwave, I set another stick and some cream cheese for frosting out on the counter. Then I pulled out the other ingredients—flour, sugar, eggs, buttermilk, baking powder, baking soda, limes. As I clattered from the pantry to the fridge and back to the small counter, both cats appeared from wherever they'd been napping, crowding underfoot in case something delicious should drop.

Miss Gloria arrived home as I finished folding the wet ingredients into the dry. She watched me pipe the cupcake liners half full of lovely pale green batter.

"How was your day?" I asked as I slid the cupcakes into the oven.

She described several of the bridge hands she'd played with her friends over the afternoon, including a grand slam that was bid and made. "Pretty good for a foursome of old biddies," she said with a cackle. "And Annie Dubisson did real well with the snacks—nothing like you'd make, of course. But at least none of us went hungry." She sat on the banquette along the kitchen wall and wiped her glasses. "What did you do today?"

Turtle's face flashed through my mind but I wasn't ready to talk about him—the memory was too vivid and raw. And Miss Gloria was tender—it would only upset her. So I told her about the interviews with the chefs and judges. And how I'd virtually stalked Buddy Higgs until he admitted he'd had a fling with Sam Rizzoli's wife.

I gathered the dirty dishes, dropped them into the sink filled with soapy water, and began to wash. "The thing is, she insisted this morning that she didn't even know him."

"So someone's told you a stretcher," said Miss Gloria, one arthritic finger waggling. "If it was me, I'd go back to her with the new information and lay it all out."

"You've become quite the little detective," I said with a laugh, piling clean bowls onto the counter. I fished a dish towel from the linens drawer and began to dry. "You'd just show up at her house?"

"We could go see her now," said my roommate, nodding eagerly. "Once the cupcakes are out. We'll surprise her and she'll spill all she knows." She whipped a phone book out of the bookcase that was tucked under the bench, laid it open on the kitchen table, and paged through until she found Rizzoli's address. "They live in Casa Marina. We could be there in no time."

I frowned and wiped the clean counter dry. "Your son would kill me. He brought me onboard to look after you, not chase around the island after criminals."

"He'd never know," she said, zipping a finger across her lips. "Besides, I'd just be along for company," she said. "And courage."

I thought this over as I settled the clean dishes back on their shelves. No way Mrs. Rizzoli had really killed her husband. She was strong, but I didn't believe she was dangerous. But on the other hand, there was a very good chance she was harboring a secret connected to his death. Something she hadn't revealed to the cops— either because it was too embarrassing or she believed it wasn't related. Or both.

"How do you feel about riding on the back of a scooter?" I asked, grinning.

"Hot dog!" she said. "Let me get a sweater."

"And you'll stay on the bike and let me do the talking?"

She nodded again.

Once the cupcakes were out of the oven and cooling

on the stove, I found the spare helmet I'd bought when my mother was visiting and ran a comb through my curls. At the last minute, I frosted four of the still-warm cupcakes and packed them into a Tupperware container. Though the melting icing was not quite up to my usual standards, I preferred not to show up empty-handed to a family in mourning. Then I drove slowly over to the Casa Marina neighborhood, Miss Gloria clutching my waist with both hands and the cupcakes nestled in the crate over the rear wheel.

"Don't let's go on Truman Avenue," she said. "Mrs. Dubisson says it's under construction—an accident waiting to happen."

"I won't," I said, trying to imagine Mrs. D on a scooter on one of the busiest streets in town.

The Rizzoli home on Washington Street was a stunner—an enormous white stucco estate just blocks from the Atlantic Ocean and Flagler's famous Casa Marina Resort. The lawn alone was larger than many of the homes in town, and the stands of tropical vegetation rivaled what I'd seen done by the garden club. A new white Mercedes sat in the driveway in front of the three-car garage, parked behind a bright yellow Hummer.

"Why would you even want a vehicle that's wider than half the streets in the city?" Miss Gloria wondered. "Haven't they heard of global warming?"

"Some people still don't get it," I said. I hopped off the scooter, took the cupcakes from Miss Gloria, and ran up the stairs to ring the bell. Mrs. Rizzoli came to the door after a long pause. She saw the cupcakes first, and it took her a moment to place me.

"You're too kind," she said politely, as I expressed condolences again and handed over the baked goods. She set them down on an occasional table just inside the door

"Who is it?" called an older woman's querulous voice from down the hall.

"I'm sorry for your loss," said Miss Gloria, suddenly materializing next to me. She'd removed her helmet and her white hair stood up like an angry cat's. "But we have something to ask you about Buddy Higgs."

Mrs. Rizzoli frowned and tried to shut the door, but Miss Gloria's sneakered foot wedged it open. "Probably better to tell us ladies than spill the whole embarrassing episode to the police," she said, ignoring my warning glare and my hand, clamped firmly on her wrist.

"Who is it?" the voice called again from the living room.

"A friend from the gym, Mother," Mrs. Rizzoli answered. "I won't be a minute." She came out onto the portico, closed the door behind her, and folded her arms across her bosom, glowering. "What do you want?"

"It's about Buddy Higgs," I said. "We've discovered that you lied, saying that you don't know him. He told me the truth today."

"I doubt that," she said, ice in her voice.

"Is there some place we could sit a minute?" Miss Gloria asked.

"Who are you?" asked Mrs. Rizzoli, but my roommate only folded her arms across her chest and planted her legs like a miniature bodyguard. In a sparkly pink sweatsuit. It was hard not to laugh. Then I thought of Turtle and the chuckle died away.

"We've had three violent incidents now," I told her, counting them off on my fingers. "Your husband was murdered. An attempt was made on one of the other judge's lives." Miss Gloria looked at me with wide eyes but I motioned her off. "And today a homeless man was beaten nearly to death."

Miss Gloria's eyes grew even wider. This was news to her, too. "And you didn't even mention the lady that got sick at the cooking show," she added.

"We need to know what you're hiding before someone else gets killed," I said to Mrs. Rizzoli. My gaze locked on hers until she finally looked away.

"Over here," said Mrs. Rizzoli, and stomped ahead of us to a grouping of Adirondack chairs partially hidden by palm fronds in the side yard. When we were all three seated, she dropped her face into her hands. "He's right. We have been involved. But it was only a way to protect myself."

"From what?" I asked.

She looked up. Her eyes filled and she dashed a tear away.

Miss Gloria rustled through her fanny pack for a tissue, and then leaned over to pat Mrs. Rizzoli's knee. "Go ahead, tell us, dear. It will help the healing to get the truth out."

"When did this start?" I asked.

Her eyes found mine and then she heaved a great sigh. "The night Sam actually brought his girlfriend into our restaurant—and practically did her right on the bar in front of all our friends and acquaintances, that's the night I went out with Buddy. He used to work in our kitchen. You know how handsome he is— and charming."

I bit my lip and nodded. Only I would never have described Buddy as charming, more like abrasive and self-absorbed. And not even all that appealing physically. I suppressed a snicker, thinking of Randy's comment about Buddy's hair impersonating roadkill.

"You said he used to work in your kitchen. Why did he leave?"

Mrs. Rizzoli said, "It's not unusual—there's a lot of turnover in this business." She put a hand to her forehead. "I don't suppose you should be surprised to learn that a man has a drinking problem if you meet him at a bar when you're both blotto," she said. "To be honest, I think he missed a number of his shifts and the manager finally canned him."

"So Buddy was unreliable?"

"That's pretty much it," she said. "I think he actually finds cooking in a restaurant beneath him. He doesn't want to fry and plate hundreds of orders of yellowtail snapper—he wants to invent crazy dishes and then boss other cooks around who are making his creations. He's ferociously ambitious."

"Did your husband know that you and Buddy were seeing each other?" I asked. "Because from what I could tell in the *Topped Chef* competition, Sam didn't seem to have anything against him. In fact, he was very complimentary about his food."

"Honestly?" Her eyes filled again, which caused Miss Gloria's lips to tremble in sympathy. "I don't think he cared. When he broke his big news the other day, I don't think he even realized that I already knew he was cheating." Her hands began to shake—sadness? Anger? Or heartsick with the sheer humiliation?

"That's not right," said Miss Gloria. "What kind of a marriage is that?"

I wasn't entirely sure her presence on an interview was turning out to be an asset. If we felt too sorry for Mrs. Rizzoli, it would get tougher to ask the hardball questions. I decided to switch direction.

"Do you remember when Sam was asked to be a *Topped Chef* judge?" I asked. "You mentioned that he's not much of a foodie."

"A couple of weeks ago, anyway," she said. "Maybe two? He was tickled to be invited. It didn't take much to pump up that man's ego. When Deena Smith called, he took it as a sign that he'd climbed another rung in the Key West culinary scene." She wrinkled her nose. "Which partly explains why he was so angry about your restaurant review. When you criticized his establishment, you pricked his balloon—and then some of his hot air ran out."

"You say Buddy's ambitious. Ambitious enough to kill someone to get what he wanted?"

Her eyes bugged out. "You think Buddy killed Sam? That's absurd."

"But does he have a temper?"

"Yes," she admitted, one hand floating to her lips. "I suppose it's possible. But I'd say he's more likely to turn the anger inside when he's frustrated, and then self-destruct."

I didn't want to come right out and say it, but wouldn't murdering someone be the ultimate form of self-destruction? A prison term for life? There wouldn't be many cutting-edge cooking opportunities in the federal penitentiary.

22

The moon glided out from its cover of
clouds, causing sparkles of light to dance
on the water like a thousand pearls of tapi-
oca.

— Hayley Snow, *Topped Chef*

After returning to Tarpon Pier and parking the scooter,
we met Eric and his dog coming down the finger of our
dock.

"You ladies are out late," Eric said, at the same time
the little Yorkie yipped his own greeting and threw
himself at my legs.

"I'm so happy to see you!" I rushed up to give him
a big hug and then scratch behind the dog's ears.

"We were doing some detective work," said Miss
Gloria, looking smug.

Eric looked at me and I rolled my eyes. "I decided it
was worth talking to Mrs. Rizzoli because we caught
her in a lie. Miss Gloria was supposed to be along for
the ride, but she couldn't keep out of it."

"Sounds familiar," said Eric. "Who taught her everything she knows?"

"And she turns out to be quite a good 'good cop,'" I said, slinging an arm around Miss Gloria's shoulders; she shivered with pleasure and beamed. "Do you have time to come in and try a key lime cupcake? We have a lot to catch up on."

"Did someone say cupcake?" Eric answered, and then patted his belly. "I've missed your cooking. Maybe I even lost a pound or two while we were away."

Once we were all settled in the kitchen, the cats closed off in Miss Gloria's bedroom to avoid double-team attacks on Eric's little dog, and cupcakes and steaming tea on the table, I caught him up on what had gone on this evening.

"Mrs. Rizzoli claimed she never knew Buddy Higgs, but that turned out to be a lie," I said. "The truth is she had an affair with him."

"Which we think was a reaction to her husband's infidelity. Mrs. R claims her husband didn't care one way or another whether she slept with another man but that's hard for me to swallow," said Miss Gloria. "Even in these modern days, doesn't a marriage mean anything?"

"Agreed," Eric said, as he bit into his cupcake. He closed his eyes for a second to chew and swallow and then blinked his eyes open. "Hayley, these are outstanding."

"Good enough for Connie's wedding?"

"Definitely. These could steal the show," he said. "Who was Sam Rizzoli's girlfriend?"

Miss Gloria and I looked at each other. "She didn't say. And we didn't think to ask."

"Whoever she is, I'm sure the cops are checking her out, because she'd make an obvious suspect."

"Oh my," said Miss Gloria. "What if he was going to dump the mystery girlfriend and go back to his wife? What if she'd rather see him dead than allow that?"

"Did you say that Henri Stentzel is one of the chefs?" Eric popped the last bite of lime cake into his mouth and licked the icing off his fingers. "Isn't she the woman you thought murdered Chad's girlfriend?"

I nodded. "She's still angry about that—and she lets me see that every chance we have to interact. And believe me, I've gone out of my way to be complimentary about what she cooks."

"She's probably not the killer, but hopefully the cops won't overlook her just because you mis-fingered her last time." He took a sip of tea. "What about the other judges?"

"Wally and Danielle and I had dinner at Chef Adam's restaurant this week. The food was very, very good, by the way. He came out to talk with us after the meal. None of us got a scary vibe, even though he has that haughty superchef air about him."

"And the third judge?" Eric asked.

"Toby Davidson," I said. "She's the one who's worried all along that someone might be picking us off, one by one."

"If there were no judges left, there would be no contest," he said. "Even one more death would kill the project, I imagine. Would anyone want that outcome?"

I shook my head. "Me." I grinned. "Not the killing part, but ending the dumb project."

I went to get my computer and typed "Toby Davidson author" into the search bar. Hundreds of links came up, many to reviews of her memoir, but also to articles about cooking that she'd written for magazines and posted on her baking blog.

"She's an old-fashioned cook's cook," I said, clicking on the link to her blog.

Eric read over my shoulder. "She says she uses cooking to conjure up folks from her past," said Eric. "Interesting."

"Here's the publisher's description of her memoir: 'Ms. Davidson absorbed her grief by cooking her way through her husband's favorite recipes, extruding the sadness into the pot roast with mashed potatoes and gravy, the coq au vin, the beef stew with beer and onions . . . ' "

"You're making me hungry all over again," said Miss Gloria. "Although I'm not sure I'd want a sad pot roast."

"I don't see a motive for murdering Rizzoli, do you?" I asked Eric.

"Not personal anyway, unless he had something to do with her husband." The little terrier whined and Eric glanced at his watch. "I've got to get home. But the question is out there: Are the judges in danger?"

"Or are they dangerous?" added Miss Gloria.

23

The first time you see something that you have never seen before, you almost always know right away if you should eat it or run away from it.

—Scott Adams

I phoned the hospital first thing when I woke, intending to ask about Turtle's condition. But once the canned "Welcome to the Lower Keys Medical Center" message began to play, I realized that I'd never heard him called anything but Turtle. Not a clue about his real name or his last name. I doubted I'd get any information with what I had, but I clicked through to the guest services line and asked the receptionist to check on a "Turtle Doe."

"Sorry we don't have anyone listed by that name," she said.

I rolled out of bed, fed the cats, and slid into my running clothes, thinking that either Derek or Elsa might know Turtle's real name. Although based on what Elsa

had told me yesterday, I worried that Derek was the
one who'd beaten Turtle to a bloody heap. I certainly
wouldn't mention that when I saw him—generally
starting out with an accusation did not produce much
new information.

I puffed slowly over to Old Town harbor, feeling every repetition of every exercise Leigh the trainer had
put me through yesterday—right through my skin to
my muscles and then down to the bone. As I reached
the water, Derek had finished washing the party boat
and begun to coil up his hose.

"Looks like another beautiful day in paradise!" I
called out.

He grunted and slung the hose onto a peg at the
edge of the dock. I stopped right in front of him so he
couldn't avoid me and watched his face carefully. "You
probably heard that Turtle's in the hospital?"

His gaze flicked up to meet mine. Then he backed
away and began to tie up a bag of trash from the boat.
"I heard."

"Tony and I found him, over at the end of Duval."

"I heard."

"Any idea what happened?"

"Someone beat the crap out of him," he said, empha-
sizing *crap*. "Knowing Turtle, he probably drove them
to it. But don't ask me a damn thing about it because I
don't know anything." He scowled and turned his hose
on again and began to squirt the dock near the boat. "I
got work to do here, if you don't mind."

I hopped back to get out of reach of his spray, which
came dangerously close to my sneakers. "Do you have
any idea what his real name is? I wanted to check on

him, but of course he's not listed at the hospital as Turtle."

"John Sampson," he said, and stomped away. He called over his shoulder: "Hope they find who did it before they finish what they started."

I headed toward the Cuban Coffee Queen, puzzling over his reaction. Honestly, he didn't look like a guy who'd bludgeoned someone to within an inch of his life. Yes, he was irritable and short-tempered. But he was more likely to drench Turtle with his hose than beat him with it.

With my tall con leche in hand, I walked back to houseboat row. Was Turtle still in danger as Derek implied? I hadn't consciously considered that, though the possibility would explain why I'd woken up worried. But surely the cops would keep an eye on a victim of that much violence—even if he was one of the throwaway homeless.

Wouldn't they?

My stomach began to churn as I faced the facts. From the glimpse I'd gotten of Turtle yesterday, the beating wasn't meant casually—it hadn't come after a small fracas or minor difference of opinion. They'd meant to finish him off, rather than teach him a lesson.

I punched Eric's number into my phone. He answered on the third ring, sounding groggy.

"Hope I didn't wake you," I said, to try to be polite. Then I told him about what Derek had said about Turtle, and all the details I'd noticed about his body language. "I used to think I was a good judge of character," I said. "But Chad lied through his teeth and I didn't pick that up until way too late. So if someone's lying, what kind of body language would you watch for?"

"Good morning to you, too," Eric said when I finally drew a breath. "Let me stagger out to the kitchen and grab a cup of coffee and then you can pelt me with your questions."

While he made his coffee, I explained again how I'd gone to talk to Derek, and how Elsa had said she saw someone who looked like Derek arguing with Turtle yesterday. But Derek claimed he knew nothing about it. "How could I tell if he was lying?"

"This is police business," he said. "Did you tell the cops about Elsa and Derek?"

"I'm planning to call Officer Torrence when I hang up with you. But the more details I give him, the better the chance he'll follow up, right?"

Eric groaned and slurped his coffee. "Probably he wouldn't make eye contact with you if he was telling a lie. Though if he's a practiced liar, that might not be true. Or you might notice excess eye movement," he suggested. "A lot of blinking, drawing eyebrows together, that sort of thing."

I sighed. "That pretty much describes him all the time. Any conversation with me, he behaves like he wishes he were somewhere else—anywhere else. I guess you don't land a job washing boats at the crack of dawn because you love working with people."

Eric laughed. "What did he say when you asked him about Turtle? Did he act defensive? Was his body language stiff?"

"He's always stiff," I said. "He mentioned thinking

Turtle brought the beating on himself. And something about hoping the person who attacked him didn't go back to finish the job." I heard Eric's dog yip in the background.

"Dog's got a lizard—I better go. Last question: Would Derek have shared his theories with the cops?" Eric asked. "Because if he didn't, you should."

"I will," I said. "I promise. Now that I've got Turtle's real name, I'm going to drop in on him at the hospital— see if I can do anything for him. Lord knows he doesn't have any family on this island. And maybe not anywhere."

I took a quick shower and drove up Route One, off Key West to the next pearl in our little string of islands, Stock Island. Though with its landfill and marine industry and trailer parks and homeless shelter, this one more resembled a misshapen freshwater pearl than a perfect white orb. Turning left before I hit the golf course, I imagined that Turtle might have taken this route many times to get to the overnight homeless shelter. Except he'd have been on foot. Every night around six o'clock, a stream of folks seeking a place to spend the night shuffled or pedaled along Route One to the Stock Island shelter.

I pulled into the parking lot of the pink and blue stucco medical center, trying to press back the unpleasant memories of my recent outpatient visit and then a visit to Miss Gloria after she'd been attacked by a would-be killer. As I approached the building, the glass entry doors slid open, releasing a blast of refrigerated, disinfected air. At the information desk, I explained to a white-haired woman in a blue jacket that I wished to see Mr. John Sampson.

She flashed through several computer screens, and then glanced up and squinted through thick lenses. "Name, please?"

"Hayley Snow," I told her, thinking they must have upgraded their system to print out personalized visitor badges.

She tapped my name into her computer.

"I'm sorry. Mr. Sampson cannot have visitors right now," she said.

"But you see, I'm his friend and I'm worried. I'm the one who found him yesterday and called the police."

She slid her glasses down her nose and peered over them. "It says here, 'no visitors.'"

"Then why did you take my name?" I couldn't help asking, feeling frustrated and disappointed.

"I'm not at liberty to discuss this," she said firmly, gripping her computer desk with both hands.

Clearly I wasn't going to get anything more from her. I retreated from the reception area and took a seat on a hard plastic chair that had been bolted to the floor. Derek's voice rang in my head: "Hope they find who did it before they finish what they started."

So I texted Torrence, telling him that I was at the hospital, had hoped to visit Turtle, and had some other information that might have bearing on the murder. As I stood to leave, I spotted a small woman signing papers at the insurance desk and recognized her as the traveling companion of the woman who had taken ill at the Mallory Square taste-off. I hurried across the room to greet her.

"How are you? And how's your friend doing?" I patted her back and told her my name. "I was one of the judges at the cooking demonstration. I've been thinking about you ever since. Is your friend okay?"

"Thanks for asking," said the little woman. "I'm Harriet Miles." She bared her teeth in a timid smile. "Of all things, they think my friend had an allergic reaction to star fruit."

"Wow," I said. "I've never heard of that."

"It's unusual," she said. "Apparently star fruit is related to mango."

"Mango?"

"A few people have a toxic reaction, and unfortunately, Sarah is one of them. She was so mad about missing the rest of the tasting." She shook her head with a wry smile. "You can probably tell by looking at her that she enjoys eating everything. She's not fussy about food the way I am. But she'd never tried star fruit before so the bad reaction was a complete surprise."

"I'm just glad it wasn't poison," I said. "That's what we were afraid of."

She looked alarmed. "You thought she was poisoned?"

Okay, foot in mouth, Hayley: I should never have mentioned that. I gave a fake laugh. "Food critic's humor. I'm so sorry you ladies missed the rest of your cruise. I'm sure this particular detour wasn't on your itinerary."

The little woman nodded. "Definitely more excitement than we bargained for. First of all, the paramedics wouldn't let me ride in the ambulance because I'm not a relative by blood or marriage. Luckily that nice Mr.

Shapiro put me up in a bed-and-breakfast on Grinnell Street. And once Sarah was stable and they weren't so worried about her, I visited the Hemingway House and saw all his cats."

"Those kitties are my favorite tourist attraction," I said with a grin.

"Sarah's getting released this morning so we plan to take the conch tour train and have a nice dinner before we have to catch a plane home tomorrow." Her face brightened. "You're a food critic, right? Maybe you have a recommendation?"

"Sure," I said. "I love Michael's for steak. Or Santiago's Bodega for tapas—it's in our funky part of town up the street from Blue Heaven. Which is also enjoyable, and famous for chickens pecking underneath your dinner table. Or Louie's Backyard for the view—though it's pricey. Or if you want the down-home Key West experience, either B.O.'s Fish Wagon or Pepe's—they're right across the street from each other on Caroline Street."

"She owes me," said Harriet. "Louie's Backyard sounds perfect. Don't tell Sarah, but I wasn't enjoying the cruise that much anyway. All those children running around shrieking, and plus I felt constantly queasy from the boat's motion. Key West is the bomb."

I exited the waiting room, relieved that the tourist ladies were alive and safe. And pleasantly surprised that Peter Shapiro had been so generous. I suppose he didn't want a lawsuit marring his show's prospects.

My phone buzzed and Torrence's name flashed on my screen. "Good morning," I said after clicking to accept the call. "They wouldn't let me in to see Turtle."

"Then *they* are doing their job," he said. "You said you had some news?"

"A little," I said. "Though mainly I called because I was worried about Turtle being in danger. But it looks like you already have that covered." I told him how I'd tracked down Derek at the harbor earlier this morning. "I might have forgotten to mention the other day that he had a photo on his iPhone of Rizzoli hanging from the mast. Turtle was kind of worked up about the whole crime thing."

"Worked up?" Torrence asked.

"Excited. Sort of. I don't know how to explain it. He insisted that Derek show me the photo. But ever since we found him all beat up, I started to wonder whether he saw something happen the night Rizzoli died. Maybe he didn't realize he saw it. But maybe the killer thought he'd seen something that would make him dangerous."

There was a pause on the line.

"You forgot to mention this?" Torrence asked.

"Sort of," I said, feeling a little sick to my stomach. In my urge to protect Derek's privacy and his smartphone, had I put Turtle in danger?

"Anything else?" he asked.

I hesitated, but then spilled the details of the visit I'd made last night to Mrs. Rizzoli, and her admission that she'd been involved with Buddy Higgs.

"Thanks for letting me know," he said.

Which sounded like a perfectly nice thing to say, only the way he emphasized "letting me know" made it clear he was annoyed.

"I would appreciate it if you'd leave any further interviews to me."

"Sorry," I said. I hesitated, but decided it wouldn't hurt to ask. "Has there been any progress on the case? Anything you can tell me, I mean?"

Torrence sighed loudly, then said: "The preliminary report on Mr. Rizzoli's autopsy is in. It appears that he didn't die from hanging. He was killed by a blow from a blunt instrument, then dressed and made up, and then hoisted up into the rigging."

"Someone put makeup on him after they killed him? That's sick."

"That's the working theory. Not that any of it should have any bearing on your activities," he warned. "I'm only telling you that because you're morbidly curious and I figured you'd badger me until I gave up something. Chances are it'll be in the paper tomorrow anyway."

24

The amateurs are not going away, which
restaurateurs once might have hoped, and
they are making chefs nervous.

—Ike DeLorenzo

A wealthy Venezuelan man and his third wife had do-
nated the use of their home for the final leg of the
Topped Chef competition. Only blocks from Mrs. Rizzoli's house on Washington Street, this place was twice
as opulent and showy. Key West is known for tiny
yards and adorable conch homes decorated with gin-
gerbread trim and inviting front porches. But Juan
Pisani had chosen to design and build a white stucco
monstrosity surrounded by a black metal fence and
elaborate plantings.

A card table had been set up on the porch outside
the door underneath an enormous portico. Two volunteers in red shirts with TOPPED CHEF KEY WEST logos
printed on them asked for my name and driver's license. Behind them, just inside the foyer, a uniformed

cop waited, partially hidden by the largest indoor ficus tree I'd ever seen.

"Got your A-team security here today," I said with a chuckle as I handed over my license.

The volunteer studied my license and then pushed it back to me. "That's right." No return smile. She gave me a badge and explained that I was to wear it at all times while on the premises. Serious business.

I entered the house, gawking shamelessly at the leather and brass bar in the foyer and after that the expansive living room filled with leather furniture and African artwork. Nothing subtle about any of it. The ceilings swept up through two full floors and some of the potted palms reached three-quarters of the way to the top. Deena hurried past me as I was trying to decipher the meaning of a twisted metal sculpture. I tapped her arm and she whirled around to face me.

"Oh, it's you." She clapped a hand to her chest. "You startled me." She looked me up and down and tweaked the fake pearls I'd put on to dress up my sleeveless black shift. "You clean up nice."

"Thanks. Hey, I have some really good news," I said. "The woman who took sick at the Mallory Square taste-off? Turns out she was allergic to star fruit. So nobody poisoned anybody." I grinned but my cheer ebbed away when I saw the worry in her expression and a sheen of sweat gathering on her upper lip. This on a woman who considered perspiration a cardinal sin.

"What's wrong?"

She glanced around the room and then beckoned for me to follow her into a small office adjacent to the living area. Once inside, she slid the mahogany pocket doors closed behind me and straightened the faux zebra-striped rug with her foot. "There's been a threat against the show."

"A threat? Good lord, what kind of threat?"

She held a finger to her lips. "We need to keep this quiet if we don't want mass hysteria. But someone slipped a note under Peter's door at his bed-and-breakfast during the night. The police have it now."

"What did it say?" I hugged my arms around my torso, feeling suddenly chilled rather than pleasantly cool, as I had when I entered this palace.

"It looked childish—made of letters cut from a magazine. 'Topped Chef Key West, where someone's not making it back for seconds.' The chief of police thinks it's a fraud, but of course it has to be taken seriously. Hence, the extra security. All the guests will have their purses searched and ID's checked."

"Shouldn't we cancel? It's not worth continuing if someone else dies. My gosh," I added, slinging my backpack off my shoulder and perching it on the shiny cherry desk, "no one looked at what I brought in."

"What did you bring?" she asked, her eyes widening with worry.

"Nothing. But that's not the point. I could have smuggled anything in. A gun. A knife. Anything. How would they know if no one is checking?"

"They are checking," she said in a soothing voice. "But you're one of the judges. Once they recognized your name, they would know you're a good egg." She smiled with encouragement. "We considered all the options, including canceling this episode of the show. The police mentioned that possibility to Peter, but they didn't push it. And neither of us felt it was the right thing to do. Especially since the cops agreed to provide extra security." She sighed. "We've come so far. We're so close to the climax. We hate to bow to some fruitcake's idea of a joke."

"But aren't you worried about the food getting tainted—for real this time?" I asked her.

"I shopped for everything personally," Deena said. "Every grain of salt, every stick of butter, every length of pasta. And it hasn't been out of my sight since I left the grocery store."

"How about right now?"

Deena smiled. "We have a volunteer stationed in the pantry and two more in the kitchen. And there are at least two cops in street clothes on the premises. We wouldn't proceed if we thought anyone was in danger." She placed her hands on my shoulders. "Look, I shouldn't have said anything. But I know you're a good observer so I wanted you to keep your eyes open. Let me know right away if you notice anything weird. Okay?"

"I guess." I shrugged my pack back onto my shoulder and followed her into the living room, which had begun to fill with guests sipping champagne from plastic flutes, even though it was well before noon.

We threaded through the crowd and finally arrived at the kitchen—a fabulous, futuristic, open-air kitchen that might have been designed for this very affair. A central island at least four yards long held a six-burner stainless stovetop, set in pink granite. It made Miss Gloria's propane stove look as though it came from Barbie's Dream House, circa 1980. Behind the stove against the window were double sinks and the biggest stainless steel refrigerator I'd ever seen, surrounded by more yards of gorgeous granite. The other wall of the kitchen was constructed of sliding glass doors so the room could be opened to a vast interior courtyard containing a pool, a hot tub, and enough foliage to keep an army of landscapers busy. Rows of folding chairs had been set up in the courtyard for the studio audience.

While the guests were getting settled and I was looking around, Toby and Chef Adam were seated on stools facing the stove and then attacked by the makeup artist bearing oil-absorbing powder. Up close they looked dusty like a dry roadbed with all that makeup, but the camera would love them. Bright spotlights had been positioned near the ceiling, casting beams of hot light onto the work surface. The three chef candidates hovered in the pantry off the back of the kitchen. Every person involved with the show looked anxious, from the contestants to the judges to the lead cameraman.

Peter emerged from the people in the courtyard and entered the kitchen. "Chop, chop, people!" he called. "Take your places. The final episode of *Topped Chef* Key West–style is about to begin." The theme song from *Oliver!* began to play from the home's fancy speakers, both out in the courtyard and inside the kitchen. The audience quickly took seats.

I sat at the counter between Chef Adam and Toby, clipped on my microphone, and submitted to a quick face powdering. Rivulets of sweat began to run down my back and chest. Behind us, I could hear the guests rustling and murmuring. I felt vulnerable and tense; I remembered hearing how a judge who handled high-profile criminal cases always sat with his back to the wall in case some loony tunes came after him with a gun.

He would not have agreed to sit on this stool.

"Welcome, welcome!" Peter called, once everyone was in place. The music faded away. "We are so pleased to present the final, thrilling installment of our contest. You've seen our contestants interviewed. You've heard about their visions for a Key West wedding and tasted their party specialties. You've watched as they pulled together a meal from secret ingredients." He rubbed his palms with feigned anticipation—or was it real? "Tonight we crown the Topped Chef of Key West! Tonight we choose the chef who will take his or her interpretation of island delicacies and spread the word to the world. This episode is all about romancing the audience. Are you ready to be swept off your feet?"

The courtyard audience roared. But inside the kitchen, the tension was palpable, as if we were all waiting for one more awful thing to happen. Peter addressed the chefs, who had gathered in a knot to the left of the double sinks. "Chefs, are you ready to leap from the frying pan into the fire?"

"Ready!" yelped Randy.

The other two merely nodded.

"We've drawn lots to select the order in which you will cook. We'll begin with chef Randy Thompson, followed by chef Henrietta Stentzel, and finally, chef Buddy Higgs will close the competition."

Randy stepped up to the counter, as the other two retreated to the pantry. "Thank you for that wonderful introduction—I adore a good romance." He winked at the camera and began to belt out the words from the song Peter had chosen as the show's theme. "Food, glorious food," he warbled as he organized his dinner ingredients. "We're all anxious to try it!"

He measured cornmeal into a pan of simmering chicken broth, shucked the shells off a pile of pink shrimp, and grated a mound of white cheddar cheese, all while chattering amiably about cooking and entertaining and interspersing his comments with snatches of song. And most appealing of all, half a pound of bacon spat in his frying pan, perfuming the air. The audience laughed and cheered at his antics: I couldn't imagine that the other two would be able to match this performance.

"Every Southern chef worth his or her salt has a variation on the classic recipe for shrimp and grits," said Randy. "And they will argue about whether the necessary secret ingredient is the bacon, the tasso ham, the green peppers, the heavy cream versus the cheese. But Key West has a supersecret weapon." He winked and grinned. "We are so lucky on this island to have access to gorgeous local shrimp—Key West pinks, they're called, for those of you who aren't local." He stopped and beckoned the camera forward to show a close-up of the shrimp.

Then, leaning toward us judges with both hands on the counter, he made eye contact with the front row of the audience. "I know it's not always possible, but fresh and local ingredients make a huge difference to your meals. Sometimes it's better to change the menu if you can't find the right stuff," he said, and then plopped half a stick of butter into the pan that now contained hot bacon grease. When the butter had melted, he dropped in some minced garlic, scallions, and green peppers, followed by a double handful of shrimp. They sizzled and spat.

"For instance, those flabby Southeast Asian crustaceans?" His lips formed a horrified O. "Absolutely deadly. Those are a never for me!"

By the time Randy had completed his shrimp and grits dish, I thought he'd won over the studio audience completely. He was relaxed and charming and the smell of his food made my stomach leap with anticipation. But Chef Adam's face looked blank and Toby's expression was bemused rather than enchanted. One of the assistants came forward to divide his dish onto three plates.

"Do not forget to have fun while you're planning the menu and cooking for company," Randy said, waggling his finger at the audience and grinning again. "It should never be a drag to entertain." He placed a plate in front of each of us and stood back like a proud father.

I nibbled the cheesy grits first, then cut into a perfectly cooked pink shrimp. "This is sublime," I said. "I adore the bacon and the bits of green pepper. So buttery and rich. And not the slightest bit fishy."

"I like it," said Toby. "But I'm not bowled over."

Chef Adam tasted and then clattered his fork onto the plate. "It's definitely heavy. Bordering on greasy," he said. "There's a month's worth of cholesterol just in this one dish." One of the cameras zoomed in on the food in front of Chef Adam, while another caught the disappointed grimace on Randy's face. "To me it tastes like a grand cliché of Southern cooking. Paula Deen squared."

Assistants rushed in to whisk away the dishes and maneuver Randy out of the way, so that Henri Stentzel could take her place and prepare to replicate the seafood fra diavolo that she'd prepared the first day of the contest. She was more nervous than she'd been earlier in the week, as I could tell from the sloppy way she chopped her onions. Her hands shook so badly that the jalapeño peppers came out in large chunks. And finally she cut a chunk of skin out of her finger and began to bleed into the onions.

Deena rushed forward with a Band-Aid and a replacement onion. Once patched up, Henri resumed chatting about the steps she was taking to make the spicy red sauce, but she stammered and stumbled over her words. It was painful to watch. When at last she was finished, an assistant produced more clean plates and ladled us each a taste.

Toby spoke first. "This doesn't appeal to me quite as much as it did on the first day we tried it. There isn't the same brightness to the dish."

"It's almost as if the chef's anxiety has infused her food," said Chef Adam. "It lacks luminosity."

"Luminosity?" I asked, and then bit into a pepper so large and hot that tears sprang to my eyes. I signaled to Deena for a glass of water, sipped, and swallowed. "Maybe go easy on the peppers next time," I suggested, trying to temper my advice with a smile. "Aside from my tongue blistering, I'm not having the same reaction as my colleagues. I find Chef Stentzel's food solid and compelling."

"But?" asked Chef Adam. "It sounds like you have a but . . ."

I tipped my head to one side and then the other, trying to press out the crackling knots of tension gathering in my neck. "But I think we want to choose a chef whose personality is luminous, along with the food. I want to see that right here in Chef Stentzel's presentation, because I have enjoyed her cooking." I emphasized *personality* and *want*, and then swallowed nervously. "But I admit that today I don't." I didn't dare make eye contact with her because I knew she'd be shooting me angry daggers of death.

"And now, chef Buddy Higgs will take center stage," Peter crowed as Henri slunk away.

Buddy strode out from the shadows of the pantry, leaned forward, looking past us to make eye contact with the studio guests just as Randy had. He began to speak. "To my mind, excellent cooking—cooking that rises to the level of a television experience—should challenge both the chef and his diners. I don't want to waste precious minutes in the lives of TV viewers by preparing something they could get by paging through the recipes of Fannie Farmer or Irma Rombauer. Allow me to show you what I mean."

He headed to the refrigerator and returned with two large, live lobsters, pincers and antennae waving. "Anyone can drop a crustacean into a pot of water and microwave melted butter on the side. With that menu, the biggest challenge is containing the diners' mess."

The lobsters scrambled for purchase on the marble countertop. The crowd looked on, mesmerized as Buddy chose a cleaver from the knife rack. There was a collective gasp as he hacked off the heads of the lobsters, and then cut the bodies into pieces. A few customers booed his brutality.

Notwithstanding the crustacean carnage, Buddy himself looked more appealing than I'd seen him this week—his toque was starched, his jacket immaculate, and his checked chef's pants fit perfectly. Even his hair was clean. Honestly, he looked and sounded professional. And utterly ruthless.

"On the other hand," Buddy said, "a grilled lobster with olive oil sea foam, jalapeño caviar, and edible sand garnish doesn't require a PhD in cutlery to consume—but it challenges even the most jaded taste buds. I promise you that those spheres of jalapeño caviar will burst with flavor in the mouths of your dinner guests, leaving a lasting impression."

He lit the gas grill next to the stove top, brushed the lobster sections with olive oil, and laid them on the grill. "In this style of cooking, there is no room for repetitive, boring food. The plate is our canvas—if we even need a plate." He chuckled. "Remember the mojito I offered several days ago? Who else would serve a cocktail in a spoon? In this case, I serve my lobster on edible sand, which is constructed of seaweed, crispy Panko crumbs, and a dash of miso oil.

"To make the sea foam, heat olive oil with glycerin flakes until they dissolve. Add salt, and then whip." He mixed his ingredients, poured the mixture into a stainless steel can that resembled a whipped cream canister, and shook it. He had the full attention of the audience now. They craned around each other to see each step of what he was doing, appearing totally wowed. By the time he'd finished cooking and arranging the plates, the dinner he'd made looked like a beach scene in miniature.

"Voilà!" he exclaimed. "Chef Buddy's seafood à la Key West."

Once his extravaganza was delivered to us, I extracted a bite of moist, pink lobster meat from its shell and dragged it through the faux sand and the olive oil foam. I cringed a little, waiting for something bizarre to hit my taste buds. Or even a gritty feeling—the fake sand was that realistic. Instead, the sample tasted delicious.

"Judges?" Peter asked, as the cameras zoomed in on the food and then our faces.

I jumped in. "I haven't been such a big fan of Buddy's work so far, but I have to admit, the lobster is amazing. And even though I can hardly believe I'm saying this, the foam and the phony sand are showstoppers."

"He's outdone himself," said Chef Adam. "He's risen to a culinary plane far above the other two chefs."

"That's a little bit of an exaggeration," said Toby. She pushed her plate away. "The meal is definitely tasty, but what home cook could replicate it?"

"Hardly a concern," said Chef Adam, with a flick of one hand. "This show is about entertainment—and Buddy Higgs is a natural."

Peter stepped forward, beckoning the three chefs to accompany him. "You have all wowed us with your food, and entranced us with your personalities, but now the moment of truth is at hand." He looked at each of the candidates. "You've heard our esteemed judges speak."

He paused dramatically. "Randy Thompson, I'm afraid you are going to have to stand over here. . . ."

Randy's face fell.

"In the semifinalists' circle!"

The audience clapped and cheered and Randy burst into a huge grin and moved closer to Peter.

"Chef Buddy Higgs," said Peter, waving for silence. "I hate to say this"—he took a deep breath—"but we'd like you join him!"

Now Buddy smiled and waved at the audience as he moved closer to Randy.

"Let's hear it from the audience for our third contestant," said Peter. "Chef Henrietta Stentzel, thank you for coming and we wish you all the luck in the world in your cooking future!"

There was a polite smattering of applause as she disappeared back into the pantry, her eyes moist and shoulders slumped. I felt instantly sorry for her, even though it seemed like the right decision.

"Now is the time we hear from you!" Peter said to the audience, his voice hoarse with excitement. "Who do you want in your living rooms for the next TV season? Randy Thompson?"

Quite a few viewers stomped and whistled.

"Or Buddy Higgs?"

The crowd erupted.

"Ladies and gentlemen," Peter shouted over the din, "I bring you our Topped Chef Key West!"

The music amped up, the viewers cheered, and Buddy waded into the audience to shake hands with the men, hug the women, and accept congratulations. A tall, heavyset man in the back row leaped to his feet and rushed forward.

"This is a setup!" he yelled. "You had a ringer chosen all along! You cheatin', lying bugger—" As he neared Peter, two security guards tackled him and flung him to the ground.

I spun around on my stool, looking for Deena, dumbfounded at how quickly this had happened. In the shadows of the pantry, Henri removed her toque and her coat. She folded it into fastidious quarters and then draped it over her arm. Randy barreled up to Peter and began to argue. On his face I could read the depth of his disappointment. And anger.

"This was fixed from the beginning." He spat out the words.

"Shall I call security again, once they take care of your friend?" Peter asked.

25

We don't just know how to play. We're not electrocuting bunnies in our lab coats. We're part of something beautiful: cooking.

—Wylie Dufresne

I retreated to the office to regroup for an hour before the Duval Uncorked event started, and to begin making notes for my *Topped Chef* article. Saturday afternoon— neither Danielle nor Wally should be there—the place would be quiet and dim. And I would not be tempted to chat with Miss Gloria or bake something tasty.

My shoulders felt like concrete blocks and the heavy-metal pounding of a major headache had kicked in. I changed my clothes, then nicked a few of Danielle's Motrin, swallowed them down with a bottle of spring water from the fridge, and went to curl up on the wicker loveseat in Wally's office. I closed my eyes and tried to breathe out the cables of tension racking my body, calmed by the scent of Wally's citrus after-shave wafting from the tropical upholstery.

As I mulled over this morning's event, my irritation with the *Topped Chef* contest crested. After Buddy's abrupt coronation, I'd tried to speak with Deena to register my concerns. The judges hadn't really had a reasonable opportunity to debate the outcome, in my opinion. Nor had there been an accounting of accumulated scores from the other cooking events.

But Deena was ebullient about the results and resistant to my complaints. After all, the final episode had gone off without any hiccups. No one had died or been poisoned or dropped to the floor with convulsions. And the chef with the most interesting food had come out on top.

But as Randy and his friend had suggested, now I suspected the contest had been rigged from the start. And despite how much I loved and trusted Deena, the producer's insistence on stirring up rancor between the contestants bothered me. I wasn't cut out for reality television, that much was clear.

Finally, it occurred to me to wonder again why I had been chosen as a judge. Yes, I was food critic for *Key Zest* magazine. But I was not well known, not yet. Why not ask one of the well-published food writers who'd worked for years for the *Key West Citizen*? And why had I been asked to join the panel so late? I realized that all three of the other judges had been tapped weeks before me. Why?

Peter and Deena would know the answer to that. But Deena was the only person who might tell me the truth. I dialed her cell phone.

"Deena, it's Hayley. I bet you're glad the week is over."

"Glad because I'm bushed. Sad because I love the stuff," said Deena. "Thanks for being a good sport and coming along for the ride."

"You're welcome, it was certainly interesting." I laughed. *Aggravating, annoying, infuriating, demeaning*— those were the words I'd have used if I didn't want something from her.

"I know you were somewhat disappointed about the results, but we're only grateful that it went off without a hitch today. That threat really rattled us," she said. "You probably couldn't tell, but Peter was a wreck. We're all relieved that the only misadventure was that crazy drag-queen friend of Randy's rushing the set. I'm so relieved that everyone's safe."

"That was Randy's friend?" I asked.

"He works and sings with him at the Aqua," Deena said.

This made sense—Randy was the kind of guy who would inspire rabid loyalty. Another reason why he would have made a magnificent Topped Chef. "Now that it's over, I've been wondering," I said. "How did you choose the judges?"

Deena cleared her throat. "Peter asked me to recommend some people since I've been living here awhile and he's not local. From those names, he chose the final panel."

"But what were the criteria?" I asked. "There are so many foodie writers and chefs in town. Who made the short list?"

"Not everyone could give up a week during their

busy season," she said. "You know what it's like in January on this island. So having the ability to take time off was critical. Since Wally was enthusiastic about the idea of a story for *Key Zest*, you were a shoo-in. And Peter wanted folks whose opinions wouldn't be overwhelming, but who would demonstrate their knowledge about food clearly."

"Rizzoli and Chef Adam hardly fit into the category of not having strong opinions," I said.

She laughed. "The results weren't perfect. First I thought of Toby Davidson. She has the foodie background because of her baking blog and the cookbooks she's written. And the memoir, of course. But I'd seen her give presentations; she seemed a little timid."

"You were looking for timid?"

Deena was quiet for a moment. "I didn't mean it that way. Peter wanted some people on the panel who would be open to considering other points of view. I think that's how he said it."

My phone buzzed with an incoming call. From Mrs. Rizzoli.

"I have to run. Thanks for telling me the truth. We'll get together soon, okay?" Although if I didn't see her for a while, that would feel perfectly fine, too.

I accepted the other call. "Hello?"

"Hayley, it's Deborah Rizzoli. I've been debating whether to call you, but I decided you deserve to know the truth. I wasn't completely honest about my husband's relationship with Randy Thompson." She sighed, and then I heard a little clicking noise and imagined her tapping her perfect nails on the phone. "It's embarrassing to admit this, but I think Sam had a little crush on him. It pains me even more to say this, but I think they may have had an affair."

"Randy and your husband?" I asked, dumbfounded. I couldn't believe she'd call to tell me this. Was she lying? What would be the point?

"Sam had eclectic tastes," she admitted. "He loved drag bars. The gay pride parade. And Fantasy Fest. He had a collection of amazing costumes and wigs and makeup that he kept on his boat. That was a side of him I didn't care to know that much about. But we've been over there cleaning things out so I can put the damn tub up for sale."

Hard to know how to respond to that. Now I truly felt sorry for her. "I'm sorry for what you're going through," I said, and then added: "Anything else I should know?"

"Well, you should know that he acted on his grudges. He wouldn't hesitate to wield his influence if someone crossed him." She cleared her throat. "If someone he was interested in ceased to be interested in return."

I tried to puzzle out what she was implying. Then it hit me like a fiery mouthful of Chef Stentzel's jalapeño pepper. "Meaning that if Randy ended things, your husband might have done something like set his eviction in motion?"

"Something like that," she said. "It's possible. Well look, Randy had a sweetheart of a deal because he'd lived in his apartment so long. Though to be fair, he had put a lot of his own money into fixing the place up. It's absolutely gorgeous. Our agent will be able to rent it for twice what Randy was paying."

Once she'd signed off, my mind spun thinking about the kind of pressure Rizzoli might have put on Randy. Housing on this island is super-expensive. He'd be in despair about losing his nest. And even more anxious to land the TV show contract. But would you kill someone over losing an apartment?

Then the photo that Derek had taken of Rizzoli the night he died flashed into my brain. And the bizarre chain of events that must have led up to that photo— how Torrence said he was conked on the head, and then makeup was applied before he was hoisted up the mast. Who would even have access to the materials, or the facility with them? Who would even come up with that? And be angry enough to pull it off?

Randy might.

I remembered his furious face when Peter announced that the contest winner was Buddy Higgs. Winning meant everything to him. And Sam Rizzoli had been dead set against him from that first day the chefs were interviewed. Suppose Randy was already seething over his eviction. And then Sam Rizzoli made it clear he had no chance of winning the contest. Made it clear he would allow Randy to win over his dead body.

Literally.

I knew better than to confront Randy myself. With some reluctance, I called Officer Torrence. Pacing up and down the short *Key Zest* hallway, I explained what I'd learned about the connection between Randy and Rizzoli.

"The thing is, my judgment was all off on this one," I said, "because I really liked Randy. And I loved his stage presence. And he made killer shrimp and grits."

"It happens to everyone," he said. "Likeability gets in the way of seeing the facts. Both personally and professionally," he added. With special emphasis on *personally*, like he was trying to send me a message in code. Pig Latin, maybe.

Ansford-Bray is an erk-jay.

26

On the far pier where the cruise ships
docked, a row of lamps cast squiggles of
light on the water, like lines on a Hostess
cupcake.

—Hayley Snow

My heart wasn't in the raucous bacchanal known as
Duval Uncorked. Starting at one end of Duval Street or
the other, each guest was given a small plastic wineglass to wear dangling from a lanyard around his or
her neck, which served as the admission ticket to the
event. Revelers stopped in at each of the participating
restaurants and shops—sixty of them, up and down
Duval—for hors d'oeuvres and a taste of wine.

A couple of hours into the evening, many of the par-
ticipants would be staggering from too much alcohol,
their taste buds dulled from too much food. I wasn't
much in the mood for drunken parties but a review of
this event was on the editorial calendar for Monday's
issue of *Key Zest*, which would focus on a roundup of

the events of the Food and Wine Festival. And Ava Faulkner, Wally's co-publisher, would be watching that calendar like a turkey vulture, waiting to pick me off.

So I parked my scooter on Petronia and began to sip and taste, making notes for next week's column. The pulled pork at Willie T's was delicious, the cheese dip at an adjoining gallery barely superior to microwaved Velveeta. I gave up drinking after the first three sips, my tired brain already feeling addled by the stressful week and not refreshed by my short rest in the office. I waved a quick hello to a number of acquaintances, sprinkled among just as many strangers. If this event was like the Mallory Square Stroll that I'd attended earlier in the week, tourists traveled a long way to participate.

On the other side of the street, I spotted Trudy Bransford. She wore a pale yellow sundress that showed her deep tan to great advantage. My breathing kicked up a notch: The detective was with her, disguised as yet one more tourist in tan cargo shorts, flip-flops, and a moss green T-shirt. I knew the shirt would have perfectly reflected the color of his eyes, if he hadn't been wearing sunglasses. If he'd been looking at me instead of at her. They were laughing so hard he spilled red wine from his plastic glass onto the sidewalk. And that only made them laugh harder. I'd never seen him so happy.

I ducked into 7 Artists to avoid being forced to wave hello, or even worse, to chat. Theoretically, I applauded his good fortune. But realistically, it turned my heart to granite.

In the process of inhaling a chip loaded with guacamole, I recognized Peter Shapiro's voice at the wine-sampling table behind me. I turned to greet him—he looked jaunty and relaxed in white pants and a blue sport coat.

"Congrats on a great week," I said, though to my ears, the words sounded less than enthusiastic.

"Thank you for your professionalism," Peter said. He clapped a hand on my shoulder and gave a gentle squeeze. "I understand that the candidate you preferred didn't win and I appreciate your patience and honesty and—well, flexibility."

If he'd heard the things that went on in my head, he would never have called me flexible.

"As it turned out, we might have had to be filming in prison, though, right?" he asked. "A friend called and said Randy Thompson was picked up for questioning in the murder of Sam Rizzoli."

"Wow, that was fast," I said, shaking my head sadly. "I really liked Randy. I liked what he did all week in the show. Except for the cake pops," I added, unable to suppress a smirk.

"My taste buds are not so well developed as yours." He grinned back. "So much goes into getting a successful program on the air. Ratings are so fluky—especially in reality TV. You imagine that a perky guy who's a good chef will draw in viewers, but the sponsors are more conservative than you might believe. Much more. Drag queens are not a draw in middle America." He looked me right in the eyes. "So thank you. Whether Randy ends up in the hoosegow or whether he doesn't, I feel certain that we chose the right man."

He fell into step beside me as I exited 7 Artists and

started down the block toward the next stop on the Uncorked program. "Did you enjoy the process?"

"I've never been through anything like it," I said, meaning I hoped never to experience anything like it again. But I assumed that, with his major ego, he'd think I meant it was amazing. "Will you have some time off before you start filming the actual show?"

He nodded as we waited for a crowd to exit the Old Town Mexican Café, our next stop. "I'll have a week or ten days, probably do some sailing. Nothing like being out on the water to help a tightly wound guy relax."

"I'm a bit like a cat," I said, flashing on that horrible plunge into the water off Mallory Square. "Even though I live on a houseboat, don't ask me to get wet."

Peter's eyes lit up. "You're really missing out. I spent several summers working as a mate on a sailboat in the British Virgin Islands. Fabulous experience! The only drawback was I'm a big guy," Peter said. "I didn't fit too well into the crew's quarters. Are you planning to stay on in Key West?" he asked.

"I love it," I said. "If I can keep the job, I can imagine settling in for the long haul. You've spent time here before?"

"Of course. I love the wackiness of the place. That's how I came up with the idea of the TV show in paradise." He grinned. "Fantasy Fest is my favorite. One year Sam and I even marched in the parade. We wore spike heels and diapers and wigs and carried spray bottles of tequila."

"Spray bottles of tequila?" I asked.

"A quick shot for any girl willing to lift up her shirt.

Such a hoot!" He laughed, then looked at my face. "Sorry, I know that's politically incorrect."

"I'm just trying to picture those outfits," I said. "I never even liked dressing up for Halloween as a kid."

Suddenly he lurched to the right, and grabbed for his back. "Good god, doesn't this put the icing on the cake."

"What's wrong?"

"My back's gone out." He winced and tried to straighten up. "I've had this happen before. It means I need a couple of days off, a bottle of muscle relaxants, and a lot of time in bed. Damn!" He took a step but grimaced with pain. "I wonder . . . no never mind."

"Should I call an ambulance?"

He shook his head decisively. "I'll be fine." He began to limp down the block toward Petronia Street and I hovered alongside him, feeling helpless. The crowd around us pressed in, seeming drunker and more boisterous by the moment.

"I hate to ask," he said. "Is it possible you could help me get to my car? I thought walking the length of Duval Street twice would be relaxing after the week I've had—bad idea. But I hate to take you away from the party . . ." He whipped the phone out of his jacket pocket. "I can call a cab."

"Not a problem," I said. "I've had enough anyway. Nobody wants to read a column listing every bite we've tasted—I'll hit a few highlights and describe the whole crazy scene. Actually I'm dying to get out of here. It has felt like a long week. Really long."

"A nightmare," Peter said. "I've tried to stay optimistic about the contest, but sometimes I wonder if it was cursed from the minute I set foot on this island."

Which reminded me of what Lorenzo had told Miss Gloria and me a few days ago during our lunch on the houseboat: Key West either embraces you, or chews you up and spits you out. Maybe Peter was finding out that he fit into the second set.

"Come on," I said, moving closer to him and offering my hand. "Let's go."

He slung his arm over my shoulder and leaned some weight on me, at the same time that I felt a sharp object poke my side. I looked up at him, startled. He laughed and staggered like he fit in completely with the crowd around us.

"Not a peep from you," he said under his breath. "If you say anything, I'll shoot you right here."

"But—"

"Not one word. It won't matter to me either way."

With one hand gripping my shoulder and the other shoving the gun in my ribs, he force-marched me down the block. Fear washed over me like a rogue wave, as I finally grasped the niggling thought that had surfaced as he told me about his sailing background. And then his love for costumes. Peter knew Sam Rizzoli well enough to play dress-up. They'd done this together in the past. And Peter was a sailor, knew his way around winches and rigging.

Peter was the killer, not Randy. Not anyone else. Peter was the man who'd had the strength and know-how to hoist Sam Rizzoli up the mast.

He'd murdered the man, dressed him up, and hung him on his own mast. And then I thought of Turtle, beaten half to death. Another loose end shifted into focus: Derek wasn't the only man with a white beard—

Peter had one, too. I hadn't cast my mental net wide enough to consider that.

With two men, one dead, one nearly dead, notched on his belt, he wouldn't hesitate to hurt me.

I tried to force my sluggish mind to churn through the options. The truth was if I went anywhere with him, I was as good as dead. He was at least a foot taller than me, and carried twice my bulk. One day at the gym would not help my chances of overpowering him. But if I shouted for help, I believed he would shoot me. The only option seemed to be to continue along Duval and hope to god I saw someone I knew. Or a cop, best of all.

"Where's your bike?"

"Petronia Street," I squeaked.

Reaching the corner, we turned up the darkened street and walked to the rack where my bike was parked. With the crowd left behind on Duval Street, Peter abandoned the pretense of needing my help. I pointed to my silver scooter and he jerked me roughly toward it. "You first, I'll get on behind."

"Where are we going?" I whispered.

"I'll tell you when we get there."

"Could you hand me my helmet?"

His only answer was a sharp jab in my back that almost knocked the breath out of me. I threw my leg over and fired the scooter up. And he slid onto the seat behind me.

"Left on Whitehead and then over to Truman," he said.

Hands shaking and mind racing, I drove as instructed. To my dismay, I'd started to cry and the tears blurred my vision.

"Take a left when you get to Reynolds and head toward the cemetery. I'd prefer not to hurt you but I will if I have to."

The scooter jiggled as we hit the first block of Truman Avenue that had been under repair for the last few weeks. The danger lights on the sawhorses that had been placed over open manholes flickered in the gloaming. Peter's grip on my waist loosened, but he grabbed me again and prodded my back with his gun. I thought of Miss Gloria's comment—sooner or later someone was going to wipe out on the road's shoddy temporary construction. Maybe then the contractors would get working. The scooter slipped on the loose stones.

"Idiot!" he said. "Pay attention to what you're doing."

With a surge of angry desperation, I realized this was probably my only way out. Lucky for me, the night had been cool enough that I had changed out of my dress into the jeans and sneakers and a sweater that I kept stashed in the office. I stepped on the gas and swerved toward the gravel and the sawhorses and the yawning holes in the pavement.

"What the hell?" Peter yelled.

The bike's tires skidded and like a slow-motion video, we began to slide sideways, finally tipping over and scraping along the pavement until the scooter crashed into the barricades by the side of the road. Peter flew off the back and slammed into the plate glass window of the convenience store on the corner. A large yellow caution sign blinked above me, illuminating the gash on Peter's head in garish Technicolor. Then the pain from my left ankle and my raw skin rushed in and I blacked out.

27

It's an unintentional master class in how to say waxy and embalming things about fresh food.

—Dwight Garner

The Aqua nightclub sat on Duval, a stone's throw from Angela Street. The door was propped open and the shutters on the windows had been folded back to reveal the oval-shaped bar, enticing customers who passed by. Though tonight it appeared that most every seat in the house was occupied. A rousing rendition of Sonny and Cher's "I Got You, Babe" bounced out onto the sidewalk. A few young coeds carrying plastic cups of beer stood by the windows peering in.

I adjusted the air cast on my right ankle, squared my shoulders, summoned my courage, and marched in. As I edged past Gassy Winds, the same tall drag queen that I'd seen the night I was here with Wally and Danielle, she glared at me. A thunk-your-head moment: I realized she was Randy's friend—the one who'd been thrown off the set on the last day of taping. In a deep bass, she growled unintelligible lines from the "Sonny" side of the duet.

At the second bar lining the left side of the room, behind the letters spelling out AQUA on the far wall, Randy Thompson was dressed as his alter ego, Victoria, in elaborate eye makeup and wide red lips. She poured drinks and belted out Cher's half of the song. I crossed the room and slid onto the bar stool at the end of the bar. As Danielle had taught me, I switched my thinking so I would call Randy "Victoria." And I reminded myself to think of him as her. Just for now.

Victoria wiped down the bar as the Sonny and Cher song wound down. "We take requests—for the right-sized tips," she said into her portable microphone as she tucked a five-dollar bill from one of the other patrons into her bustier. She did not look at me or ask if I wanted a drink. But when she came to my end of the bar to page through the songbook I said: "I'd like a Coke, please. And do you know Brenda Lee's 'I'm Sorry'?"

She rolled her eyes and poured the soda, then called out a series of numbers and letters to the sound engineer. She slammed my drink in front of me and moved away again.

"I'm sorry, so sorry," she sang in a powerful voice that could have been Brenda herself. When she finished, I pushed a ten-dollar bill across the bar. She lit a cigarette, blew out a stream of smoke, and stared me down.

"I am sorry," I said, the words coming out in a rush. Wanting to get everything in before she walked away.

"I read the situation completely wrong. I thought you felt trapped here." I waved my hand to indicate the nightclub, the bar, the sound man, the other drag queen. "And that you'd never find an affordable place to live after you were evicted. And that Rizzoli would block you from winning Topped Chef. And then when Mrs. Rizzoli told me that Sam had a crush on you—"

She cut me off. "You thought I was psychologically damaged. Sick enough to kill a person and try to kill two others because I might not get what I wanted from that ridiculous contest."

"I'm sorry," I said again. "I didn't get the whole drag queen thing—that you're an entertainer and that you love what you do."

"I thought I was pretty clear during my interview on that stupid show that I have some bigger aspirations. And there's some good news on that front, too," she said and huffed down the length of the bar to take the drink orders of a couple who'd just wandered in from Duval Street. Across the room, Gassy, the other drag queen, began to warble "It's raining men."

When Victoria was back within earshot, I said: "I'd love to hear about it. Your news. Really, I would."

"I get a break in ten minutes," she said. "Meet me over there." She pointed across the smoky dance floor to the tables on the other side of the room. I grabbed my Coke from the bar and took a seat. Victoria joined me shortly, sat, and lit another cigarette.

"I know, they're bad for me, so don't waste your breath," she said and blew a stream of smoke out the side of her mouth. "So here's the deal. When the *Topped Chef* show blew up this week, the executives at the company did some exit interviews. So I got the chance to pitch an idea to Shapiro's boss at the TV station. It would be a cooking show called "Sing for Your Supper."

"Brilliant," I said. "Did they love it?"

She nodded and broke into her first smile since I'd arrived. "He pitched it to his boss. They want to start filming in a couple of weeks. They're still not sure whether they want me in drag, so we may film it both ways. During a mini-segment within each half hour, I'll give advice about parties and decorating and what to serve to a crowd. That will be called 'Entertaining Shouldn't Be a Drag.'"

I reached for her hand and squeezed it. "I'm so glad."

"And there's more." Her smile grew wider. "I'm appearing as a guest on *Emeril*. Watch the show Friday night."

She squinted and sat back in her chair. "You have quite a road rash there. I read in the paper how you scraped that bum off your scooter and nearly killed yourself to boot."

"It was the only thing I could think to do. I knew if he got me somewhere alone, I was toast. He'd figured out that he'd told me too much and pretty soon I was going to realize he was the real killer."

"And not me after all." She scowled.

"I'm sorry," I said again. "And I'll say it as often as I need to until you forgive me."

A sly smile played over Victoria's face. "So what's going on with you and the hunky detective?"

"Every time I think we're getting started, another

case comes along and somehow I get involved and mess things up and he gets mad." I blew out a heavy sigh. "Although this time was even worse because his ex showed up. She's a knockout and she makes him laugh. So I think we're pretty much a bust."

She reached across the table to touch my cheek, exactly where my face had scraped along the pavement. And where a slash of brown shadow on her face created the illusion of carved cheekbones. "Don't give up so easily. I know a thing or two about what men like. I could help with your makeup for example. And cleavage, girlfriend. Men love cleavage." She laughed and batted her long false eyelashes.

"Of course, you'll never look like me. And where the detective's concerned, that's probably not a bad thing."

I was relaxing on the deck of Miss Gloria's houseboat with a glass of wine and my foot propped up on the railing when I saw a figure coming down the finger, headed for our boat. I was already tired from a stream of solicitous visitors today—Deena, who apologized for putting me in danger. Toby Davidson, who brought a signed copy of her memoir to read during my convalescence. And Chef Adam with a gift certificate for a return visit to his restaurant.

This time it was Detective Bransford. Dressed like a professional cop, not his absurd imitation of a tourist. My heart fluttered, but the rest of me stood on alert, ready for bad news if it came. And my roiling stomach told me that it would.

"Come have a seat," I said when he reached our boat, trying to sound casual and upbeat. Not utterly rattled, the way I felt. I patted the cushion on the chair beside me. "Would you like a drink?"

He shook his head, remained on the dock. "Can't stay." He pushed his sunglasses up above his forehead, peering at my face. "Are you feeling okay?"

I nodded, my hand touching my cheek, exactly where Victoria had touched it an hour earlier.

"I'm sorry we didn't put things together sooner. Once your friend Turtle regained consciousness, he started mumbling like a crazy man. How he'd seen the big guy with the white beard hoisting the pirate up the mast. And how the man had beaten him senseless after he offered to keep quiet in exchange for a couple packs of cigarettes."

"He *is* crazy off his meds, poor guy; I'd think you trained professionals would recognize that."

"We were a little late, I admit," he said with a nod. "When I went over to interview him Saturday morning, among his other ramblings, like I said, he mentioned a big guy with a white beard. After I passed you on Duval Street with Shapiro, the pieces fell into place. I called for backup and ran after you, but by the time I reached Petronia Street, he was already on the back of your scooter and you were riding away." He grimaced and crossed his arms over his chest. "We were right behind you. We would have stopped him before anything happened."

"But I didn't know that," I said fiercely. "I couldn't count on someone swooping in to save my bacon." If he was going to blame me for wiping out . . .

"You did what you thought you had to," he said. "Shapiro confessed this morning when one of our of-

ficers confronted him with the goods on his financials.
He was deep in a hole—bankruptcy, foreclosure on two
homes, three ex-wives suing him for alimony and in-
creases in child support."

"So he was desperate about coming up with a show
that would be a hit," I said.

"Then it turns out that Buddy Higgs's uncle is a network executive. He promised Shapiro a job and a show,
if he could deliver the right man as the star of *Topped
Chef.*"

"Buddy Higgs," I said. "Henri Stentzel didn't have
the zip to carry off hosting a show. And Randy was
simply too risky. Even if he was the best chef in the
world, Peter must have worried about his sponsors."

"It wasn't just what was right for the show—it was
nepotism, pure and simple. Shapiro thought he'd
picked a panel of judges who would agree that Buddy
Higgs had what it took to go all the way. But Sam
wouldn't promise to follow the script. So he added you
to the judges' roster, just for insurance. That night after
the first taping, Shapiro went to see Sam on his boat.
They got stinking drunk and dressed up in Sam's Fantasy Fest costumes. But the drunker Sam got, the more
he dug his heels in about voting for whomever he
wanted. Shapiro says Rizzoli chased him up to the deck
and then came at him with a knife. He hit him with the
bottle of Jim Beam in self-defense. That's what killed
him."

"Self-defense? A likely story," I said. "The jury will
have to figure that one out. How did he end up hanging from the mast?"

"Shapiro panicked and thought he could make it

look like he'd been hung as punishment. To muddy the trail," Bransford said.

"So he got me on the show because he thought I'd be a pushover," I said, frowning.

The detective grinned. "Big mistake."

"What about the shooting incident with Toby on Mallory Square?"

"He admitted to shooting at her," Bransford said. "But only to scare her so she'd start really doubting herself. Not take a big stand against Higgs."

"She'll be relieved to hear it wasn't her imagination," I said.

The longer we talked, the more truly awkward I felt, with him two feet above me on the dock, looking uncomfortable. "Sure I can't tempt you with a glass of wine or a beer?"

He shook his head, slid the sunglasses back on, even though it was too dark to need those tinted lenses.

"I wasn't going to come by," he said. "I'm not sure this is the right thing, but Torrence insisted I had to clear the air. He's like the departmental shrink these days." He wiped his lips with his hand. "First of all, Trudy's decided to stay awhile. We need to figure out whether there's anything left between us."

"Fair enough," I said, working to keep the tremble out of my words.

"Even if she wasn't sticking around," he added, "you're ten years younger than I am. Sometimes that feels like an eon. And then it seems like I'd be dating one of my younger sister's girlfriends."

"And what else?" I asked, tapping my good foot furiously on the deck. "There's not a damn thing I can do about my age. You're only young once but you can be immature forever."

He busted out laughing. "I do love that sense of humor. Trudy's funny but she's also more sensitive. I feel like you can take care of yourself, even with the boneheaded things you get yourself into. Like skidding that damn scooter across the construction area."

"Is that supposed to be a compliment?"

He grinned again, a lopsided smile that pushed into my belly. "Trudy needs me more. She needs *me*." He tapped his chest with two fingers. "But I'd love to stay in touch."

I thought of Lorenzo after my last tarot reading, then rose to my feet and puffed out a breath of air. And shook my head. "I don't think that works too well from my perspective. How about you two figure out what you're doing. If you decide to break things off, then we'll talk. If you stick it out, I wish you well."

I saluted him, then wheeled around and limped a retreat into the boat.

28

You bring your own weather to the picnic.
—Harlan Coben, *Caught*

I patted the chicken dry, daubed on dots of butter, and sprinkled the skin with coarse kosher salt and slivers of Miss Gloria's fresh rosemary snipped from the big pot on the back deck. Then I slid the bird into the oven, followed by the pan of potatoes scalloped with leeks, cheddar cheese, and cream. Everything would be golden and bubbly about the time that Randy's appearance on *Emeril* came on the tube. We knew he'd make us hungry and we were going to be prepared.

I put the bowl of slippery gizzards and other innards in the fridge, to use for my cat training session later. Since Trudy Bransford had made the decision to extend her stay in Key West and see if there were any live embers in her marriage, I had the feeling my social life would dribble down to a trickle. Filling my spare time watching cooking shows with my roommate and training cats would be better than nothing. Maybe.

I started working on mixing the chocolate cake, an easy recipe that had come from my mother's mother. One bowl, one pan—but a recipe that produced heavenly, light warm chocolate cake that went perfectly with ice cream. Any flavor really. I set out a stick of butter to soften, then measured out cocoa, sugar, flour, baking soda, and salt.

Eric called just after I'd scraped the batter into a bundt pan. "If you have a minute, I wanted to give you an update on Turtle," he said.

"I'd love that," I said, wiping my hands on my apron and limping to the chair on the back deck.

"The psychiatrist over at the hospital managed to stabilize his medications, and now he's agreed to move to the Florida Keys Outreach Coalition halfway house program," Eric told me. "They'll make sure he takes his meds. He'll have a real bed to sleep in. And people who care where he is at night. He'll attend AA meetings and they'll help him look for work. And I'll see him in outpatient therapy."

My eyes filled with happy tears. "That's honestly light years better than I could have imagined."

"He's been out on the streets a long time but he might have a fighting chance," Eric said. "We'll give it all we have."

Once I'd thanked Eric profusely, and the kitchen was back in good order, I called Mom on Skype and positioned the computer and Miss Gloria on the couch as my live studio audience. Earlier, I'd gotten the idea for trying to teach Evinrude some of the Cat Man's tricks when cleaning out the cavity of tonight's roasting chicken. We had borrowed a wooden stool from Miss

Gloria's best pal up the dock, Mrs. Dubisson, and fashioned a large wire loop out of a flimsy coat hanger. We propped up the loop with soup cans in the middle of the room.

"Are you going to set the hoop on fire like the Cat Man does?" Mom asked.

"Not the first time out. He's got a lot more experience with this stuff." I laughed and scooped up Evinrude, placed him on the stool, and set a small Pyrex bowl of liver on the other side of the loop. Evinrude sat on the stool, tail twitching.

"So far so good," I said.

Miss Gloria clapped with enthusiasm. "He's better looking than Dominique's cats. A few of them have some awfully ratty-looking fur. But not Evinrude. He's a real star."

"He hasn't done anything yet," I said, walking across the room to tap the bowl of liver. "Come on, kitty."

Miss Gloria's black cat, Sparky, sprang off the couch and bolted over to gobble the entrails.

"This is harder than it looks." I snatched up the little cat and handed him off to Miss Gloria, then replenished the treats. "Here, kitty, kitty."

Evinrude twitched his whiskers and blinked. Then he hopped off the stool and strolled around the wire loop to sniff at the liver. He grabbed the treat and trotted off toward the back deck, tail held high. Both my mother and Miss Gloria broke into peals of laughter.

The seaman's bell outside Miss Gloria's front door chimed, signaling the arrival of a visitor. "I'll get it," I told her.

Wally's familiar boxy shape was framed in the doorway. "Am I coming at a bad time?" He sniffed the air, now perfumed with the scent of roasting chicken and potatoes.

"Not a problem," I said, feeling a pang of apprehension. Since when was it good news for your boss to show up at your home unannounced?

"Who is it?" asked my mom from the computer screen.

"I don't mean to intrude," he said. "I'm sure you're busy—"

"Come on in," I said, opening the screen door and stepping aside so he could make his way into the living area.

"This is my boss, Wally," I explained to my housemate. "And this is Miss Gloria. And my mom's on the computer."

Wally waved to them both. "A pleasure to meet you ladies."

"We're just about to watch Randy Thompson's guest appearance on *Emeril*," Miss Gloria twittered. "Come watch with us? It's not so often we get male visitors."

"Thanks a lot," I mouthed behind his back.

"Actually, I just came to check on you," said Wally, turning to me. "You scared us half to death. Take a few more days off if you need them."

"Thanks, but thumbs-up," I said. "I'll be in tomorrow morning." Suddenly I was acutely aware of my yoga leggings and ratty KEY WEST—ONE HUMAN FAMILY T-shirt.

"Come on," Miss Gloria coaxed. "Hayley's roasting a chicken. A couple of little ladies can't possibly do it justice. She's made scalloped potatoes, too. With leeks and cheese and tons of butter. And a chocolate cake is going into the oven shortly." She patted her belly. "I've gained five pounds since Hayley moved in."

"That's the absolute worst part of joining them by Skype," said my mother. "I don't get a thing to eat."

"We were afraid we'd get hungry watching Randy on *Emeril*," I said. "I may have gotten carried away."

Wally licked his lips and pushed his glasses up the bridge of his nose. He looked younger than he did at the office, wearing a faded T-shirt and jeans with holes where the knees used to be. *Hog's breath is better than no breath at all*, his T-shirt slogan read.

"If you really don't mind," he said. "It smells amazing."

"Settled!" said Miss Gloria. "We love company. We don't get that much of it. Last man we had in here was the tarot card reader—and he's not of the right persuasion, if you take my meaning."

Embarrassment flooded me from toes to the roots of my hair. I was saved from any further comments from my roommate as the theme song from *Oliver!* tinkled out from the TV screen. A teaser about Randy aka Victoria announced the show and then the program broke for an early commercial.

"Quick, quick," Miss Gloria cried, herding us over to the couch. "Beer, sir?" Within minutes, we were settled on the couch, Sparky on Miss Gloria's lap, Evinrude on mine, Wally in the middle. We watched Randy's lively introduction and then he explained that he'd be cooking shrimp and grits. "We have a secret weapon in Key West," he said slyly. "And I'm going to share it with you. Here's a hint: It should never be a drag to enter-tain!" He two-stepped across the little kitchen. The tele-vision broke for another commercial.

"Hayley," said my mom from the computer screen, "could I speak to you in private for a minute?" I dropped Evinrude to the ground and carried the laptop into my bedroom.

"What about Wally?" she whispered once I'd shut the door. "He'd make a great boyfriend. He's way cuter than I imagined from the way you described him."

"Mom, he's my boss."

Mom chuckled. "You wouldn't be the first girl to sample that recipe."

Recipes

Tim Boyd's Mediterranean Cod Soup

My friend Tim Boyd is an amazing cook who inspired his son Adam to become a chef. (And yes, Adam Boyd is the inspiration for Chef Adam, though he's much more pleasant and handsome and less churlish than the character in this book.) Tim says this is a good meal for entertaining, either as a first course or main. He makes the soup ahead and then poaches the cod in the soup at the last minute. It's even better with a toasted baguette crouton on the side. Hayley had the chunky basil sauce made up ahead of time and frozen, which made her dish a snap to prepare for Lorenzo and Miss Gloria.

Chunky Basil Sauce
2 tablespoons olive oil
1 large shallot, chopped
1 tablespoon minced onion
1 teaspoon each: dried oregano, dried basil, garlic, and salt
1 (35 oz.) can Italian whole tomatoes

Heat oil and sauté shallots, onions, and spices. Pour off about 1 cup of the liquid from the tomatoes and set aside. Chop the tomatoes coarsely and add to the oil/spice mixture. Bring to a boil and simmer for 35 minutes or so. If sauce gets too thick, add a little of the reserved tomato liquid.

Soup

1 Recipe Chunky Basil Sauce
1 can (35 oz.) crushed or diced tomatoes
1 cup chopped onions
2 green zucchini cut into ½-inch dice
¼ cup sliced black olives
2 teaspoons chopped fresh tarragon—or less (taste this first—it can be strong)
⅔ cup white wine
⅔ cup chicken stock
1 cup water (optional)
1½ pounds fresh cod cut into 2-inch chunks

Add the crushed tomatoes to the Chunky Basil Sauce along with the onions, zucchini, olives, wine, and stock. Bring to a slow boil, then reduce heat and simmer until zucchini is soft. Add water to the desired thickness. At this point the soup can sit overnight (and the flavors usually improve) or longer, if chilled.

To serve:
Heat the soup to serving temperature and add the cod chunks. The cod will cook quickly so test every few minutes. When the cod is done, remove the chunks with a slotted spoon and place in the serving bowls. Ladle soup over the fish and top with a toasted baguette crouton.

Lime Cupcakes with Lime Cream Cheese Frosting

Henri Stentzel made these for the wedding challenge portion of the reality TV competition. This was adapted from a Buttersweet Bakery recipe in *Bon Appetit* but Hayley tweaked it to be less sweet, with fewer ingredients, and no food coloring. They are so light and delicious and they freeze beautifully! (As I found out when I had the date wrong for a potluck party and arrived two weeks early. . . .)

Cupcakes
2 *cups all-purpose flour*
1 *teaspoon baking powder*
½ *teaspoon salt*
¼ *teaspoon baking soda*
1 *stick butter, softened*
1 *cup sugar*
2 *large eggs*
2½ *tablespoons fresh lime juice (2 to 3 limes, depending on size)**
1 *tablespoon finely grated lime peel*
¾ *cup buttermilk*

To make the cupcakes, preheat the oven to 350°F. Line a cupcake or muffin pan with paper liners. Sift first four ingredients together in a medium bowl. In another large bowl, beat the butter with a mixer until smooth. Add sugar and beat well. Add eggs one at a time, beating after each addition. Beat in the lime juice and lime peel. Add dry ingredients and buttermilk alternately to the butter/sugar/egg mixture in three stages. Divide the batter between twelve cupcake liners. Bake 20 to 25 minutes. (Mine took 22 minutes—check with a toothpick to see if they are done. And don't overcook or they will come out dry!) Cool ten minutes and then remove from the pan and cool completely.

Icing
1 (8 oz.) package cream cheese, softened
1 stick butter, softened
1 cup powdered sugar
1 tablespoon finely grated lime peel (zest of about 2 limes, depending on size)
½ teaspoon vanilla

Beat all the ingredients together until soft. Then frost the cupcakes—this is a very generous helping of rich icing. If you like less frosting, you can reduce the amount of cream cheese and butter, or freeze the excess for another use. Refrigerate the frosted cupcakes if not serving immediately, but then serve at room temperature.

*Note about squeezing limes or lemons: Did you know that the jaw is one of the strongest parts of the body? If you are willing to taste the tartness of the lime and lemon skins, the most effective way to squeeze juice out of a fruit is to cut it in half and chomp down—juice will release into bowl.

Lucy Burdette's Go-Anywhere Granola

Ingredients
4 cups rolled oats
1 cup slivered almonds
1 cup broken pecan pieces
¾ cup shredded unsweetened coconut
¼ cup, plus 2 tablespoons dark brown sugar
¼ cup, plus 2 tablespoons maple syrup (use the real stuff!)
¼ cup vegetable oil (I use canola)
¾ teaspoon salt
1 cup dried cherries (or raisins if you like them better)

Preheat the oven to 250°F. Mix oats, almonds, pecans, sugar, and coconut in a bowl. Combine syrup, oil and salt, and then mix into the grains and nuts. Now comes the only time-consuming part: spread the uncooked granola on baking trays. Bake for 1 hour and 15 minutes, stopping every 15 minutes to stir the mixture so it browns evenly. Cool and add cherries or raisins. Store in an airtight container, but don't expect it to last very long. It also freezes well. Serve with milk or yogurt.

Lucy Burdette's One-Bowl Chocolate Cake

When it came time to pick a pen name for my new
Key West food critic series, I didn't hesitate. I
chose my maternal grandmother's name, Lucille
Burdette, aka Lucy. I don't know if she was ever
called Lucy, as she died when I was only five or
six. But I do have a few oil paintings that she did
and a few memories of her as a sweet, warm
grandmother.

I imagine that she might have been a good
cook, as my mother and both of her sisters loved
to get together for dinners and holiday meals.
And recently, when sorting madly through my
messy (ulp!) drawer of recipes, I found a recipe
for chocolate cake from Nana, aka Lucille Burdette. I tried the cake out on two confirmed choc-
oholics. They both had seconds.

½ cup Crisco (I am not a fan, so I use a stick of butter)
1 cup sugar
½ cup Hershey's cocoa
1 egg
½ cup sour milk (or sweet, with 1 tablespooon vinegar added)
1 teaspoon vanilla
1 teaspoon baking soda
1½ cups all-purpose flour
¼ teaspoon salt
½ cup boiling water

My grandmother's instructions were as follows: Put all ingredients into bowl and mix. Bake as usual.

Here's my interpretation: Preheat the oven to 350ºF. Beat softened butter and sugar until well combined. Add the other ingredients one at a time, mixing after each. Grease a bundt pan, add the batter, and bake for about 30 minutes until cake springs back when touched. Cool for ten minutes and then invert onto a cake plate.

Sift powdered sugar over the top when completely cool and serve with ice cream!

Read on for a sneak peek
at the next Key West Food Critic Mystery.
Coming in early 2014 from Obsidian!

1

*I'm in an open relationship with salt and
butter.*

—Michele Catalano

Faster than a speeding KitchenAid mixer, I scraped the
freshly squeezed lime juice and zested lime peel into
the bowl and beat the batter to a creamy pale green.
Inside the oven, the first set of cupcakes rose gracefully,
releasing their sweet citrus fragrance into the tiny galley of our houseboat.

Then my cell phone bleated: Jim Snow. AKA Dad.

My father isn't big on phone conversations. My father isn't big on conversations, period. Clients, he has
to butter up because he needs something from them.
But I could count on the fingers of one hand the times
we'd chatted since my near-arrest for murder last fall.

So when his name flashed on the screen, I set down the whisk, abandoning the "do not answer" policy I'd adopted in order to survive the week leading up to my best friend Connie's wedding. Something had to be wrong.

"Hi, Dad. What's up?" I asked, trying to sound cheerful, when wary was what I felt.

"Good news, Hayley Snow!" he said with the faux heartiness he reserved for business associates. And using my full name, which he reserved for times I'd gotten into trouble. "The whole family's coming to the wedding."

I whooshed out a breath of relief—he was just lagging a beat and a half behind his wife. "I know. Allison RSVP'd weeks ago. You're all set with a corner suite at the Casa Marina. You'll love everything but the bill." My stepmother, Allison, was organized to a fault. She had to be as a chemist, though why that didn't translate into an ability to follow a simple recipe was beyond me. Hopeless in the kitchen, my mom always said, when she couldn't restrain herself from an edgy comment.

The oven timer began to ding. I donned a red silicone mitten, pulled the cupcakes out, and slid them onto the stovetop.

"The whole family," my father repeated. "Rory's coming too."

"Rory's coming?"

My fifteen-year-old stepbrother. To be honest, I was already stressed about the upcoming week, visualizing how I might handle the family dynamics between my mother and her new boyfriend, whom I hadn't met except on Skype, and my father and stepmother. Not to mention juggling a high-strung bride while baking two hundred cupcakes for her wedding reception. A surly, pimply teenage boy would not, no way, be an asset.

"I was hoping you could find him a place to sleep. Otherwise he'll end up on the couch in our sitting room." Dad's voice rolled out ominously, like the music from *Jaws*. I was pretty certain he didn't care much for Rory either—only he didn't have the luxury of saying so.

"I don't think I can, Dad. You guys are arriving today. It's spring break. The hotels in Key West have been sold out for months. I might be able to get a bead on a bunk in a youth hostel. But between us, I think that's asking for trouble."

He cleared his throat. "Might there be room on your houseboat? I know he'd love to have some special time with you."

"No can do," I said briskly. Rory and I had never lived together long enough to bond like sister and brother. After my parents' divorce, I spent only alternate weekends and Wednesdays with Dad. And the weekends dwindled further once he remarried and moved two towns away.

"Think Airstream trailer on the high seas. The smallest model. Between me, Miss Gloria, two cats, wedding favors, and hundreds of cupcakes, we don't have room to spit." Was I being uncharitable? I looked around at the common spaces of our tiny houseboat, the counters in the galley covered with cupcakes, cupcake batter, zested limes, dirty pots and pans, and Evinrude, my gray tiger cat, eyeing it all from a stool beside the stove.

My father fell silent, which made me feel awful. "What about Eric Altman? Didn't your mother stay in his guest room in January?"

I groaned. How did he even know this? When I moved down to Key West from New Jersey last fall, I'd assured my old friend Eric I would only ask this kind of favor in case of emergency. He'd insisted on hosting mom, because she'd been so kind to him when he was a troubled teen. It wasn't fair to foist Rory on him.

But then I pictured messy, grumpy Rory camped out on our single couch not five feet from the room where I'd be desperate to sleep. This was definitely an emergency.

At exactly that moment, Miss Gloria's black kitten, Sparky, launched himself up onto the stool beside the stove, chasing Evinrude onto the counter. The two cats sprinted across two trays of pale green cupcakes waiting for icing, tipping them up perpendicular to the counter. They crashed onto the floor and splattered into a million pieces. "Shoo!" I shrieked. The bowl of green batter rocked and then tilted, dumping its contents down the front of the stove.

"Gotta go right now," I said to my father. "I'll ask Eric."

I hung up the phone and lunged for the cats. Evinrude slipped through my fingers and vanished down the hall. "*Et tu, Brute?*" I yelled after him.

2

And somewhere, a soufflé has just fallen.
—Charlotte Druckman

I swept up the shards of cupcake, mourning their perfect texture and delicate green color. As I dumped them into the trash, Evinrude peered around the corner into the kitchen, his gray ears and white whiskers twitching.

"Bad kitty," I said. "You're supposed to be helping, not making things worse. That's what pets are supposed to do." He trotted over and wound his lithe striped body in figure eights around my legs, purring as loudly as the engine that had given him his name. I snatched him up and rubbed my cheek on his head, then set him back down on the banquette against the wall of our little galley kitchen. My smartphone buzzed, clattering across the kitchen table, onto the floor, and into the Key lime cupcake batter.

Staff meeting at noon, the flashing text on the screen read.

I groaned, scooped up the phone, and wiped it

down. My boss, Wally, had been crystal clear about how I needed to be ready to pitch story ideas for the next few issues of the magazine.

"We need more structure," he said. "We're getting bigger, with a bigger audience. They expect us to act like professionals and produce a professional product. We can't continue with an editorial calendar that consists of 'Oh crap, we have an issue coming out Wednesday. What can we write?'"

Danielle, his administrative assistant, had giggled, but Wally glared at her, looking fierce and serious. I was willing to bet the scolding stemmed from his co-owner's pressure. Ava Faulkner had despised me ever since her sister's murder last fall. Even after I was cleared of all suspicions, the slate wiped clean, the real murderer jailed, she still despised me. Whenever we met on the street (and Key West is a small town—crossing paths is inevitable), she looked right past me, her thin lips drawn to grim lines, her eyes frosty like the color of Arctic ice floes. If we'd been the only survivors on the island, she'd still have acted as though I didn't exist. Hers was a hatred based on that small but piercing connection in our past, and the memory of it festered inside her like a puncture wound.

Eric, a friend since childhood and a clinical psychologist, liked to remind me that her toxicity was eating at her more than it scalded me. I should ignore her. Challenging wisdom.

I zipped down the hall to change into my *Key Zest* uniform—a yellow shirt decorated with little palm trees, a pair of clean jeans, and red sneakers—all the while hunting through my head to come up with a pitch. But the only thing that came to mind was the ruined cupcakes.

Cupcakes! Why not kill two birds with one stone by pitching a story on wedding desserts? At the same time, I could pick up samples for Connie and Ray to try. I had no time to waste, with the wedding only four days away. The thought made my heart gallop with anxiety.

I googled "wedding cakes Key West" and came up with a list of possibilities that I tapped into my smartphone: Key West Cakes, Amazing Cakes and Creations, and my old standbys for cupcakes and cookies, the Coles Peace Bakery, the Old Town Bakery, and the bakery department in the Fausto's supermarket. Then I packed up six of the lime cupcakes, which had survived the onslaught of the cats, as bribes for the staff meeting. Even Ava Faulkner might weaken when she saw these beauties.

I scribbled a note for my roommate, Miss Gloria—"Had a CAT-astrophe in the kitchen, will clean up later"—and pinned it to the fridge with a Fast Buck Freddy's magnet, yet one more Key West shopping landmark that had bitten the dust since I'd arrived in town. It was not that easy to make a living here, whether you were a restaurant owner, an upscale souvenir shop owner, or, especially, a writer. I jogged down our finger of the dock to the parking lot, where my silver scooter was parked, and bungied the box of goodies into the basket behind my seat. Then I revved up the engine and chugged over the Palm Avenue hill, which led into town.

Once I got to our office—the attic "suite" above Preferred Properties Real Estate on Southard—I dashed up the stairs, stopping at the door to finger-comb my curls and take a calming breath. Which didn't do much for me, especially once I pushed the door open and heard the not so dulcet tones of Ava Faulkner, already ensconced in Wally's office. Danielle, our receptionist, rolled her eyes and tapped her watch.

"Better hurry," she whispered. I glanced at the clock—only two minutes late. But late was late in Ava's book and I should have known better.

After stuffing the cupcakes into the mini fridge, I swung around the corner into Wally's office. "Morning, everyone," I said, my voice quavering with faux cheeriness—after all, my father's daughter. I slid onto the metal chair close to Wally and pulled a pen and paper and my phone out of my backpack. Danielle appeared at the door, poised to take notes too.

"Nice of you to join us," said Ava, tossing a hank of golden hair over her shoulder but keeping her gaze pinned on Wally.

"We were about to start with the editorial calendar," he said, tapping a finger on his computer keyboard. He read off the notes on his screen. " 'Off the Beaten Track—How to Avoid the Spring Break Crowds.' "

"Is that even possible?" I asked, and then laughed. No one answered.

"That's been done by every publication on the island," Ava said.

"How about 'Key Zest Dishes on Cats—Hemingway's Other Legacy,' " Wally tried. "Everyone talks about his writing, but not about the cats. And there's been that whole controversy about the height of the fence and whether the cats should be allowed off the property."

"I heard that story on NPR!" Danielle exclaimed.

"Imagine the great photos we could get to go along with the text," Wally added, his head bobbing.

Ava shrugged. "It's a little goofy, but fine."

Wally jotted my name beside the new article's title. I could only hope he didn't need the draft this week. "I'll let Hayley speak to the food features." He nodded at me.

"I'll be reviewing 915," I said, mentioning a casual restaurant at the far end of Duval, almost to the Atlantic Ocean. "Small plates, reasonable prices, a comfortable window on the Duval Street zaniness."

"I don't want small plates for this issue," said Ava, again looking at Wally, "especially from a restaurant that's been here since the Stone Age. What else have you got?"

"I've been meaning to try Paseo," I said. "It's Caribbean food—on Eaton Street where Paradise Café used to be?"

She sighed and shrugged her shoulders, which I took as a yes.

"And maybe I can pull together a sidebar about breakfast on the go. I had the most amazing sticky bun from the Old Town Bakery this week."

"OMG—those are heavenly!" Danielle said.

Ava delivered her a look that would have melted a weaker woman to a puddle of caramel.

"What else?" Wally asked briskly.

"My bigger feature will be a review of wedding cakes. I was thinking I could include a couple of bakeries plus Fausto's, Coles Peace—the regulars. Kind of focusing on how you can pull together a gorgeous pièce de rèsistance even if you've decided to get married at the last minute."

Ava laid her silver pen on Wally's desk, her perfectly painted lips curling in disgust. "Wedding cakes in March? You'd have to be insane to plan a Key West wedding in March. The island is thick with spring breakers. The streets are disgusting by morning. I won't even mention what I saw on Duval on my way over. No one in her right mind would choose that. And no one would be interested in a piece like that." She slapped her notepad on the desk next to the silver pen. "Unacceptable."

I felt my neck and face flush a deep, hot red. My mother and I share the reddish curls and pale skin of her Irish grandmother—and it's never pretty when we get mad or embarrassed. Now I was both. Wally's lower lip twitched. He couldn't side with me directly—he'd spent too much capital simply insisting that I remain on staff.

"If you don't like weddings, let's brainstorm," he said. "What do you think of when you think spring break? I think beer. Wet T-shirt contests. Edible meals on the cheap. Battles of the bands."

I glanced over at Danielle, who hovered in the doorway, where Ava couldn't see her. "Wet T-shirt contests?" She mouthed. "He's lost his marbles."

I scratched a note on a scrap of paper. "Excuse me a second," I said to Wally. "I'll be right back."

Out in the hallway, I passed the note to Danielle. Then I grabbed the cupcakes from the mini fridge and arranged them quickly on a white plate Danielle kept to use for occasional snacks and various celebrations. They looked gorgeous—cream cheese frosting the pale green color of early-summer leaves with a sprinkle of lime zest on top. I delivered the plate to Danielle and motioned to her to slide the plate onto Wally's desk, in between him and the fire-breathing dragon. Then I returned to the office and took my seat again.

"'How about taking a sweet break with a cupcake— find the best of the island,'" Danielle read off the note I'd given to her. Any ideas would have a better chance of surviving coming from her mouth than mine. She passed out napkins with dancing hearts on them, leftover from our Valentine's Day party, which had been a tad morose since we'd had to produce a whole magazine issue aimed at lovers when none of the three of us had a valentine.

Wally's face brightened. "Everything could be Key lime. Or maybe some coconut thrown in. That makes the piece obviously Key West-y for the tourists, but Hayley would of course hit places that aren't on the tourists' radar."

He peeled the paper liner off the cupcake nearest to him and took a bite. "These are amazing. Where did they come from?"

"Fausto's," I lied. Ava would never eat something I'd baked.

She picked up a knife from the plate, cut one of the cupcakes in half, and then in quarters. She dipped a finger into the frosting and nibbled. "Hmm, pretty good. Though I like mine a little sweeter."

She'd probably prefer the icing on a supermarket

bakery cake, chock-full of artery-clogging trans fat and overloaded with powdered sugar. I managed to force a smile and say nothing.

A few minutes later we'd agreed on a list of articles including breakfast on the go, the Hemingway cats, Paseo, and the spring break cupcake roundup—all due at the end of this week. Although how in the world I would manage that with my family arriving today . . . and Connie's wedding. I could feel a tiny bubble of hysteria rising up.

"One more thing," Ava said, laying her palm flat on the folder in her lap. "We're way over budget on the meals and entertainment line. This month, I want that number cut in half."

"I can explain that," I said. "I like to try to visit each place I'm reviewing three times—twice is my minimum." I leaned forward, grinning foolishly, and tried to meet her eyes. "I feel like I give the establishments a fair shot that way."

Ava looked at Wally. "We don't have the funds for multiple visits. If your restaurant critic needs to eat three dinners to make up her mind about whether the food is any good, I'd suggest you advertise for a new employee. Besides," she added as she slid her papers and her iPad into a purple leather case, "a restaurant should always be on its game. After all, if a customer has a lousy meal somewhere once, chances are they aren't going back." Now she smiled as my grin faded. "And besides that, negative reviews are good for our traffic. Conflict brings in readers. Even novice journalists know that."

My jaw dropped open in disbelief. How could I count the ways she was wrong?

"What if the line cook broke his arm that night? Or the dishwasher quit midshift? Or the shipment of avocados came in black? Or the steak gray?" I took a deep breath. "Ruth Reichl used to visit places six times before she wrote a review."

"Ruth Reichl was the food critic for the *New York Times*. And the editor of *Gourmet* magazine. And the publisher of umpteen bestselling books. You're no Ruth Reichl—not even close," Ava snapped, then focused back on Wally. "Bottom line is, if we don't have the money, we can't spend it."

Then she stood up and stalked off, leaving a cloud of cloying perfume in the office and a sour taste in my mouth.

Wally sighed and reached for another cupcake, refusing to meet my eyes. "All I can say is we have to pick our battles. At least we got the okay on the cupcake gig, right?"

"And the cats!" Danielle peeled the paper liner away from her treat and began to lick the icing all the way around its circumference. "I can't stand that woman, though. She makes me so tense. I feel like a wet dishrag every time she leaves."

I wolfed down a second cupcake, which I knew I'd regret as soon as I'd finished. It was hard enough to keep my weight in check as a food critic—anxiety eating was a habit I couldn't afford. Danielle wasn't the only one who didn't do tension well. And I was facing an entire week of eggshell-walking between handling the details of the wedding and managing the various factions of my family.

My phone buzzed with news of an incoming text,

this time from my stepmother, Allison. Which meant my relatives must have arrived on the island. The cupcakes in my stomach growled and whirred.

FYI, Hayley, Allison's text read. *Rory is dying to ride one of those Jet Ski things. Do you think that's a good idea?*

Of course it wasn't a good idea. Teenagers and speed—what could be worse? Teenagers and speed and alcohol maybe. But what was I supposed to do about it? I wasn't his mother. I eyed the remaining cupcake, but heaved a sigh, wiped my lips, and texted her back.

Can you interest him in fishing? Or paddleboarding?

Then I headed out to face the music.